It wasn't ever
dead man's s

Had more than a ~~~
She didn't feel refreshed. Rather groggy, actually.

The room was dark, but a line of moonlight traced across her leg. Immediately she sensed danger. A twitch of the muscles in her jaw. The scent of…something familiar. A tingle in her wrists…

Rachel jerked completely awake. She tugged her hand but it was fixed above her head. So was the other hand. Cold metal bound her to the chrome bed frame – handcuffs. She tugged, but the steel dug into her flesh.

"How the hell—" Rachel stopped abruptly, knowing there was only one way this could have happened, and guessing whoever did this was still around.

A familiar scent crashed upon her senses. Masculine and edged with Bay Rum spice.

Rachel turned her head slowly. There beside the bed, his eyes level with hers, squatted the one man she'd hoped never to see again.

Available in June 2007 from Mills & Boon Intrigue

Ricochet
by Jessica Andersen
(Bear Claw Creek Crime Lab)

The Rebel King
by Kathleen Creighton
(Capturing the Crown)

The Hidden Heir
by Debra Webb
(Colby Agency: New Recruits)

In Protective Custody
by Beth Cornelison

Duplicate Daughter
by Alice Sharpe
(Dead Ringer)

The Spy Wore Red
by Wendy Rosnau
(Bombshell)

Honeymoon with a Stranger
by Frances Housden
(International Affairs)

Once a Thief
by Michele Hauf
(Bombshell)

Once a Thief
MICHELE HAUF

MILLS & BOON®
INTRIGUE

DID YOU PURCHASE THIS BOOK WITHOUT A COVER?
If you did, you should be aware it is **stolen property** as it was reported *unsold and destroyed* by a retailer. Neither the author nor the publisher has received any payment for this book.

All the characters in this book have no existence outside the imagination of the author, and have no relation whatsoever to anyone bearing the same name or names. They are not even distantly inspired by any individual known or unknown to the author, and all the incidents are pure invention.

All Rights Reserved including the right of reproduction in whole or in part in any form. This edition is published by arrangement with Harlequin Enterprises II B.V./S.à.r.l. The text of this publication or any part thereof may not be reproduced or transmitted in any form or by any means, electronic or mechanical, including photocopying, recording, storage in an information retrieval system, or otherwise, without the written permission of the publisher.

This book is sold subject to the condition that it shall not, by way of trade or otherwise, be lent, resold, hired out or otherwise circulated without the prior consent of the publisher in any form of binding or cover other than that in which it is published and without a similar condition including this condition being imposed on the subsequent purchaser.

MILLS & BOON and MILLS & BOON with the Rose Device are registered trademarks of the publisher.

*First published in Great Britain 2007
Harlequin Mills & Boon Limited,
Eton House, 18-24 Paradise Road, Richmond, Surrey TW9 1SR*

© Michele Hauf 2005

ISBN: 978 0 263 85728 3

46-0607

*Printed and bound in Spain
by Litografia Rosés S.A., Barcelona*

MICHELE HAUF

has been writing for more than a decade and has published historical, fantasy and paranormal romance. A good strong heroine, action and adventure, and a touch of romance make for her favourite kind of story. And if it's set in France, all the better! She lives with her family in Minnesota and loves the four seasons, even if one of them lasts six months and can be colder than a deep freeze. You can find out more about her at www.michelehauf.com.

This one is for the little girl who once
dreamed of becoming a cat burglar.
(Me.)

Acknowledgements

First, I must admit I've always had the secret desire to be an international jewel thief. Blame it on the first Pink Panther movie that featured David Niven sliding across a museum floor to steal the jewel with the dancing panther inside it. It is a thrill to finally live vicariously through my heroine, and realise that the dream is probably much better than reality.

Readers who have read my stories will know I have an obsession with Paris. I've yet to visit the city that frequents my dreams, so I must rely on others to help with the details that make it come alive. Nita Krevans has helped with the French translations.

Lisa E Spencer, aka FF, is my French connection, cyber-answering all my odd little questions, from what the French prefer when they drink beer to when nightclubs are open and just how the heck does *le périph* work and what, exactly, is it? Thanks, ladies!

And for the Britishisms
I have Paul Fisher to thank.

Prologue

French countryside—Location: undisclosed
5:55 a.m.

Sooty, the sunless morning sky. Rain beat upon a dented metal awning scrolled over the study windows. A yard light mounted on a rusted flagpole sketched a haze of blurry gold across the grassless, muddy courtyard.

The limestone facade of the Lazar compound offered a sheer three-story rise facing east. The windows were matte gray, no lights behind them. Raindrops pattered the tin air vents spotting the red-tile roof.

Off-road tires had impressed fresh parallel trails in the mud; the household crew—but a cook and groundsman—had left for the nearest village half an hour earlier to collect supplies for the week.

The day always began before dawn. Rachel could not remember a time when it had not. Hop from bed, meditate with tai chi, down a protein breakfast and then to run laps, or—if raining like today—go to the gym to lift weights. Routine kept her body hard, her mind sound and her vision focused. Vision, having nothing to do with eyesight and everything to do with the purpose of her life—to follow orders and to be nothing less than the best. A machine. Christian Lazar's pretty machine.

Today, a sporting match of blades had been offered—in the usual you-know-better-than-to-refuse tone. Refusal hadn't entered her mind. Rachel enjoyed the rain. The challenge and exhilaration of the weather had spurred on both opponents.

Now Rachel crouched in the center of the courtyard. Cold November rain beat down from the lightening morning sky. Her long black hair, secured tightly in a ponytail with a wrap of thin leather strips, sat heavily upon her right shoulder. Her Doc Martens were slick with mud, as well as her black pants. The ultrathin jacket she wore as protection against a swift and cocky blade—fashioned from gabardine and Kevlar—repelled the rain in speedy rivulets.

Propping her elbows on her knees and bowing her head, Rachel closed her eyes. A shiver encompassed her body. She was not chilled, but unsettled.

In the shadows of the timber soffit Christian sat—no, he didn't sit—he had collapsed.

Could he be dead?

Water dribbled off Rachel's nose and in the curve of her upper lip. Splaying one hand over her knee, her fingertips shot out pearls of rain. Concern niggled, beating out a reluctant empathy. So difficult to show compassion, yet the compulsion was there.

Snippets of last night's conversation with Christian eddied inside her skull. He'd quietly entered her small, spare bedroom. Rachel hadn't realized he'd settled next to her on the ironwood bench until he'd remarked on the absence of koi in the pond outside her floor-to-ceiling window. Garland, the groundsman, had been cleaning the pond and had removed the three giant fish for the winter.

Levity had softened Christian's tone. A rare occurrence. *Beware.*

After moments of silent reflection, the two of them sitting facing the window, staring at the still pond, he'd cleared his throat. Then, with a slow start, but gaining confidence, he'd actually asked what Rachel had wanted to be when she was a child.

The question had stunned her. But she had learned long ago to simply answer, never argue a query, no matter how conversational it sounded.

"I don't know," Rachel had answered. Had she ever been a child? So much he had taken from her. *You allowed it to be taken.* "Doesn't matter anymore. I am…what I have become."

Christian leaned forward and pressed a palm to the cool glass—the window spanned one complete wall of her room and viewed the miniparadise outside. His fingers were long, elegant, but powerful. Capable of cutting off breath, of snapping a collarbone. He remained beside her, too far to touch, too close to disregard. Breaths moved in soft rhythm from his chest. Always, his presence was impeccable, precise, tainted only by the warm spice from the soap he used. Rachel could feel him on her skin, taste him in her throat. Predatory, his sensuality, and so dangerous.

"What of you?" a destructive curiosity had made her wonder. The little girl lost inside her cringed. "What made you the man you are today?"

He'd answered after a few beats. "The same thing that made you what you are."

She had suspected as much. Trained. *Don't falter. Concen-*

trate. You cannot achieve success without sweat, struggle and yes, blood. This is what you are meant to be. Brutal mastery of a naive and frightened teenager. *No one cared for you. I do. Only I love you, Rachel Blu.*

A cruel love, that.

And then she had dared ask, "How did you...get away from him?"

She had *heard* Christian's grin—a little exhale of air from his nose, and then that slight lift of his mouth on the left side. Evil, that grin.

"I killed him."

Now Rachel tucked her head down and twisted to search the rain-distorted shadows dancing against the east wall of the compound. Was Christian dead? *I killed him.* No, she would not think it. She was no murderer. Life was too precious. The machine that she had become had not been programmed to kill.

She and Christian had been fencing. Not a friendly spar, but instead a no-holds-barred teaching experience that ever impressed her of Christian's skills. *Still more powerful than you.*

Fencing wasn't a practical skill—not in this age of high-caliber weapons and extreme martial arts—but it did teach balance and build stamina, and it forced you to prethink your moves, to learn to anticipate the opponent's next move, or two. The slightest miscalculation could result in injury; as the scar on Rachel's jaw attested.

When the downpour began, Christian had reveled in the challenge. As had Rachel. She liked to test her body's limits. The mud and cold did not disappoint. Mud suctioned every footstep, and intermittent spots of wet grass tested her balance. They'd been fencing for half an hour; had ignored the crew's leave for market.

Then it had happened—jaw tight, Christian had let out a yelp and clutched his forehead.

Rachel's initial thought was to run to him—brief, that moment of compassion—but conditioning had taught her to staunchly stand back. Hide emotion. Hold your war stance. Never let the opponent see there may be weakness lurking within.

I am not weak. I am a survivor.

In the next instant, Christian began to fall, the rapier still gripped in his outstretched hand, ready to deflect the riposte Rachel hadn't finished. His shoulder hit the ground first. Mud splattered his eyelids. A spasm rocked him to his back where he now lay half in, half out of shadow. His legs were visible in the glow beaming down from the rusted metal yard light.

Tentatively, Rachel had stepped across the courtyard and bent over him, extending a hand to touch—

—retract.

Wide, empty blue eyes. Unblinking. Dark lashes deflected the raindrops. Did he see her? What had happened? She hadn't completed the riposte. Her blade had gone nowhere near his face, yet he'd clutched his head.

Could it be? The migraines. At rare times Christian would closet himself away in his room. No entrance. Punishment waited should she make noise.

The cook had reluctantly revealed Christian's debilitating secret years earlier after Rachel had threatened her with a hot frying pan. *He doesn't want you to know about them. One of these days one of those nasty head pains will kill him.* Rachel would not have hurt the woman, but she knew the value of a threat.

Still squatting, Rachel lifted her head, keeping her back to the fallen man. Sweet, the rain's fragrance, like a wide-open field. Lightly, it fell in her heart.

After all this time, had the moment finally been granted?

This is it! You've been planning for this day. Ever since...

"I know you love me," Christian had said one night many

months earlier. (Or had it been years? So difficult to track time here in Christian's world away from society.) The last birthday she had celebrated was her sweet sixteen. Not so sweet, she recalled. Calculating in his devotion, Christian's ice-blue eyes held a flame frozen in their centers. "As well, I know your hate for me is equal to the love. That's the way it should be. Black and white. No gray. Never think you can walk away from me, Rachel Blu." Whenever he used her middle name it cemented the fact he knew so much more about her than she could begin to know about him. Rachel Blu, spoken in his claiming whisper, had become a vile oath over the years. "I made you, Rachel Blu. I *am* you."

Always he held the upper hand. She had believed in him. She loved him. Yes, he had made her. Christian had taken her from an ugly life and placed her into his own. A machine, he often admiringly said of her. "My pretty machine."

But for all he had given Rachel, the one thing he'd denied her—intimacy—cleaved at her soul.

Just one kiss, please?

Always denied. Sex was required—a tool used to gain advantage over a mark—but to press together their mouths violated the invisible boundaries Christian kept secured about him.

And so Rachel had begun to make plans. To invest in hope.

Everything was ready. She needn't much. A change of clothing, some cash and her passports. The few other necessities she had inventoried were locked in Christian's safe—an easy crack.

Decisive, Rachel stood and eased back her shoulders to stretch the muscles chilled by the rain. Realizing she still held the rapier, she thrust it forward. It landed in a growing puddle with a tinny splash.

"Touché?" she whispered, so unsure of this gift of victory.

How much time before the cook and Garland—more a periphery guard than the gardener, for he did pack heat—returned? Another hour, tops. They'd taken the off-road, but the Clio remained in the car shed.

Escape? She needed but ten minutes.

Twisting to face the fallen man—her teacher, her mentor, her lover, her tormentor—Rachel shrugged off the Kevlar jacket and dangled it in her left hand. Rain soaked through her thin cotton muscle shirt. Two paces placed her over the prone body of a man she truly did hate as much as she loved. Love confused. Hate, well, that was a prime bit of high, wasn't it?

Lifting a boot to toe Christian's leg, she paused. A touch might wake him from a mere faint. Too risky.

She ran her palm up her left arm and shivered. Short breaths misted before her. Strange, she'd just noticed how cold the rain actually was. Beneath her palm she felt the raised lines in the bulge of her bicep—two inserts half an inch long and thin as a toothpick—just below her skin. Tracking devices implanted when she had first arrived at the ranch.

I'll always know where you are, Rachel Blu.

Slipping a hand over her sodden clothing, she glided her fingers into the back pocket of her pants. The small leaf-shaped push dagger fitted into her palm and with a flick, she exposed the blade.

Now, to forever remove Christian Lazar from her life.

Chapter 1

Eight months later—a Midwestern metropolitan city
Monday—2:11 a.m.

The brushed surface of the steel door bore minute lines in the cold metal. The antipenetration plate proved an unwanted tactile sensation, which made concentration initially frustrating. A full minute passed, her fingers idly twisting the heavy dial that moved like a dream upon its well-oiled tumblers. With a TL rating of 30-6, this safe was comfortably resistant to tool entry.

Which is why the old-fashioned method proved tried-and-true.

Easing into the feel of the box, taking in its density and seeking its secrets, the moment of connection suddenly hit. Eyes closed, Rachel settled into focus. One precise *dumpf* vibrated against the tips of her fingers. The beat of a heart. The heart of the combination lock had begun to answer to her manipulations.

Fingers extended and forehead pressed to the steel door, she twisted slowly to the left. Nothing to hear; ten thick inches of steel beneath her fingertips. Just…sense.

Smooth roll. Twist quickly. Spin for the feel. Grip the stop and…*dumpf.*

One number remained.

Easing out her right leg, Rachel counteracted an oncoming cramp. Crouched on her left leg, she wiggled her toes within the black nylon rubber-soled creepers. She should have worked out this morning but lately it was easy to slack. Why push her body to its limit when there was no longer anyone to force that maniacal control?

Concentrate.

Final spin. Rachel pressed the side of each hand—pinkie fingers inward—to the dial and rotated steadily. So close. Feel for the final wheel to click into place.

Crackin' boxes, you're a natural, sweet. A whisper from her past, flavored with a British accent.

A few notes of a hummed tune visited her memory. She didn't know the words, only the rhythm. How many times had she replayed that tune in her head? And always when on a job. What was the song? It was familiar, but—

Focus!

Chasing off the seductive slip into memory, Rachel nodded once as each number passed with her rotation. Counting, waiting, anticipating…

Dumpf. The gate and fence mechanism dropped into place.

Letting out a breath, Rachel paused, fingers of both hands splayed flat before the safe door, but not touching. Too easy? No, just out of practice. Not accustomed to the hands mastering the method before the brain comprehended. And likely, interference from her past joggled her expectations.

Rachel moved her forehead away from the steel door, stretched her right arm to the side and spun the five-spoked spinner wheel. And…

…*click.* The bolt retracted and the inner suction breathed out, pressing the thick steel door into her shoulder.

Repressing a smile—a smile! Imagine that. It was a new thing within the past few months—Rachel peered inside the box, tilting her head to focus the tiny laser light snaked over her left ear.

A walk-in safe about six-by-eight feet, walls approximately eight inches thick and rimmed with inner lighting activated by opening the door. Fire sparkles glinted with each pass of her headlight over the rows of glass shelving. Colored stuff and diamonds, little flames dancing in the sudden shock of light. Nothing was concealed. All items were laid out for display upon black velvet trays.

A check of her watch: 2:19. A little over seven minutes to crack the box. Not bad.

Drawing the laser light across the rows, she spied a thick rope of pearls. Not flashy enough. Colored stuff was her fix—rubies, emeralds and sapphires. Instead, she selected a strand of canary diamonds. A single pear drop weighted the piece nicely. Ten carats? She studied the heft of the feature stone in her palm. Close. Enough to make a point.

She tucked the necklace inside the nylon waistbelt fit snug around her stomach, then closed the door, spun the spoked handle, and began to backtrack. A stretch of her arm touched the camera over the door to the safe room—a wood door with little more than bolt locks placed at top, mid and bottom. The same key opened each lock—stupid mistake. (As if the wood door would prevent an ax from cleaving it open?) Tilting the camera back into position, she shook her head at the ease.

Did no one test their security systems? And if they did invest in cameras, why were there no on-sight guards to watch the monitors? Sure, there were videotapes, but that after-the-fact evidence always proved too stale. Arrests were difficult because the thief was long gone by the time a positive identification was made.

Mentally tallying key security hazards, Rachel slid down the hall in the darkness, a shadow incarnate.

Five more cameras were avoided on the way to the back door. Yes, the back door. No sneak entry into the ultrachic main street jeweler by way of the duct system or roof ventilation. Access had been all too easy.

Tilting the final camera back into position, Rachel then ducked into focal range and gave a wave to the camera lens. A thumbs-up gesture provided necessary proof.

Bending to reset the trip sensor at the base of the door, she shouldered open the metal door and scanned the alleyway. The heavy July air settled on her face with a muffling hug. It hadn't cooled much with nightfall.

The camera across the street, mounted in the shadows of an office-supply factory, had been disabled with a rock. No functional damage, merely redirection to sight in the battered yellow station wagon parked behind a Chinese restaurant down the alley. There were no on-site guards to answer any commotion the cameras should spy. The nearest security office was a three-minute drive to the south. The police station? Twenty blocks to the east.

Closing the door securely, Rachel stepped lightly across the street and wound her way through a labyrinth of passages until the tempting scent of kung pao chicken had segued into other scents of the night.

Entering her loft, Rachel crossed the expanse of hardwood floor, her path unhampered by furniture. She stripped off her long-sleeved black shirt, the waist belt with the diamond necklace, and tugged down her dark jersey pants. Toeing off her creepers, they landed on the sisal rug before her bed. The necklace clunked as it hit the floor. A toss of her shirt landed on the only item of furniture she cared to own, a bed, the organic mattress set upon a low Swedish pine platform. Piles of shiny hardcover books had begun to form a fortress on the opposite side of the bed from the window-lined brick wall that overlooked a quiet warehouse neighborhood at the edge of the city.

A beeline for the bathroom and a warm, scented bath had become ritual following a heist. A luscious reward for a job well done—box cracked; sparklers in hand.

The whole reward concept was new to Rachel. But she found resistance more difficult than expected. There was no one to say she couldn't reward herself. So…why not? Secretly she experienced a moment of worry before plunging into the tub. Like someone would know, and would punish her for such reckless indulgence. But that feeling only lasted momentarily.

Twisting the hot-water knob to let out a rush of water, she then tapped a few beads of vanilla oil into the tub. A flick of the cold water would keep the heady brew from scalding her weary muscles. Twist, twist. Cracking boxes was similar to adjusting the perfect bath. Precision, know-how and attention to detail led to a satisfying experience.

Thick, straight curtains of dark hair spilled over her shoulders as she unwrapped the leather strip and set it on the bathroom vanity. Removing her watch, she checked the time: 3:09 a.m.

With a hissing protest to the heat, Rachel settled into the sweltering bliss. From toe to breast her flesh reddened and her heart pounded, but within seconds she adjusted, settling her head against the Istrian-tiled wall. Using her toes, she twisted both knobs to off. The sudden whimsical thought to try and crack a box with her toes made her smirk.

"Never say never," she murmured, and then immersed her head. Bubbles from her nose surfaced. She emerged, slicking her hands over her hair. Hot water fogged from her arms in steaming vanilla mists. The bright yellow rubber duck she kept perched at the tub's edge wobbled in the center of the sweet-smelling water.

"You have spoiled yourself," she said. "What next? Beauty-shop hairstyles and perfume?"

Well, she wouldn't go quite that far. Vanity did not register on her radar. Many of life's privileges were new to her. Until a few months ago she had not ever taken a bath. (Since she was a child.) Had never been allowed time to preen herself beyond the quick cleansing scrub of a hot, then icy-cold, shower. Now bathing had become the greatest luxury. One she allowed herself almost every evening.

And why not? She had done it. Escaped her past. Freedom was hers. No man would ever again control her.

"The future can be perfumed and styled if I wish it."

Hands floating upon the surface of vanilla-oil-riddled water, Rachel began to meditate.

An hour later Rachel reluctantly emerged from her lagoon for dry land.

Wrapping an Egyptian-cotton towel around her wet body, Rachel, bare feet slapping the polished hardwood in wet splatters, went to answer the taps at her door. Not demanding, but just there, the knocks—an identifying clue her neighbor who lived across the hallway stood on the other side of the heavy metal door. It was the two of them, and an old elevator that no longer worked, occupying the upper level of a warehouse that had once housed architectural reproductions. Access to the loft level was a three-story trek up clanging metal stairs. Even Rachel had difficulty maintaining stealth climbing the noisy stairs.

"Hey," Oscar offered as she slid back the factory door hung on four squeaky rollers. His sun-streaked hair stood at odd angles, surrounding bushy brows and a smooth grin.

A writer, who rarely left his apartment save to buy groceries or run to a movie, Oscar was not a threat. Threat level must be assessed within the first seconds of meeting someone. Once a criminal, the self-preservation thought process never went away, no matter the lack of desire to ever again commit a crime.

It didn't even surprise her that it was so early in the morning. Rachel had learned Oscar slept as little as she, just a few hours in the wee shadows of the morning. Oddly, their sleeping schedules almost paralleled.

Oscar was handsome in a scruffy, just-tumbled-from-bed way. But what else to expect when he basically lived in flannel bottoms and a torn T-shirt? Kind, and trustworthy, Rachel liked the man. (Though his gentleness still startled her.) He was her first, and only, male friend.

She eyed his arms, loaded with grocery bags. No keys dangled from his long fingers.

"I think I locked myself out again."

"He thinks?" she muttered as she dashed for a robe hooked on the back of the bathroom door. "What is that, three times now since I've known you? And I've known you all of eight months."

"But you love me, yes? I never think when I leave," he offered as he stepped aside to follow her across the hall to his door. The hallway was an open stairwell, concrete walls and a dusty ceiling networked with exposed ducts and ancient pipework.

"I *do* think," Oscar corrected, "but it's usually a conversation with a killer or a mad scientist or a time-traveling adventurer. You know? I suppose I could get one of those rocks to set by the door."

"Very effective device," Rachel said about the fake rock key-hider she had learned so many catalogs offered for the amazingly low price of $19.95, plus shipping and handling. "Especially when placed outside an *inner* door."

He offered a snarky sneer at her sarcasm.

"Do you always grocery shop after midnight, Oscar?"

"Hell, yes. Roberta works the graveyard—er, uh… That's when they put out the fresh fruit and there's usually no one else in the store."

"Really?" She'd have to remember that.

Grocery shopping made her uncomfortable. The first time she had walked into a grocery store she'd lost four hours roaming the aisles of multicolored food and had only left with one full bag. It had been a strange sort of sensory overload standing there amidst the manufactured smells of sweetness and the glossy cardboard packages. Not once had she purchased food for herself, as a child, or when living with Christian. How to choose from such an abundance? What did she like? Was pasta boiled or baked? Juice boxes and yogurt in tubes? And what in hell was a bakery product called a beehive?

She reached high and retrieved the bent paper clip she'd placed atop the door frame the last time Oscar had needed her help. Shaped into waves like a snake's body, the end of the fine wire had been bent to allow her to gently rake the pin tumbler-style lock on the door. A common lock used on houses and old factories, it merely required a fine touch and patience. She wasn't about to whip out her pick set and risk a writer's curious questions.

Squatting, Rachel poked the clip inside the keyhole.

Oscar set down the grocery bags and rummaged inside one of them for a piece of candy. A sucker stick always poked from between his lips. Kept his thoughts moist, he claimed.

Moist for what? she always wondered. Was moistness required when typing one of his historical-horror thrillers?

"Hand me one of those," she said.

He did, and, first biting the stick to flatten the end, she then stuck it into the base of the keyhole to use for tension.

"You're very good at picking locks," he observed casually.

"Childhood hobby."

"You said that last time."

"Then I guess I'm good at keeping my story straight."

Oscar had introduced himself to Rachel the first night she'd moved in. Standing in the middle of the big empty loft, thinking she'd certainly gone and done something horrible—leaving behind the only life she had known—she'd looked up to him and he'd seen her blink tears from her eyes. For one moment she'd instinctively stiffened, prepared to take out a new enemy with a high kick and a chop to his throat. But his hand, extended in sympathy, had wiped away her suspicion. Only when he'd embraced her had she been able to pull herself up from the drowning black hole of what the future held and push him away. She wasn't much for conciliatory contact. Life was either black or white.

Box cracking: black. Survival: white. Hugs? Too gray for her hardened sensibilities.

Sucking on what smelled to Rachel like a grape sucker, Oscar rubbed his palms together expectantly as she worked the lock. She'd rake the pins and have the door open in a jiffy.

He leaned against the door. Surprisingly, his brown loafers were immaculate; an odd smoothness to the remainder of his grunge look. His crisp oceany cologne invaded Rachel's nostrils. Nice. But…gray.

"In the bath again?"

"You're very perceptive." She checked to ensure the robe wasn't gaping open. Not that it mattered, but…well, it did. She'd never tease Oscar. Though, certainly she would not deny a curiosity for him. A handsome, single man, living but ten strides across the hall? Why not?

Because you don't do gray, remember?

"I think you're part mermaid for all the time you spend in the bath. You were in a towel last time I needed your help."

"Maybe I'm a nudist."

"Don't tempt me, Rachel. You're talking to a man who gets out very little."

"Yet it seems you have lots of parties."

"Gotta bring the friends to me. Speaking of which, I'm having one this Thursday. I'm celebrating the completion of my first historical epic. You will come."

"I don't know." Bending her head, she closed her eyes. Focus. A twist of the paper clip moved another pin up to its shear level. Two remained.

"There she goes again, avoiding human contact. What is it with you, woman?"

"I don't avoid humans. I'm just cautious."

"Yeah? Well, I won't take no for an answer. If there's a bigger hermit than myself, it's you. What do you do with yourself all day, Rachel? You have no furniture or homey decorations to speak of, so I know you don't shop. No music, so I know you don't indulge in the fine arts. No TV—I won't even bother with that one. I've never seen you date—"

"You keep tabs on me?"

"Er, of course."

She lifted a brow.

He waved dismissively and readjusted the sucker to bulge out his left cheek. "Kidding. I don't spy on you. You think I'm a spy?"

"No—"

"You know the acoustics up here leave little to be desired."

Indeed. Toilet flushes were heard, backed-up sinks clanked in the pipes, as well, the occasional song carried overhead when Oscar showered. (Disney movie tunes, he'd once explained.) Disney? She vaguely recalled something about a princess sleeping in a tower, but Rachel's memory for television and movies didn't go much further. Christian hadn't allowed television. Mindless media redirected focus, he'd claimed, and was ninety-nine percent junk. When Oscar held his parties, she usually left for a quiet coffee shop. Loud music debilitated in ways she didn't want to think about.

"I've yet to hear anyone escort you home," he said. "And trust me, I'd hear any earth-shattering orgasms. Unless you're the silent, whimpering type?"

She shot him arrows, but soft-tipped ones. If he knew how elusive an orgasm was— Hell, what did a man care? "I've yet to hear any blissful moans from your place."

Hands splayed up in defense, he offered, "Touché. Blame it on the writer. I'm just trying to peg you. You're so gorgeous, Rachel. Kinda quiet, but not offensively so. A little strange when it comes to decorating, but everyone should be allowed their quirks."

"Such as the stuffed dachshunds populating your living room?"

"Don't throw stones, Ms. I Like Ducks on my Toilet Seat."

She smirked. Oscar had provided the screwdriver for that little adventure into domesticity. For some reason the little yellow quackers just made her smile. What would he think of her duck-emblazoned lucky bra? The thought led her toward that bit of grayness she wasn't prepared to consider. Not yet.

Back to business. The final pin slipped up to shear level and Rachel twisted the sucker stick, torquing the tension, which opened the door. "The castle gate has been pillaged."

"My thanks, fair lady." Oscar lifted a bag. "The king shall expect your presence at his next fete."

"Really, I—"

"Or he'll bring the party to you."

Rachel sighed and stood. She fiddled with the thick terry

robe. She didn't have anything against parties. Quiet parties. But forget mingling. She didn't know how to mingle. Well, she did, but only in the sort of covert indulgence focused on luring a mark into her web. Common, chatty, party mingling fell under the heading "torture." And she had known torture in her lifetime.

"I'll hold your hand," Oscar coaxed. "There's this guy I want you to meet. You'd be perfect—"

"Oscar."

"Just meet. I didn't say you had to have sex with him. Yet. He's a nice guy, and handsome and, well…he doesn't go out a lot and is kind of unsure around women."

"So you think pairing two social misfits will suddenly spark a rousing conversation and future bliss?"

Oscar leaned in to kiss her forehead. She didn't mind his kisses. They were just friendly, after all. Never even close to her mouth. Good that way. Completely white with no shades of gray.

"Thanks, gorgeous, you're a sport. Thursday at nine, yes?"

What could she say? *No, I prefer to sit across the hall in my big empty loft staring out the window and wondering when I'll finally feel like a part of this world? Sure, I'll talk to the "prospective man," but don't expect me to do anything more than fidget and wish for a natural disaster so I don't have to drown in the "meet" thing. Or worse, watch me dart when the music reaches the uncomfortable-decibel level.*

Oh yeah, so sexy.

"It won't hurt," Oscar offered around his sucker. "Promise."

"Fine. Nine o'clock. I'll be there."

Chapter 2

Tuesday—9:05 a.m.

"Ms. Anderson...I...hadn't expected you."

Her business card simply read: Rachel Anderson—Security Expert.

Rachel had never told Christian her last name, but still felt compelled to use a false name—some version of the Swedish Lutheran surname she had once used, like Larson or Nelson or...Anderson. It was required she appear legit amongst her competition, which included former policemen, special-investigations officers, insurance surveyors and a long list of experts with an alphabet soup of letters following their names. Of course, her passports—all four of them—listed a variety of international surnames.

Entering the mahogany-paneled private office, she laid a black velvet pouch on the desk before the owner of Finley

Jewelers. Smoothing a hand down her simple sleeveless black dress that buttoned almost to the neck—business attire—she checked her composure. This part always made her a little nervous. She wasn't much for confessing to a crime—even if it was a legitimate job.

Finley's wide eyes spoke loudly through the swirl of musty cherry cigar smoke curling before his face. He suddenly comprehended why Rachel was here. His store had been violated, and he—likely—hadn't even been aware.

"But the window we had discussed—" Finley stammered. He clutched his silk necktie. Ashes tumbled from the stub of his cigar. "That was agreed upon, Ms. Anderson. My security was to be on alert starting tomorrow."

"Exactly." She pressed her palms onto the cold granite desktop. A bit of eye contact, subtle flirtation, would ease his apprehensions. Manipulating his emotions was key—she couldn't risk an irate customer. "Is that a cherry cigar? Mmm, it has such a sensual fragrance."

Over the top, she knew, but minimally effective.

Gaining confidence from his softening gaze, Rachel explained, "Forgive my tactics, Mr. Finley, but I wanted to visit the store during normal security awareness. If you had planned to place security on ultra alert during the four-day time period I gave you, it makes little sense to fall back into a lacking security mode later. It is extremely important the simulated theft occur during *normal* operating conditions."

"Well..." Shock always made acceptance slow in arriving. Her tactics were crude, but once she got them over the initial distress, understanding clarified.

A tilt of her head offered an optimistic expression. Rachel traced a finger along the blunt ends of her hair, an unobtrusive tucking away of a loose strand that wasn't there. Mouth held partly open, soft and inviting, she allowed the silence to steep.

Finley eyed the stub of his cigar...then nodded subtly. A short step toward trust.

"My technique matters little now, the task is complete." She tilted the velvet bag and out slid the canary diamond necklace. The silver setting clicked deliciously upon the stone desktop.

"You took such a valuable piece?"

"And now I am returning it." Rushing to calm the panic she always saw in their eyes, Rachel continued. "Along with a comprehensive report on your security faults. There were not many, I might add. The Finley employs state-of-the art safes that would easily scare off the average thief."

The administrator reached for the necklace and tugged it hastily to his grasp. "Average?"

"I entered your facility at approximately 2:00 a.m. and vacated the premises before two-thirty."

"It took you but half an hour to steal the finest in our collection? But the safe—the security company promised—it's a TL rating of...what was that again?"

"The rating is 30-6. Yes, and most effective against drills and sophisticated torches and burn bars."

"And yet you...?"

"I work exclusively by touch, Mr. Finley." She tapped her middle finger against her thumb in display. A stroke of her tongue over her lower lip recaptured his flitting attention. "Less complicated, a bit more time-consuming, but ultimately overcomes any challenge a safe should present. An expert thief will not fool around with gadgets when his fingers will serve."

"Expert? Yes. Oh..." The droplets beading on Finley's forehead clued her he was near fainting. Or choking on the smoke curling thickly before him.

Unlike other security investigators, Rachel did not stride through the complex with a manager or owner by her side while she surveyed and assessed. She simulated an actual break-in. There were so many tangents a visual tour could miss. The entire scenario changed after the employees punched out and the cameras were left to roam in peace. Most companies hired her on a whim, never expecting she'd pull off a heist, false or otherwise. They always smiled ingratiatingly as Rachel would explain her modus operandi, then push for the job. She offered personal recommendations from half a dozen local jewelers and a major New York museum. But infiltrate *our* security? Sure, give it a go. *You silly woman,* was the unspoken part.

"Now." She pushed a thin violet file folder across the table, smearing the ash. "I've detailed my every move and commented on each and every security breach. While the safe is impressive, I'm more worried about the perimeter sensors and alarms. You want to stop a thief from entering the building, Mr. Finley, because once inside, three-quarters of the battle has already been won. And not by you. I'd like to take you on a walking tour, if you would allow. I find to point things out and allow for questions alleviates much of the shock."

"Sure. Yes." He tapped the file folder and sighed. "Your...invoice?"

"Is in the file."

He peered inside the violet folder.

"I believe you'll find my charge reasonable. Half of all proceeds is donated to charity."

"Oh?" A smirk of machismo stiffening his jaw, he swept the air with the cigar. "So I am funding some fireman's ball?"

"Foster care," she stated bluntly "My preferred charity."

"I see. A fine cause, I'm sure. And yet, as you say, the charge *is* reasonable. How do you make a living, Ms. Anderson?"

"It's not the money that keeps me at a job I enjoy."

"I see."

No, he didn't see. He likely suspected she got some sort of rush from playing cat burglar without the worry of criminal conviction. She didn't.

Well…

No. Any high Rachel experienced during the heist was from pushing her body's limits, both mentally, when determining an entrance plan and cracking a box, and physically, the climbing, creeping and sneaking part. The sparklers were no prize. A challenge met was all she needed. And enough cash for food, rent and a bit to give back to the foster system. A system that had failed her.

She was no hero, but given the opportunity, she'd do what she could to ensure at least one child received the proper care.

Jerking her thoughts from a past that mattered little and could never be changed, she reassumed business mode. "I will ask for a recommendation though."

"Certainly. In fact…" Finley toggled the necklace before him, admiring the multicolored sparkler. "I believe I know of a curator who could use your hands-on expertise."

"Excellent. In the city?"

"Yes, an established museum. But I won't provide details until I've spoken with the curator. You'll leave your card? How does one contact you, Ms. Anderson? There is no phone number on any of your paperwork."

"I'm currently changing residence. I rely completely on recommendations, so if your curator has an interest, I will contact him after having touched base with you."

"Fine. Shall we take that tour now?"

"Certainly."

"And you understand, I must do an inventory before you are allowed to leave the premises?"

"Of course. I wouldn't have it any other way."

Tuesday—11:00 a.m.

"Have I got a mark for you."

"Really? I've been searching for weeks. How'd you score that one?"

"The how is not important. Only that this is the break you've been waiting for. She'll contact you tomorrow for information."

"She?"

"Yes. Ms. Rachel Anderson, security expert. A real looker, too."

"Why no contact number?"

"Some excuse about being between residences. I don't buy it, nor should you. But you don't have to. She'll work nicely, I promise."

"I trust you. Send her my way."

Wednesday—1:00 a.m.

Rachel twisted the hot-water spigot to off and leaned over the scalloped bathroom sink to splash water over her face and neck. The July heat purled sweat droplets down her scalp and between her shoulder blades. The muggy Midwest summer, along with high temps pushing the upper nineties, had hit the city with spot power outages for the past few days. A thief's dream. A former expatriate's nightmare. She wasn't accustomed to the humidity or the mosquitoes. The French countryside had offered pleasant summers; not that she'd spent much time outdoors engaged in pleasant activities. Of course, running wasn't unpleasant, just more like work.

She was used to hard, muscle-stretching, heart-pumping movement. A good daily workout. But it was more difficult to meet her workout goals in this heavy air that teased one to forgo the effort and simply stretch out and relax. It would be impossible to install an air-conditioning system in the spacious loft. So she prayed for an early fall.

She spat out a spray of water and smeared the fog from the vanity mirror. A weary smile winked back at her. So she'd managed half a workout today. Smoothing a palm down her stomach she noted the muscles were not so pronounced. She hadn't been taxing her body as much as she should of late. Gone was the hard armor of muscle that had once wrapped her torso and arms and legs. The loss of strength had been noticeable when she'd squatted before the safe in the Finley jewelry store. The position had stretched her quads until they'd burned.

Time to step up her workouts. She had to stay in top form if she wished to continue on this road she'd taken.

It wasn't as if she had much choice in what to do to earn a living. When it came to office and real-world applications, her job skills were nil. She hadn't the first clue how to type. Hunt-and-peck worked well enough for any security system that required keyboard access. Sitting enclosed in a cubicle all day before a computer screen reeked of torture. While she could ferret out the cut wire in a digitized security system, to begin to understand office applications challenged a part of her brain she couldn't comprehend. E-mail? No problem. But spreadsheets and pie charts? Not going to happen. And to begin to develop her lacking social skills? Ugh. Gray stuff.

Rachel knew how to lift rocks and sparklers. And she did it well. But she wouldn't go to jail for it. Nor did it make sense to profit from another's inept security, that's why she kept her price just low enough without crossing the too-low level where prospective employers may consider her a cheap wannabe. Tack on a percentage to cover the charitable donations, and she earned enough for a simple life.

Her respect for personal property clung to the gray edge of the black. She had stolen millions' worth of jewels over the years because that is what she had been trained to do. And for a while, she had begun to believe it was right. But just for a moment. Always, the niggling at the back of her skull—*it is not yours to take*—had kept her from completely surrendering to Christian's twisted morals.

Picking up a bath towel from the toilet revealed the clear acrylic toilet seat embedded with dozens of little yellow ducks with orange beaks. The sight made her smile.

Lately, Rachel was finding more and more of interest, curiosity and even amusement. She couldn't remember a time when laughter had been easy. Cracking boxes was serious stuff. But just yesterday morning she'd laughed at a joke overheard at the bus stop when a little boy had asked his mother: How does a farmer count cows? When his mother shook her head in dismay, he'd laughingly answered, "With a cow-cu-lator!"

Kids were sweet. Completely trusting. Adults tended to overlook their innocence.

Twisting the towel about her hair, she flipped the wrap back as she straightened. Thinking to air dry, she strode naked out into the massive expanse of her loft. Some freedoms were too good to resist.

Resistance was one of those easy states she'd learned to embrace. Resist failure, resist defeat. Resist forming emotional bonds with anyone—though certainly she had failed when it came to Christian.

Now, something so simple as purchasing a piece of furniture challenged her sense of entitlement. Did she really need a couch to serve as a catchall for a lazy body? Nope. Nor was a dining table and chairs necessary when the kitchen provided a stainless-steel countertop with two matching steel bar stools. Wall decorations seemed senseless, though she knew, instinctively, they were part of making a home...homey.

What did a home feel like? To summon an image of her ultimate home proved impossible. Once home had been hers—when she was a child. But that image was marred by five years of being shuffled from bed to bed in the foster system.

Rachel assumed home was an emotional thing. Like maybe...just feeling safe. Secure. Happy? Yes, happiness was a requirement for a home. As well, a feeling she belonged, that she *deserved* to belong.

It had been eight months since she'd left France. Soon enough she would begin to feel comfortable in her surroundings. She hoped.

Striding past the only item of furniture she could justify—the low platform bed—Rachel flapped her arms and did a quick jog step to hurry the drying process. It was late, but she felt antsy. Anticipation for tomorrow's job simmered in her veins.

Tomorrow the Lalique museum received the Rousseau ruby into inventory—a flawless Burmese ruby worth two million dollars. It was only eight carats, but transparent rubies without flaws were oftentimes worth more than diamonds. The museum planned to put it out for public display next Tuesday.

Just this morning she had met Sidney Posada, the curator of the Lalique, for an interview thanks to a recommendation from Mr. Finley. A handsome man with dyed black hair and sunbaked creases in his forehead, Posada had flirted gregariously with her. But Rachel had avoided the trap of allowing him to think her a silly woman with ludicrous ideas. His intimations they might have a drink later were matched with a businesslike manner that, while not cold, left the curator pleased to have met her but duly aware she wasn't available.

Rachel had given Posada a window of Friday through Sunday for her investigation. Tomorrow was Thursday. The ruby should be received and set in its display in the West Corridor, a high-tech security extravaganza reserved exclusively for special showings.

Posada had offered her a tour of the layout—which she'd refused; no need to point out what she should discover herself. Instead, she'd spent a leisurely afternoon walking the grounds, casing the single-level structure. It would present challenges. Interior walls were smooth marble, lasers at eight-inch intervals located at every doorway, ventilation ducts narrow (too narrow for a body), an armed guard and—what she suspected, but couldn't verify until she was inside the security box—a redundant backup line should the security system fail, perhaps during a summer-heat power outage.

But challenge was what Rachel lived for.

If it's not a struggle then it is not worth it. Think about it, Rachel Blu, you need to give blood for this. It is required.

Still that stern voice visited her thoughts. It was difficult to erase. She supposed it would never completely be abolished. Not that she wanted it gone. Christian Lazar had been everything to her. He fit like a puzzle piece into her soul. Even with his death, his presence had merely diminished, but would never be obliterated.

Rachel's parents had both drowned during a cruise-ship fire when she was eight. With no relatives or even a friendly neighbor to assume guardianship, her life had been taken over by the court system. At fourteen she'd just run away from her fifth foster home. With the wisdom of hindsight, she suspected a home with a child or two might summon the time and effort to care, but she'd never been so lucky. Always she was squeezed into a bed with one or two others, rounding out a group of six, seven, or even more. Enduring the horrors of so many angry young personalities all tossed together, the neglect was inevitable. Wary of the looks and less-than-discreet touches her last foster father had given her, escape had been inevitable.

She'd spent two nights in a public park crying, cursing her parents for abandoning her, wondering if she should join them by jumping into the city's lake, and yes, even dreaming. How to start this thing called life all over?

It had been an overcast Wednesday afternoon when Christian Lazar had approached her, his bold blue wink and charming manner instantly winning her crushing, love-hungry teenage heart. Young, handsome and whispering promises of a new life—in the exotic country of France!—Rachel had followed Christian like a lost sheep toddling behind a shepherd.

"I will teach you things," he'd said. "I will take care of you. Love you. I will make you strong and powerful, irresistible to men."

And he had done so in a master/slave relationship. She had been conditioned to obey—an act as natural as breathing—for Christian Lazar, she had learned to love and trust and rely upon.

How long had she hated to love him?

Over a decade, her entire stay with Lazar, from what Rachel could figure now. Calendars and clocks weren't necessary, save a stopwatch to time jobs. When one quit celebrating birthdays the years began to mesh together, the passage of time becoming less significant. And without television to watch the news or a radio, she had slipped into a numb routine of simple existence. Certainly world events had been reported to her. The millennium, the reelection of the current American president and the tumultuous war in Iraq. She guessed she was about twenty-four or twenty-five, but couldn't be positive. Didn't matter.

Now, what she'd thought would be easy—escape, and starting over—was proving more difficult than a Samson 3000 glass-plated safe surrounded by razor wire and a pack of rottweilers.

Oh, the physical part was easy. She'd relocated to a Midwestern city, large enough to provide fodder for her profession but small enough that the criminal underworld would not ferret her out and recognize her for who she really was. The loft had been a choice find; it was secluded in a warehouse district, no close neighbors for blocks—save Oscar. And she was generating income. Grocery stores were still a challenge, but she found to write a list beforehand lessened the sensory overload. And buses, while she had been trained to be highly cognizant, taking in all faces, conversations, etc., now she could sit in a crowded bus and meditate.

The emotional part of adjusting to a new life though...that proved a struggle.

I should be at home here, she thought. Standing in the center of the two-thousand-square-foot loft, Rachel stared out the dusty window to the equally dull brick warehouse across the street. *Shouldn't I become...domestic? Want a family? Want to start a career?*

You have one.

No, a real career, one that does not involve illegal operations.

On the other hand, someone had to do it. Hands-on security investigation was an untapped market, to judge from the bemused grins Rachel had initially received. But after dozens of successful jobs she had proven her worth, and that she could be trusted. Finley's recommendation had been a coup; the Lalique was a major museum.

But was it right to employ criminal means for noncriminal gain? To donate to charity?

There were very few, she guessed, with the skills she had honed over the years. Why not use them to better herself? And to give back to those who really needed it.

That was the crux. Bettering herself. If only she could step beyond the past and become the person she knew lingered deep inside. For there in her depths lived a curious young woman, eager for life and all the adventure it offered. The life she'd been denied because she had only ever strived to comply.

Still, she was a survivor. Every day she survived.

Slowly she was becoming more relaxed. Accepting. And curious.

There's this guy I want you to meet.

A guy? To meet? As in, to possibly become a boyfriend? Sounded adventurous!

A boyfriend would be different than a Christian Lazar. Yes? Not all men were predatory, so possessive and power hungry. Oscar was proof men could be, well...just friends.

And gentle. Rachel still felt goose bumps whenever Oscar did something nice for her, such as bringing up her mail from the box below (always junk mail; she paid her utilities yearly). Kindness wasn't a practice she was overly familiar with.

And the missing experience of knowing a man as a loving partner intrigued her. She hadn't the first clue how to be someone's partner. Not unless it involved swinging a roundhouse kick into a thug's face and laying him flat for questioning. Or scaling a steel wall and cracking a high-security box to claim some sparklers for laydown. Or submitting to Christian's demands for sex. Unemotional, mechanical sex.

Prove to me your alliance. You are mine, Rachel Blu.

She didn't want to be any man's "mine" anymore.

She just wanted to be Rachel.

Thursday—1:00 a.m.

Full moon. Fog settled atop a fine mist. An alley cat had noticed a squirrel and now pawed at the base of a power pole half a block down the street. Set at the edge of a residential section, the Lalique building would have sparkled in the sixties. The Frank Lloyd Wright design is what kept the aging museum so popular.

A peripheral scan sighted a neon Hogshead bar sign that flickered a block north. A thick row of elms lined the back of the block, sheltering the residential houses from the business traffic, while the street side offered a lamp shop, a dry cleaner, a pancake house and two bars. Three blocks down, an aging Holiday Inn, painted a Miami turquoise, added a colorful touch to the neighborhood.

Perfect setup for a fly-in job. Hotel nearby? What thief could ask for more convenience?

Rachel crouched on the roof of the Lalique museum. Freshly tarred maybe a month earlier, she guessed, for the thick layer of loose pebble gravel that crunched with every careful step and the dull odor of asphalt.

Museums were unusual jobs. Jewelry stores could always be done at night—that's when ninety-five percent of thefts occurred. The other five percent was attributed to the idiotically bold smash-and-dash jobs. But museums, they were hit both at night and during business hours. Rachel planned to survey the building tomorrow during the lunch hour—the busiest time. She had balked when the curator had suggested she take an item to test security. There was no reason to, and what could she take besides the ruby? A painting? An Indian artifact? Too bulky, all of the choices. Together, they had eventually agreed it wasn't necessary.

There were two security cameras attached to the cinder-block roof walls. The first scanned the north half of the roof, the second, which she approached from the side, wasn't moving at all.

Strange.

Bending beside the camera, she assessed the mechanism. Oftentimes cameras were obscured by weather or bird droppings. This one was clean, well cared for, and yet, the lens did not rotate the expanse of the rooftop.

She leaned in closer to inspect the strange pink substance tucked beneath the black shell. Gum?

She poked it. Still pliable. Sugar-stickiness clung to her fingertip.

"What the..."

The only way the gum could be fresh— Heartbeats began to pound against Rachel's rib cage. Impossible.

A scan of the roof surface sighted in two central vents of curved tin; both looked in proper position. But there, what was that beyond the first vent? It was...a flat circular shape. A piece of roof? Cut out from its whole?

The click of a rappelling hook sounded. Rachel's heart

lunged to her throat. A black-capped head emerged from the circle cut into the roof, facing away from her.

Rachel stifled an oath.

Chapter 3

Thursday—1:04 a.m.

A prepared thief anticipated the presence of alley cats poking about the garbage, birds nesting in access vents, and the hazard of people living their lives nearby the sight of a planned heist. The arrival of the police was even planned for, but hopefully, never experienced. It was all part of the job.

But the presence of another thief had never before been on Rachel's radar.

This was her job. And a legitimate one, at that. What were the odds the very night she had chosen to work the museum another thief would be planning the same heist? Phenomenal, surely.

For a moment Rachel considered the possibility of a frame. Had the museum hired another thief? A backup plan? Or, a test to challenge her assessment? Made little sense. Mr. Posada was concerned for security for this showing. He'd hired her without brandishing a bemused smirk; Finley had convinced him her credentials were solid. She had for a moment considered the job too easy to gain. Less than three days following the Finley job? But Posada had spoke highly of Mr. Finley; he trusted his recommendation implicitly.

None of that explained this thief. And the fact, if indeed he was robbing the place, her job description just took a one-eighty. That realization kept her from turning a real one-eighty and getting the hell out of there.

Rachel was responsible for anything that was removed from this museum and she would be held accountable. Not the best way to advertise her credentials.

He'd cut a hole into the roof. Stunning, in a simplistic, low-tech sort of way. Made a heck of a lot more sense than snaking oneself through a ventilation system. But the noise of such an entry? Must have used a battery-operated handsaw, virtually silent, and small enough to be easily stowed.

None of her deductions mattered at the moment. There was only one truth—she couldn't let the thief get away.

As the man emerged from the hole, sneaking up onto the roof, a shadow figure with wide shoulders and spider-long legs, he turned to replace the circle cut out from the roof. He did not scan his surroundings. Why should he? He wouldn't expect another thief to be working his job.

Using the few moments of surprise she would have before he sighted her, Rachel scampered along the edge of the roof, moving behind his line of vision. But the loose pebbles crunched no matter how much stealth she tried to employ.

As he straightened, she lunged into his sight. A swing up of her leg connected the side of her foot with his jaw. He went down with a yelp and a spray of saliva. Pebbles shifted and caught his body.

Poised to strike, Rachel stood over his prone body, hands

loose but ready for a side slice to the neck. She hadn't knocked him out; his groan made that apparent. He lay facedown, his palms bracketing his head but his body tense. Anticipating and planning, likely.

She bet he hadn't planned on encountering her.

A small leather bag sat propped at the edge of the roof just touching the corner of Rachel's peripheral sight—tools, likely. He hadn't time to cross to the bag, so must have whatever it is he stole on his body. No doubt tucked in a waist belt or pocket. It had to be the ruby. It was the only jewel in the building. Paintings, Egyptian pottery and New Age sculpture made up the Lalique's offerings. To take any of those required a grab-and-run day job, or two-man night job to remove something so large.

As Rachel bent to grip the back of his collar, a hand shot out, spraying pebbles, and circled her ankle. A yank effectively defeated her balance. She hit the roof, one shoulder first, and rolled. Her jaw clacked with the hit, but the pebbles softened the landing, although they didn't prevent an unladylike grunt. She couldn't right herself, for the thief scrambled on top of her body.

A fist of black leather pulled back. It began ascent to her face. A jerk of her shoulder placed her head a whisper from a direct hit. Shoulders moving one way, her knee followed, and Rachel jammed her thigh up into the man's crotch. Not enough force to do more than make him growl.

A return fist cracked her nose. The sting of pain momentarily overwhelmed all. Strong bit of pride-buster. Her eyes watered. The taste of blood—vile and feral—always ignited the simmering anger just beneath her surface. Anger at an unjust life. Anger for her loss of freedom—

You *are* free.

Let's see if you can keep it that way.

An elbow knifed into the man's kidney brought him down

on top of Rachel's prone body. He landed on hands and knees. His hiss of pain sprayed a splatter of saliva across her forehead. Perspiration sweetened the misty night air.

As he drew back a fist to strike, Rachel cannonballed her head into his throat. Arms splayed, he flew away from her. She followed his plummet to his back. The predator pinned her prey. Two fingers to the sensitive nerve at the base of his neck forced out a hacking spurt. A drop of blood from her nose stained his cheek.

Let it not be said a kick to the crotch doesn't hurt a woman as much as it can hurt a man. Wincing at the crush of knee bone to her groin, Rachel faltered. Electric tingles shimmied in her loins—not a particularly sensuous feeling. That breach of her armor opened her to failure.

Two gloved hands shoved her shoulders to the roof. The jar of connection drew the pain up from her groin to spike in her neck. Again she lay prone.

"Qui vive?"

A Frenchman? Just her luck.

Literally lying in a pod of light cast from a street lamp—not wise, but presently she hadn't a vote—Rachel used the opportunity to memorize her opponent. He wore a black skullcap pulled down over his ears, but his beetled black brows and tight jaw revealed determination. A broken-but-healed nose separated two clear green eyes. Everything about his bone structure seemed urgent. He raised a fist over her.

"Cease!" Rachel hissed, conscious to keep her voice low.

Two stories down and half a block away a diner had let out the final bar rush. Though blocked by trees, surely somewhere in the residential area that backed this street a person might view their tussle. And the street lamp beaming like a stage prop made it easier for witnesses.

She thought of their antics being captured on camera. Well

out of range of the bubble-gummed device, but a clear capture for the other—no, the vent blocked view.

"Let me go."

"Je ferai," he said, and then switched to a choppy English. "I then will get up to walk away. You sit. Do not move, *oui?*"

"No deal. Whatever you've got is mine."

"Ah?" Moonlight brightened his cocky smirk and glittering eyes. A tilt of his head revealed a dark scrub of razor stubble along his fierce jaw. "You think to claim what I have marked as my own? Without the work? Is that how the American cat burglar succeeds? He waits to spy another thief then jumps in at the end? No effort but to assault the real winner?"

It wasn't the fairest of deals. But it wasn't as if there was a thieves' code of honor, either. He'd claimed whatever it was he held, fair and square. But life wasn't fair. And Rachel was playing by a new set of rules. Should he make off with one single shard of ruby, the only truth was that Rachel had been invited to rob the place, *without* removing an item. Should something go missing? She became the only suspect.

"You are a woman." No surprise in that declaration.

He released her shoulders, his hand gliding over her chest. The nylon jacket she wore—no bra underneath, just a thin cotton muscle shirt—allowed the tactile sensation to attack her skin. Her body prickled to a new alertness, distinctly sensitive, but not to stealth.

Rachel didn't move. Let him relax, forget his guard. The pressure of his fingers moving over her groin stirred up irritated disinterest, mixed with the tiniest bit of curiosity.

Here she lay on a rooftop under a beam of light, getting felt up by the enemy. Men were so primal. Their intentions diverted so easily.

"Maybe there is a bargain we can strike for trade, *oui?*"

Oh, she was good at striking bargains, especially when it

involved getting a man to strip off his clothes. Once naked, it was the cock not the brain giving the orders.

You don't need to use sex as a weapon anymore.

Logically, she knew that. But her newly forged, still-not-dry-so-don't-touch-the-paint reputation was at stake. As well, her freedom.

Use whatever works.

"Right here?" she coyly asked. Not the most conducive to seduction, or safe. Likely their actions were being recorded at this very moment, if not by the cameras, by curious eyes peering from the depths of suburbia.

"You agree to bargain?" he asked.

"You willing to offer the ruby for trade?"

He made the sound Frenchmen do, a sigh mixed with a *tcht*ing noise that signaled he thought himself the one in control and woe to the woman who deigned to fool him.

"You assume I have a ruby, *chérie*."

"There is nothing of greater value to be taken from the museum, or anything so small as to hold on your person. I cased it yesterday."

He pressed his palms to the roof at the sides of her shoulders and lowered himself over her. The seams of his jacket toggled one of her nipples. Cinnamon-tainted breath heated her lips. Not a handsome man, but neither ugly. Just…French. And on top. And so reeking of memories she'd rather erase.

"Give me one reason I should not knock you out and alert the police?" he said.

A purse of her lips invited his greedy attention. He lowered his head.

His diverted attention allowed her to grip his crotch. His pants were thin and stretchy enough that she secured a good hold on one or maybe both his testicles. A squeeze drew a gasped oath from his mouth. Not painful—just warning. She didn't want him to pass out. Yet.

"Give it your best shot," Rachel challenged. She held the ball, so to speak, in her court. Nothing would make her release the prize until she saw a ruby sparkling beneath the street lamp.

"Those are not—" he choked out a gasp "—the jewels you came for."

"No, they're not. Enough play. Let me see it."

"You've got it in hand, *salope*."

She hated being called a bitch—men resorted to the slur when their masculinity was challenged—so she torqued her grip. Just like picking locks. "The ruby?"

"Oooh, careful. *S'il vous plaît!* The rock…in my…trousers."

A discerning grope of her handful discovered the man's crotch proved more valuable than she could have guessed. Put a whole new spin on the phrase *family jewels*. What was it with men and their obsession with their sexual parts? The world reigned there. Or so she had learned from years of predatory seduction, both on her part and Christian's.

"So you see," he managed through a tight jaw, "we will have to tend that bargain after all."

He wanted to get into her pants?

"Very well."

The beginning of a surprised utterance from him was halted by Rachel's kiss. She connected so hard with the thief's mouth their teeth clacked. Call it lack of practice and the need to jump into the fray. Kissing was not her forte. But he didn't need persuasion. Forcing his tongue over her bottom lip, he occupied himself with whatever he could get from her. So he didn't notice her slip her hand down inside his pants—until she grazed her fingers along his hard cock. Much as she should be focused, the girth of the thing surprised and stoked her curiosity.

Sloppy kisses abandoned, he reached down and closed his

hand over hers. Green eyes sparkled with anticipation. His rigid muscle pulsed in her fingers.

"You are tricky," he singsonged.

A firm squeeze silenced him. Drawing that firm hold up and down the shaft, Rachel milked a few moans from him. A trick she'd accidentally learned one night when curious about Christian's body. Rarely had he allowed her the upper hand sexually, unless his lust had already been stoked. Now she smiled to herself as her hand slid to the base of the heavy rod and she touched something even harder. Success.

One beat of time clicked.

One deft movement. Rachel grasped the jewel (the real jewel).

The kiss broken—with a moan her thief looked down, bewildered at the switch.

She withdrew her hand and lifted a knee to his lust-tender testicles.

Counterattack—he slapped down a shield of his hand just as she should have connected.

The thief palmed her knee and twisted. The abrupt movement stung all the way up to her hip. Rolling into the pain to shorten the twisted muscle, with a shove of her shoulder Rachel knocked him off balance. Pebbles sprayed her face as the thief landed on his back.

Ruby in hand, she sprang up and into a run across the crunchy surface. She spat a pebble to the side. Five strides took her to the roof's edge.

"*Non!* You will not—"

Rachel pumped her arms—her toes pushed from the roof edge—and leaped. She knew there was a building close, a pottery shop sporting a wide brick chimney at the back of the store. Planning for any situation, on arrival she'd remarked the distance. A tricky leap—maybe eight feet.

While she was airborne, the mist-fogged night kissed away

the sticky residue of the thief's frantic kiss. As her trailing foot took to air, Rachel's heel twisted. He grasped for her, but couldn't secure hold. But the fleeting touch tugged, drawing her forward motion to an abrupt halt.

The notion she could thrust herself onto the roof worked mentally rather than physically. Much as she pushed out her chest, Rachel did not succeed in adding length to her jump. The roof was close. But not close enough to land.

Chapter 4

Bittersweet, the abrupt jar of landing. Tendrils of electrical pain spiked from fingers to arms and shoulders then vibrated straight down to toes. Fabric tore as Rachel's arms slid over the brick edging the roof. At the last moment she hooked her palms and caught herself from a free fall to a nasty death.

Legs swinging like a pendulum, she concentrated on keeping her hold. Inching her toes up the wall she tried to gain a better hold with the creepers. The dot-rubber treads were designed for ease when climbing. The ruby—still in hand, and precariously clutched between two fingers that should be better utilized to save her butt—challenged her stamina.

Her body stretched down the wall. Every muscle strained. Her pack was still slung over her left shoulder. Couldn't drop that; it held her credit card and pick tools.

Rachel pressed her cheek to rough brick. Not like this, she thought. I'm not ready to die.

Overhead, the thief took the same leap, but without the hindrance she'd been served. He plunged to a rolling landing on the rooftop where she clung.

Moments later a French-tinged voice bellowed down to her. "We have to stop meeting like this," he rasped.

A hand slapped around her right forearm.

"I don't need your help!" She did—but she wouldn't let him know it.

Rachel felt him manipulate the ruby from between her numbing fingers. The grip about her arm released. He'd no intention of helping.

The weight of her body began to drag her down. Left knee giving way from the sharp brick, her leg slid about half a foot. Her jersey pants tore, but she didn't sense a cut to her flesh. It was difficult for her toes to find purchase in the aging brick worn to the mortar. But for its smoothness it was still brick, and it cut into her palms. Her fingers were quickly losing sensation.

"Help" teased her tongue.

The noise of their antics should have stirred some interest from below. And it did. A curious *mew* carried up from the floor of the alley. Below, a cat sidled along the Lalique building. The mangy beast was the only thing that had taken an interest in what was going on high above. And keep it that way, Rachel thought. The last thing she needed was a gregarious drunk or even a helpful diner eager to call for the police.

She managed to tilt her head up. One hand gave free. She slapped it back to a shaky hold. Cuts on her palm pulsed with pain but she ignored the fiery ache.

The thief stood tall and made show of holding the ruby up to the street lamp. Bloodred glints fired in his eyes. Something about him was— Did she know this man? She had encountered many a thief in her short lifetime. Most wore disguises, hoods or face masks to camouflage scars from their deadly trade or outstanding facial features. It was his strongly boned face and the angle the light hit his nose that suddenly reminded her of a previous meeting. Brief. Christian had been there. He and this thief might have been buying or selling to one another. Rachel had stood behind Christian, his thug. A position that had once filled her with pride.

For her very life, she could not summon a name or fix an exact deal to this man.

Just as well. Who had the leisure to ask names? Familiarity would not soften her fall.

The thief tucked the ruby inside the front pocket of his pants. A vulgar pat and a triumphant smile. Then he pressed both palms to the brick ledge and leaned over her. "Didn't catch your name, *chérie*. I should have a name to give the coroner when they scrape your body off the pavement."

Saving her reply, Rachel let go with one hand. Pressing up with her toes she grabbed one of his arms, and then released hold to grab the other just above the elbow. Cinnamon breath *whoofed* into her face as he plunged forward, slamming into brick with his chest. He shook at her dangling body, but her bloody fingers remained glued to the hard muscles wrapping his arms.

"If I splatter," she hissed, "so will you."

"A challenge to separate the remains," he mocked.

"You Frenchmen are so romantic."

He tried one more shake. The width of his muscles did not make for an easy hold. Rachel surprised herself with her ability to cleave to the lightweight cloth that hugged his arms. But if she was going down, he must come with her. The ruby would be found on his body. Not hers.

"Put your feet to the wall," he demanded. "I will pull you up."

Should she accept help?

You can't dangle here all night. Much better than splattering.

Walking her way up the serrated brick wall, Rachel worked

with the thief to gain the roof. One final tug—she, still attached to him like a barnacle—and they landed on the loose pebbles in a lovers' embrace. The stench of tar assaulted her senses. The entire block must have been reroofed.

For a moment Rachel lay there atop the length of the man's heaving form. All hard muscles, flexing and tightening; a physical weapon, this man. Certainly a challenge. They could exchange punches and roll about on the rooftops the entire night without coming to accord. But there were ways to overcome a man bigger and bulkier than she.

Rachel released her iron grip on his forearms and spread her hands in preparation to pounce, but neither made a move. Her muscles were stretched, and her usually solid nerves were shaken. Exhaustion tapped at her brain. She hoped he was feeling the same—not sure, just a bit off his game. In her next thought, she reminded herself to never allow the enemy to see her weakness.

Pushing away from his huffing breaths, she squatted back on her haunches. Their separation allowed him to scramble backward, virtually swimming through pebbles. With a protective slap over his pant pocket, he made a mocking kissing noise, defiant even with Rachel's blood dribbling across his cheek.

"You're not shucking me until that ruby is mine," she said.

"So sorry. I do not have another ticket."

"Ticket? You leaving the country?" Of course he was. And France was her first guess. "You can't sell what you don't have."

"You can grope my jewels all you like, *salope,* you're not going to win this one."

"Then I guess I'll have to do some more damage."

Lunging forward, she punched him, hooking a fist up under his right jaw. A return slap to the left side of his face drew blood from his nose.

"You like to slap your men around before you do them?" He gave a gargly laugh.

Rachel shoved his chest. He settled onto the roof, submissive, but still grinning.

"You think you're going to get lucky, asshole?"

"I know it. The only way you'll ever lay your hands on the ruby is to make a trade."

He considered having sex with her fair trade for a two-million-dollar jewel? This guy was easy.

A slide of his hand over his head pushed the knitted skullcap to the roof. A crop of short black curls eased into their springy design. Attractive—in a thug sort of way.

"You are thinking about it?" he said. "What is there to consider? It is not every day I find myself pinned to a roof by a female intent on groping my privates. Take a chance, *oui?* You might gain a ruby."

The rush of the moment fired all parts of her that wanted more. More, as in a high. A release. Contact with a stranger promised the prize. You've got to sweat for it, give blood.

What had she to lose?

Your freedom.

"You want a deal?" Rachel stood and held out her hand to assist him up. "Where are you staying?"

"Not far. At a blue hotel."

Blue? Just down the street, then.

Whimsical in his bouncing steps, he worked with a kinetic energy, dancing in place. "So, here is the deal."

Braced to hear a ridiculous offer, Rachel wasn't prepared to react to the high kick that connected with her jaw. Her head snapped back. Blackness killed her senses.

Chapter 5

Thursday—1:21 a.m.

Slapping a palm onto the brick ledge, Rachel levered her body up to kneel and peered down onto the street. She scanned the alley—no sign of the thief, just the twitching white tail of the waiting cat. Her own personal mascot?

With a furious shake of her head, she chased away the woozy remnants of that remarkable kick. Must have knocked her out for a few seconds but no more.

He couldn't have gotten far. She knew how far, because he'd made the mistake of telling her he was staying in a blue hotel. Only one option, unless there was another turquoise monstrosity in the vicinity.

Creeping over to the iron access ladder curled over the roof edge opposite from where she had jumped, she stood, and in that moment, sighted the black shadow of her prey strolling casually down the street. A couple leaving the all-night pancake house, their hands entwined, parted to allow him between them. He did a scan, left to right, and when she saw his shoulders twist, Rachel ducked.

Breathing three counts, she then scrambled down the ladder, skipped down the alley between the pottery shop and the restaurant and peered around the corner.

He was headed toward the Holiday Inn. Cheeky of him, staying so close to the scene of the crime. If the police got whiff of the theft this night and began investigating, the hotel would likely be their first target. Doubtful. No interior alarms had been tripped, or she would not have made the roof without an entire posse of patrol cars rounding up below. That meant the security cameras were unmonitored. Unless the thief had dismantled them. Surprising. After touring the facility, she had guessed the Lalique's security would be formidable.

And she was still stunned about the hole cut into the roof. Bold fellow. Almost as bold as a daylight smash-and-dash, but not as idiotic. His mistake had been in letting down his guard.

Hell, what was she thinking? It wasn't as though *she* held the ruby right now. Her nameless thief, for all he knew, had been ludicrously successful tonight.

Insinuating herself onto the main street, she remained wary. The thief had already stepped through the hotel door, but she wasn't yet safe from his notice. A couple walked in her direction with hands joined, and but ten feet behind them, a man wobbled drunkenly.

Gripping the binder at the back of her head, Rachel tugged it from her ponytail and gave a shake to disperse her hair. Her dark attire was designed to make her blend, segue into the night, but the fact she was dressed neck to toe in black and there was not a crowd to hide her would make an easy mark for the thief. As well, her bloody hands would draw attention.

Thinking to give him time if he needed to check in, she stepped into the doorway of a closed camera shop and shrugged a hand down her arm. Her pack was still slung over her shoulders—she hadn't lost a thing. Save the ruby.

And some pride.

The couple passed her by, both glancing at her, then moving on.

Rachel touched her jaw. It stung, but nothing felt broken, nor did any of her teeth wobble. The tear in her pants revealed her knobby knee but no blood, though the flesh was serrated and red. Blood slickened her hands. There were at least two shallow cuts on each palm, but thankfully not on her fingertips. Scars would make touch-cracking all the more difficult.

Pressing her palms to her thighs to soak away the blood, she chanced a look toward the hotel. Street lighting shone through the plate-glass windows. The lobby clerk sat behind his desk, chin in hand. Time to make her move.

1:37 a.m.

"That handsome man who just walked in?" Holding her pack clasped behind her back, more to avoid showing the blood on her hands than the physical effect it had of pushing up her chest—but she could work with that, too—Rachel smiled her warmest at the droopy-eyed clerk. "If I could get the room above him?"

"There's an empty one right next to his," the clerk offered with a cursory glance over her body. Heavy black bangs fenced his bloodshot eyes.

Rachel stepped forward and shook her head, drawing him back to her eyes. "Above," she murmured, and touched his hand briefly before slipping her fingers through the tips of her hair.

How he managed to reach back for the key and slide it onto the counter without removing his eyes from hers was remarkable, and laughable. Stifling an inappropriate giggle, Rachel observed as he slid her credit card—again, all eyes on her—and handed her the receipt to sign.

"Thanks, sweetie." Sashaying toward the stairway, she didn't lose the swing to her hips until she'd rounded the corner.

Then she dashed for the stairway door and jogged up three flights. Room 317, directly above 217. Sliding the key card through the electronic lock, she entered the humid room, tossed her pack and the key card to the bed, and crossed the darkness to the patio door. It glided noiselessly open and she stepped out, but paused when she heard a voice below.

"Tomorrow, *oui*. It'll have to be late," the voice spoke in French, but Rachel was fluent, even with a few of the provincial dialects. He stood on the deck below her.

She crouched and snuck forward on her hands and knees, being careful, should any of the boards creak. The deck was fashioned from woodlike plastic. Should be safe for no noise.

"My flight doesn't leave until 7:00 a.m. We meet at 9:00 p.m. at number 17 behind the Trocadéro? *Très bien. Oui,* I have it. *Merde!* Hmm? *N'importe.* The window is stuck and the air-conditioning is out of order. What? Of course I know how to operate it!"

Pressing her body flat to the deck, Rachel tried to see through the fake boards but they were tightly placed. She thought to poke her head between the iron railing and peer over the edge, but that would be too risky. She could hear just fine.

The Trocadéro? She knew where that was. In Paris.

A surge of nervous anticipation flooded her breast, making her gasp as if being smothered. Rachel hated Paris. Too many bad memories there. To return would be like stepping naked onto a stage surrounded by voyeurs. So exposed and unsure.

It was imperative the thief not leave the States with the ruby. She did not favor occupying a jail cell for the rest of her life.

"Eh? Nothing I could not handle. Finally I have the ruby in hand. No one will take it away ever again. *Au revoir.*"

The phone clicked off, but Rachel didn't sense the thief walked back inside. The creak of iron clued her he stood right below her, hands on the railing, most likely looking over the dimly lit pool that paralleled the back of the hotel.

Paris? Not if she had any say.

Tracing the inside of her mouth with her tongue, Rachel tasted remnants of their brutal kiss. In that moment adrenaline had ruled. *Do whatever is required to win.* Even offer sex.

He'd decided sex was no deal. Formidable, the man. But he wasn't yet free.

"Shitty air-conditioning."

She heard him kick the base of the iron railing, setting the whole to a rattle. Two footsteps and then nothing; he'd stepped inside. The glide of the patio door did not come to a suctioning close. Had he left the door open to let in the breeze? She glanced at the door to her room, it was fit with a slide-lock screen door. Perfect for sleeping if one wanted to let in a humid summer breeze for lack of air-conditioning.

Could her luck get any better?

Yes, it could. This night could have never happened. She could be home by now, writing up notes on the security job in preparation to report to Posada tomorrow morning. Oh yes, her luck could be a hell of a lot better.

Rachel checked her watch. One forty-five. If his flight left at seven in the morning, he'd have but a few hours to sleep. Why sleep, when he had an eight-hour flight to do so?

Why then the hotel room? He could have easily stashed his gear in an airport locker and waited out the flight there.

Something did not figure right.

Of course, he could have arrived early, and had needed a place to stash his tools. What had he done with the saw? Amateurs often gave themselves so much extra time. Rachel had learned to time her heists to the second. Once she'd flown to Germany, landed, half an hour later she had entered the Swaropski warehouse—a chicken factory in disguise. Two hours later she sat nervously sweating on a return flight to Paris.

Was he an amateur? Physical skills aside the hole in the roof would say yes.

Prepared to wait it out, Rachel pushed up and sat in the open doorway, one foot inside on the matted shag carpet of a color indefinable in the darkness, the other outside on the fake wood decking.

Best bet would find him showering then catching a few winks. Worst would see her on a flight to Paris at dawn.

The clock just ticked 1:58 when Rachel heard the first rumbling snore from below. Sleeping already? He hadn't showered.

Bending to slide out onto the deck, she flattened her body on the deck floor and pressed the side of her head against the railing. Catlike movements came easily after years of tai chi and yoga.

She listened. If she didn't know differently, she could make a case for a hibernating bear taking refuge in this Holiday Inn. Her mark was definitely asleep.

A shake of the iron railing moved it a good quarter of an inch back and forth. Not a secure hold. Inspecting the steel hex-bolts securing the railing to the deck planks, she decided the base of the railing would hold for the few moments she would need it.

The fall was two and a half stories—she'd most likely snap her neck. The pool was too far to leap for a wet landing.

But she wasn't about to fall.

Retrieving her pack from the bed, Rachel slid her arms through the canvas straps. She swung a leg over the railing, put herself on the opposite side and balanced to hold her position, rather than clinging to the loose rail. Envisioning the jump, she bent, and kicked out, moving her grip down the iron railing to the base at the same time. While she dangled freely, her sight was blocked by the floor of her deck. She swung her legs forward and neatly landed at the center of the second-floor deck in a crouch.

Crouched tight and hands spread for balance, she held there for a few moments. The screen door was closed, but the glass door was not. No air-conditioning. One reason to appreciate the humidity. The snoring continued.

Common folk would reason a second-floor room would deter theft and would see no harm in leaving a door open. But one in the know doing such? That a thief would leave himself so open!

Slipping her credit card from her pack, she jimmied the screen-door lock. Checking first for a portable laser that might have been placed at the base of the wall, she spied not a single beam. Pausing, half in, half out, she surveyed the semi-moonlit room. The bed sat three steps to the right. The wall immediately to her left held the television, a writing desk and the requisite lamp screwed onto the desk to prevent theft. Beyond the bed an expanse about six feet square was open. The bathroom door stood down a short hall opposite a long sliding-door closet.

Crouching, Rachel crawled by the bed. A snort alerted her. Like a cat arching its back to danger, she stiffened and peered over the end of the bed. She spied a cap of curly hair. Right there, but eight inches from her face. The scent of cinnamon teased her nostrils. His feet were on the pillows?

Wondering if her pounding heartbeats could be heard, she reasoned such a feat would be impossible over the incessant snores. And where there was snoring, there was a certain safety.

Relaxing, she worked her shoulders, easing at the strained muscles in the center of her back. Blowing out a breath, she crawled forward. She was accustomed to working vacant sites. Very rarely were there others—security or occupants—in the building.

So long as he snored, she was safe. And should he stop? She'd make a quick escape before he could summon his senses.

One sign of a professional thief is they never traveled with any more than a single bag. Just the necessary, yet inconspicuous, tools—nothing to wait for in customs. The bag in question sat against the far wall, dimly spotlighted by the stream of moonlight the patio door cast in her wake. So maybe he wasn't an amateur.

Kneeling over the bag and twisting her body so she faced the bed, Rachel slipped a hand inside the unzipped canvas pack. Rope and clamps, no other tool that could be ruled questionable by airport security, or deemed part of a thief's arsenal. He must have dumped the saw.

There…a small velvet pouch.

The shape of the jewel fit inside her palm. It wasn't large, about the size of a walnut in shell.

Standing, Rachel stepped into the hall facing the closet door and weighed the velvet bag in her palm. Better check before leaving; it could be a switch. Always suspect the worst; think like a criminal.

Even if you no longer are one?

You bet.

And the only way to keep it that way was to get this jewel back to the museum. They'd have her head for the hole in the roof. She performed unobtrusive security checks. No cutting, no holes, no drilling through safes. If she determined a safe was untouchable by hand, she would take a few moments to work the drill scenario, so she could report on that. But never did she damage anything beyond a snipped security wire.

The ruby fell into her cut palm, a thick cold lump. Even in the darkness she knew she held a treasure.

"That is not yours, *salope*."

Chapter 6

The hands clamped about her neck were the first clue she'd lost track of the snoring.

Dropping the velvet bag and ruby, Rachel, instead of trying to flip her attacker over her head, lifted her feet, kicked the wall and pushed them both backward to the floor. Their hard landing released the chokehold. She flipped her hips, straddling the man on the floor. A hand to each shoulder pinned him. His head conked the wooden bed frame.

"You are persistent," he hissed. "But you have not won a single thing."

When he made to lift a knee, she stretched out a leg, not effectively pinning him but delaying his move.

"I don't want this fight," she warned.

In the moonlit grayness she suddenly realized he wore very little. Just underwear, the boxer-briefs sort that revealed every bulge—said bulge obvious against her thigh. Jumping a prowler gave the man a hard-on?

Momentarily releasing him, she then shoved him hard, fitting her forearm against his neck. The sharp dodge of his Adam's apple gouged her arm.

He smelled like strong soap, likely the hotel's offering. It wasn't offensive. Nor was his breath, still cinnamon and huffing against her face.

"I want what I came for," she said, "then I'll leave you to get back to your beauty sleep."

"The ruby is mine." He shifted to sit up a little higher, but didn't touch her with his hands. They remained at his shoulders, splayed out but far from surrender. "Mine. I took it. I cut into the roof. I disabled the security. I cracked the safe. I—"

"I don't care if you dug it up from the mine and cut it yourself, I am responsible for it."

"Responsible?" A tilt of his head caught the moonlight shining through the patio door on the corner of his smirk. "You say so?"

She wasn't about to explain. Nor hold a conversation.

But three feet behind her lay the ruby. To grab it and run would see her struggling with him before she could reach the front door. And to rush out the patio door promised a death drop. A pool-landing trajectory would be impossible. A fight could see her the victor, but then again, she had tested this guy's mettle once, and he was no wimp.

Time to try a different approach. One that always saw her mark condescending to her seductive demands.

Sidling up onto his lap, Rachel felt the heavy weight of his erection fit against her groin. She pressed both hands on the mattress beside his head and leaned close enough to kiss. "Let's see if we can interest you in something a little…prettier."

He lifted his face, nudging his nose aside hers, a soft, coaxing movement that tested her determination. "The only pretty thing in this room," he cooed "is the ruby."

What was the French word for bastard?

"Yes, but..." Stubborn, Rachel reached down and stroked him through the thin cotton briefs. "...can it satisfy?"

He chuckled low and greedily. One of his hands slid to the small of her back. He pressed her hips to his, tilting her breasts to his chin level. He nuzzled into her bosom, biting teasingly at the thin jacket she wore. Her nipples quickly responded. "You did mention a deal earlier."

"I don't do deals. Obviously—" she moved her jaw against the minute reminder of pain from his unexpected kick "—you don't either. You change your mind?"

"Maybe."

"All right then."

"So..." His breath played across her nipples; they tightened mutinously. "You are going to fuck me and make off with the jewel while I am in the throes of passion?"

He wasn't, for one moment, going to make this easy.

"About like that."

His throaty laughter upped the challenge. "You are welcome to try."

Try? Oh, she'd do more than try. Give her five minutes and the man would be on his knees whimpering for more, more, and more.

He pulled the zipper on her jacket down and slid his hand over her breast, clutching and growling satisfaction. She wore no bra tonight; she didn't like the added weight when on a job; the muscle shirt was thin as a layer of skin.

Tugging the stretchy cotton low, he kissed her breast and laved his tongue across her nipple, setting her adrenaline-filled blood to a different kind of race. Rachel had conditioned herself to shrug off the pleasant sensations of sex. Actually, Christian's maniacal training had done it for her. Under Christian's direction, the sexual act was kept to a businesslike transaction with frequent slaps to warn and dissuade a creeping pleasure. A woman could only be denied orgasm so many times during sex before her desires deadened. But his methods had worked, allowing her to concentrate on the job and not the menacing complications of foreplay. The man—rather, her mark—was the only one allowed to slip into the clutches of bliss. Once engaged in such a reel? The jewel could be easily palmed.

Sex was a game Rachel never lost.

She would let him take the lead until she could read him, pinpoint his idiosyncrasies, determine if there was a specific move she could make to render him senseless to any covert moves toward the ruby. Right now, she had to do but two things. Allow him to think she was focused on his pleasure, and…focus on the location of the ruby. Against the wall on the floor, her very life sat waiting for her to make the right move.

Shrugging off her jacket, she tossed it back, hoping to land it near the ruby.

"I saw that," he singsonged.

"Tell me—" Standing and drawing the muscle shirt over her head, she coaxed him up and onto the bed. Her flesh prickled in the sultry air. Leaning over his legs, she moved her head slowly up the length, from knee to cock, breathing heavily upon his erection. "You like this?"

"You have to get a firm grip on my jewels, *chérie*. Show me you mean business."

"Soon enough. Let's play first. Come here." Moving onto her side, she stretched out a leg and thrust back her arm, lifting her breasts high, which lured him like a puppy to kibble.

The thief climbed on top of her and pressed his groin against hers. There was plenty to deal with.

Her feet hitting the wooden headboard, Rachel pushed her body up, moving her head closer to the bed's edge. Perfect view of her target. But if she didn't pay attention, her mark would soon grow bored.

So she slid her hand inside his briefs and inched down the clingy cotton until she gripped his derriere and gave it a promising squeeze. The strong soap smell segued to a thick perfume of cinnamon and lust. Like most men, he didn't say much once engaged in activity with a half-naked woman. Fine with her. Let him focus completely on the task; should keep his brain occupied.

Arching her back at the sensation of a bite to her nipple, she ground her hips against his.

"*Jésu*, you want more than the ruby?"

Still thinking about the jewel, the prick. "I want this." A firm squeeze of his cock milked a moan from him.

"You are in so much of a rush. You don't know how to play this game properly. What of you, *chérie?* Let's get you more comfortable."

Her pants were tugged down with a few frantic pulls. Roaming her stomach with kisses and nips, he murmured a protesting grunt as Rachel seesawed her legs to kick off her shoes and pants. The clothing landed on the side of the bed next to her jacket. Everything must remain close at hand.

"Is it getting hot in here?" she teased.

"No air," he muttered. "This foreign climate is hideous."

Talking about the weather? Oh, but she had her work cut out for her.

"You don't seem very interested. Am I not enough for you?"

"We shall see soon enough."

She cried out as he slipped a finger into her mons. He announced his delight with a nonsyllabic growl. Wet already, she startled herself that she'd so easily become ready for this stranger. Since when did a few kisses to her breasts loosen her inhibitions? She was not attracted to this foulmouthed idiot. His obvious burglary skills impressed, and the novelty of cutting through the roof intrigued, but he, well, the man was not physically attractive. No man called her a bitch and summoned an ounce of respect.

Pressing her fingers against his scalp—ready to shove him off her—Rachel paused. Use the aversion. Triumph over his simple male lust by turning his idiocy back on him.

Her fingers stroked down the back of his skull and traced his neck, thick with strain. Muscles glided under her searching fingertips and they topped his buttocks and slid lower. His thighs tensed. Groans—*I am pleased*—filled her ear. And there, his cock was thick and hard; he would fill her completely.

To feel a hard column of man inside of her, captured, a slave to her discretions, always ratcheted up the power scale. For once inside a woman, all men were at their weakest. They were home, bathed in such heady sensations Rachel could not fathom the force. She could bring him to climax. Just a simple squeeze of her muscles would reduce him to mumbling fits.

A shock of sensation alerted. Rachel forgot her train of thought. A firm touch high at the apex of her groin slipped over the usually covert bit of herself that always eluded coaxing. *You're one of those nonorgasmic women,* Christian had once murmured. *So difficult to get off. So I will not bother.*

This man did take the time to bother.

He played her slowly. One stroke firm and lingering, followed by another, lighter and faster. He glided like a skilled skater marking out a design on the icy borders of her control. Arching her back to move into the shudder rippling across her flesh, Rachel realized she moaned softly. The sound wasn't a farce, orchestrated to urge on her mark—it was an involuntary moan.

You're not supposed to do that! Don't moan unless it is planned.

Concentrate. You are the aggressor...

Where was it? His cock. There was her power. She needed to get it in hand.

The man's body, sinuous and ripped with muscles, fit against her lithe but equally muscular curves. Hot lips suckled at her nipples while his finger worked a stunning mastery to her libido. His manipulations were deft, sure, like a seasoned box cracker owning the safe with but a few expert moves.

Rachel turned her head to look for— An expert stroke coiled her muscles and she pressed her head deep into the nubby blanket. She had seen it. The ruby was there. By the wall. It wasn't going to walk away— "Oh!"

Suddenly aware she balanced on the verge of orgasm, Rachel lifted her head. Dark curls hovered above her stomach. An ear pressed to the safe door? She clawed her fingers into the man's curly hair—she didn't even have his name. He must have a name?

Names complicate.

Where's the... What was she doing here? Having sex with a stranger? Why?

Just knock him out and run! An easy decision. She was skilled, could lay a man flat with a kick to the jaw or a fist to the solar plexus.

He's breached your security, whispered somewhere in the depths of her straying thoughts.

His mouth, it wasn't where it should be, sliding lower—closer to danger. Pulling, she directed his tongue to stay at her nipple. Yes, deflect his concentration. This safe would not be cracked!

Relentless, he dizzied her head with another expert stroke to her wet depths. Clinging, Rachel clenched her stomach muscles. Fight it. Don't give up the prize. Orgasm is a reward. You can't have it. You are working!

You don't deserve such a reward, Rachel Blu.

That voice in her head. It wouldn't go away. But for once she was thankful. It worked to momentarily redirect her thoughts. The ruby. Her life—

But the steady strokes easing in and out of her body were even more persistent.

Don't give them the upper hand. *You don't want them to control you.* Use their lust.

Yes. I am in control. He's just playing. She had him in hand. If only…

Wanting to push this nameless man away, to flee to a sexless safety, a more desperate part of her wanted to release.

And…she did.

"*Oui*, that's good, *chérie*," he cooed in her ear. "Give it all to me. Now this is the way to play the game."

Bucking against his hard chest, Rachel clung to his forearms with tearing nails. Safe cracked. Offer up the booty. The ride was short, but it suffused her system with a soft, resonant warmth and put a strange smile to her face.

He'd dizzied her. Stolen something he'd no right to take. A true thief—of her soul?

"Another?" he whispered.

Sensing his smile, she panted to take in air, to clear her thoughts. Speech was impossible. *Just breathe. Calm your center. Don't allow the eddying remnants of orgasm to smear your concentration.*

"No," she gasped. A push to his chest made him chuckle, followed by an even more intense focus on her aching body. So sweet this ache. An elusive quest mastered. Impossible if he thought she could come again so quickly. She would not.

Or…could she?

Rachel clutched the bedsheets and pulled as her shoulders lifted from the bed and another wave overtook her.

Protests turned to gasps of "yes."

So softly she begged for another.

So softly the third orgasm slid through her body, coaxed by a gentle stroke, light as a feather.

So softly, she drifted to sleep.

Chapter 7

Friday—6:25 a.m.

An unladylike snort woke Rachel from a deep sleep. She startled upright on the bed, stretching her hands across the rumpled sheets. Hazy sunlight poured across her bare legs. The room smelled humid, like a long shower spent slicking her skin with cinnamon soap. The taint of grass leaked through the patio screen door. The obnoxious noise of a lawn mower clued her it must be day.

Day?

"No." Instantly aware, she slapped the bed. No male body lying at her side. The sheets were cool. "Gone?"

Feeling like a shell-shocked toddler sitting abandoned at the edge of a bombed village, Rachel stared at the empty side of the bed. The pillow was still indented from a head.

Squinting and focusing, she scanned the small room.

Alone. She listened for the shower, noise, any clue he was still here. While her hopes stretched for the impossible, she knew better. He was gone.

"To Paris."

Wrestling with the sheets tangled between her legs, she scrambled out of bed. No ruby sitting on the floor by the wall. He'd left her pack, half-open, the contents spilled. Her credit card—the only identifying piece of information she had on her—lay on top.

He hadn't taken it? Great, but now he knew her name. Albeit, a false name.

A quick check of the bathroom found it empty. The toilet seat was up. Thinning white towels were lumped on the floor in soggy hills.

What was that? Something had been smeared on the mirror. Rachel flicked the light switch and read the French words scrawled in soap. *Faites profile bas.*

"Lie low?"

What could he—she hadn't any reason to—well, she did. But she wasn't about to lie low!

Overwhelmed by a sudden lurch in her gut, Rachel pressed her back to the door frame. She closed her eyes and opened her mouth to swear—but didn't. That she had allowed the man to get the better of her— Three orgasms? Unbelievable. Amazing, and absolutely the most incredible sexual experience. Ever.

But so devastating to her future.

Scrambling for the phone next to the bed, she punched the button for the front desk.

A cheery female voice answered, "Hello? Front desk."

Where was her watch? She never removed it. It lay on the floor near her pack.

"Can you tell me what time it is?"

"Er...it's 6:30 a.m., ma'am."

Rachel recalled the thief saying his flight to Paris left at seven. No time to make it to the airport for that flight; the security check alone would eat up half an hour. "Can you connect me to the airport?"

"Which one?"

There was more than one? Right. She knew that. "I don't know. The big one."

"One moment."

Gather your wits, woman! "Wait! Can you also call me a cab? I'll be down in five minutes."

"Certainly, ma'am. Hold, please."

Ma'am. Wasn't that what polite children called people older than the dirt beneath their toenails?

Why was she allowing a simple courtesy to upset her?

Pacing the length of the bed, phone to ear, Rachel looked out the patio door and scanned the grounds. The lawn mower wasn't to be seen. Must have been the rumble of traffic or something else. The splash of water from below clued her someone indulged in an early-morning swim.

Heartbeats rapping in her throat, a clear summation of what had happened came to her.

The thief was gone. With the Rousseau ruby.

She had failed. A first. And likely, the last if she allowed herself one moment to feel deficient.

She rubbed a palm up her arm, then, realizing she stood naked in the doorway, stepped back and settled onto the corner of the bed. Searching every inch of the room, her eyes did not land on a ruby sparkler. The dresser and bed met the floor, and there was no room for anything to slip behind either of the pieces.

You let him get away.

Strange to be shivering, for it wasn't cold. Hot already even.

Christ, she was shivering because she was shaken. This had never happened before.

The orgasms or the dupe, girlfriend?

"Both," she muttered. With a frantic plunge to the floor and a twist this way and that, she realized another defeat. "The bastard took my clothes."

Thinking to slam the phone receiver against the wall, she stopped just before causing damage. Shrugging her fingers through her hair, she caught her forehead and blew out a tremendous breath. "This is not happening."

Six-thirty. Friday morning. Within hours the Lalique would begin to fill with employees. They would certainly notice a hole in the roof. Unless there was a subceiling. She prayed for that small mercy. Even if it wasn't scheduled for display until Tuesday, the missing ruby would surely be discovered. Inventory must be taken. If she was lucky, and the ineptness quotient of the museum staff was high, she might have the entire morning before anything suspect was noticed.

Unlikely.

Which meant...

"I don't have time to dash off to Paris!"

"Ma'am?"

"Yes?"

"I'll transfer you. Hello?"

"Is this the airline? I'd like to book a flight to Paris."

Minutes later, her charge card had been approved. A second flight to Paris departed at 9:00 a.m. Two hours later than the thief's flight, but the early flight had a layover in Philadelphia, and hers was in New York, which would prove much shorter. She would arrive in Paris approximately forty-five minutes after he did. Worked for her.

It would *have* to work.

Now, what to do about clothes?

Stomping into the bathroom, Rachel sloshed some water over her face. Lie low. It was an eerie message. The thief could have no concern for her well-being. Did he intend to place a hit on her? Didn't make sense; as far as he was concerned, he'd won. Unless he suspected she would follow him?

She shook her head at her reflection. "Put all the obstacles you want in my path, I'm not backing away."

Even if the first obstacle had been a night of incredible sex. Rachel glanced away from her guilty reflection.

There was a pile of wet towels on the floor. He'd showered and she hadn't woken? Risky move on his part. She bet he was wallowing in his ability to reduce her to a simpering pile of mush with a mere few strokes of his finger.

"Cocky French bastard."

She stomped out to the main room and tugged off the top sheet from the bed and began to toga it around her body. She wasn't about to put into thought what she was feeling. That he'd been so damn good. Never had she experienced so much sexual pleasure, and with such ease. It was as if he'd known her body, had studied the map beforehand, and had walked straight to the treasure, avoiding the snaking red line that always led to the X, but had never quite got her there before.

Wise of Christian when he'd denied her orgasm to keep her at the top of her game. While she'd always wondered what she was missing, she knew it was for the best. For look what a few moments of pleasure had done to her.

Those moments just might be the lock to her jail cell.

Hooking her pack over a shoulder, Rachel yanked up the tail of her toga and strode out from the room and down to the lobby. She'd already given her credit-card number—and had left her key on the bed of her third-floor room—so she wasn't required to check out.

"Hey! Ma'am?" A female clerk called to her, but Rachel didn't slow as she spied the yellow taxi pull up outside the front doors. "Isn't that— You can't take that sheet with you!"

"Charge it to room 317!" she yelled back. And, nearly toppling a waiter with silver tray in hand, she dodged, but swiveled back. A cinnamon roll with thick frosting called to her. Grabbing it and taking a bite, Rachel murmured as she stepped outside, "Charge this to the room as well!"

The taxi driver did a double take as she slid into the back seat.

Rachel wasn't in the mood. "Drive," she said, and took another chomp of the roll. Cinnamon? How utterly ironic.

The cab rolled off, and after a few nervous glances from the cabbie, she gave him the address to her home. Once there, she asked him to wait.

His effusive nod and greedy smile told her he wasn't going anywhere. He intended to stick around to see what happened next.

Friday—7:10 a.m.

Rachel tugged up her makeshift toga and took the metal stairs two at a time to the top level of the warehouse. An empty beer bottle sat a lone sentry at the top stair. Had someone been partying? Ah! She'd completely forgotten Oscar's party.

Actually, she hadn't forgotten, but had known her plans would not coincide, and so had slipped from the warehouse with the intention to plead business to Oscar today. With luck, she wouldn't even see him—

"Rachel?"

The clanging stairs always gave her away. He crossed the hall and followed her into her loft.

"Oscar, I'm sorry…" She let her words hang as she traversed the hardwood floor, flinging her pack to the bed.

"I think you've got your signals crossed," he said, strolling, hands in loose flannel pant pockets, to the center of the loft. "It wasn't a toga party."

"I had…an appointment last night."

"I see. With a Roman emperor?"

She shot him a confused glance.

"Much as I'm disappointed I wasn't able to introduce you to Ryan, at least your *appointment* was with a man."

Shedding the sheet, she tramped over to the open closet that lined the outer wall of the bathroom, the only enclosed room in the loft. The loft was blissfully cool and goose bumps surfaced on her arms. "Why would you assume I was with a man?"

Did she bear the thief's mark? His scent? Had the bastard put a hickey somewhere on her body?

"Well—mother of mercy! Rachel! You're—"

"Oh, come on, Oscar." She sorted through the clothes rack and selected a minidress with a black-and-white houndstooth design and wide black leather hip belt. It zipped up the back, and a few decorative buttons closed the front to either discreet or sexy. "You've seen naked women before."

He kept his distance standing in the center of the loft, but—well, it was a wide-open loft—so he couldn't help but watch her dress. She could have slipped inside the bathroom to dress, but there was no time for discretion.

"Yes, many a naked female body," he finally said. "Christ, a guy learns new things about you every day."

"Such as?"

"You're not a prude. That's a nice tattoo."

Her back to him, Rachel pulled the dress up her legs and slipped her arms in through the cap sleeves. "Haven't seen it."

"What?" he literally shrieked. He took a few cautious paces toward the bed. "You've got a tattoo the size of a baby octopus on your back—in blackest of black ink—and you've never seen it? Why would you get something like that and not look at it?"

"It's a long story. I just...never had any interest in looking at it."

"Uh-huh."

Stretching an arm around her back, she gestured at the unreachable zipper. A twist of her head over her shoulder saw he stood there, jaw open, utterly stunned.

"Could you help me?" She pulled aside her hair. When he didn't move, she tucked another look at him. "I'm in a hurry, Oscar. The cab is waiting."

"A cab? Sure." He touched her at the base of her spine where the zipper started, but she didn't hear any zipping.

She knew the tattoo was huge and black and snaking this way and that in a tribal design Christian had selected—no, he'd *designed* the monstrosity. At the time she'd been eager to please him, to prove her love to him by inking her body. A celebration ritual, he'd deemed her inking. She had mastered the skills he'd taught her. She had become a phenomenal instrument. *A machine.* And because it was he who had made her, he wanted to sign his work.

"That's weird."

"What? Oscar." She shrugged a shoulder, hinting for him to zip. "I'm in a hurry."

"Yeah, okay. It's just, the middle of the tattoo here, on your spine, looks like it's missing a piece, like a slot or something." He slid up the zipper and turned her about by the shoulders, gripping her so she was forced to stand in his arms and look at him. "Is something wrong? Can I...help? What went on last night?"

"Nothing." Had her voice slipped the tiniest bit?

"Nothing? You came home wearing a sheet, Rachel. What happened to your clothes? Did he...?"

"There was no *he,* Oscar."

"I don't believe you."

"And what do you believe? That I picked up a strange man, took him to a hotel room and let him have his way with me, then allowed him to take off with all my clothes?"

He lifted a brow.

Oh, but she was so unskilled at making a joke.

Michele Hauf 81

"I just...don't have time to explain. I've got a plane to catch."

"Where to?" He followed her as she knelt beside the storage box in the closet and began to stuff necessary things in her backpack. "Your passport? You're leaving the country?"

"Just a quick trip to Paris. There's, um...a relative."

What should the story be? Thinking on her feet was a talent Christian had always encouraged. Not that Oscar needed an explanation, but, well...yes, he did deserve something.

"I have a sister."

"You do?"

"Yes. She...needs a blood transfusion. I need to get there right now. Don't worry, Oscar, I'll be back in a few days." She hoped.

"That's cool. I wasn't aware you had family. Of course you have to go. Don't worry, I'll lock up for you."

"Thanks, Oscar."

A T-shirt, brown suede pants (armored, and capable of stopping a 9-millimeter slug), her lucky bra and some good running shoes were shoved into the pack. Her passport, credit card and a toothbrush and toothpaste were retrieved from the bathroom. Emergency Gummi Bears were kept on top of one of the book stacks—she tucked a Ziploc baggie filled with chunks of gooey sugar bears into the pack. She vacillated about bringing the small leaf-style folding push dagger. Nope, never make it through airport security.

A dodge to the platform bed—Rachel stuck a hand under the mattress—produced a black address book. That was tossed in the pack as well.

"You've got my phone number?" Oscar asked as she slipped into a pair of low black pumps with chunky heels. She didn't want to look like a tourist when arriving in Paris; the simple dress and shoes would say "Parisian."

With a glance about the loft, Rachel decided all was well,

and started for the door. "You want me to call you from Paris? Whatever for?"

"No, I—Rachel."

She stopped at the door. Her sensibilities knew some sort of goodbye ritual was required between friends. She wasn't that dislocated from society. *And shouldn't you be trying harder to fit in?* But she'd lied to Oscar about having a sister, and the deception affected her sense of right and wrong more than it should. He didn't deserve lies.

Oscar swung around in front of her. Tousled hair and rumpled shirt, he was easy and comfortable, but his concern frightened her. She could take care of herself. Hadn't he figured that one out?

"It's nothing, Oscar."

"Nothing? You said it was your sister! Aren't blood transfusions an emergency?"

"Yes, but…she's with family. My…other sister is there with her."

"You have two sisters?"

"I've got to go." Before she created an entire make-believe family.

"Sure, but you do have my number?"

"What is it?"

"Hell, you wouldn't use it if you were in trouble."

"What could you do for me, Oscar, all the way in Paris?"

"I could…" He nodded, seeing the logic in that statement. "Right. The woman remains a mystery. And I won't ask for your number 'cause I know you don't do cell phones."

"Too difficult to keep track of."

"You're going to be fine?"

"I always am." Sensing this was the moment for connection, Rachel leaned forward and planted a kiss to his forehead. That little bit of grayness felt all right. "Just a few days."

"I worry about you," he called as she ascended the stairs.

Stepping out into the sky, Rachel couldn't help but think she worried about herself, too. She should not be in this mess. It was entirely her fault things had gone so wrong.

Who would have thought a night of fabulous sex would be her downfall?

Chapter 8

"It's gone."

"Good. I suggest you allow twelve hours before reporting it to insurance. Tell them it didn't occur to you to look in the safe until later in the day. It's not like you do a daily inventory."

"Why?"

"You've got to give the thief a head start."

"He doesn't need one. He's free and clear."

"True. But it might look suspicious if you did not."

"Very well. And then, I'll contact the police."

Friday—8:45 a.m.

Boarding an airplane required more courage than standing down a thug with a 33-caliber aimed at her heart. Both situations were life threatening. The thug promised a quick standoff. The other stretched out over eight hours.

As the 747 began its ascent, Rachel decided she much preferred the thug to an airplane. Ears popping and fingers clutching the skinny foam seat arms, she closed her eyes and began her inner mantra. "Relax, relax...relax!"

First class had been booked. Rear seats were the only available. Close to the bathroom: good. But as well, always a bumpy ride, and the very reason for needing the close bathroom in the first place.

At a touch from the right side, Rachel let out a frightened squeak.

An older woman with white hair and a crocheted shawl smiled meaningfully at her. "First time flying?"

Rachel swallowed, trying to keep back her stomach. She shook her head. *Don't talk to me,* she thought. *Just let me die in peace.*

"Want some gum?"

She took the proffered stick of cinnamon gum—oh, the irony—hoping her acceptance would shut the woman up. The seat-belt sign dinged to *off* and, unlatching herself, Rachel made a fast trail to the coffinlike horrors of the bathroom.

Two hours later and two more frantic trips to the bathroom, Rachel's nerves were so stripped she couldn't even think to be frightened. She hadn't eaten a decent meal in over twelve hours. Her stomach was completely empty. Now, she was woozy, drained and couldn't sleep. And she was only a quarter of the way through the flight.

The woman in the seat next to her slept.

Refusing lunch, Rachel had pulled out her pack from the overhead compartments and tried to occupy her discombobulated brain.

The contact book was one of few items Rachel had determined would be a good snatch when she'd escaped from Christian's compound that rainy morning in November. She had a few times glimpsed the innards, tiny entries made in precise black marks. So small, in fact, they looked like ant tracks from a couple feet away. One had to look closely to decipher. Every thief, cracker, thug and fence Christian had ever dealt with was listed within. There were also drivers, cleaners and moneymen. Christian didn't trust computers, though it had been an absolute requirement she learn the machine inside and out, for no security system worked without one. Computers can be broken into. Viruses destroy records. She should be cautious about computer usage; know the machine, how to master and manipulate it, but don't feed it any of her valuable information.

Computers, Rachel had eventually figured out, were also a link to the outside world. A universe beyond the six-acre compound she had been imprisoned in for—was it over a decade?

Imprisoned was a harsh word. Initially it had been a dream vacation. When Christian had introduced himself to her that day in the park, she'd looked into hard blue eyes and had fallen in love. Yes, love.

Christian Lazar had promised her power, strength and riches. She'd followed him to France without looking back. With no family, no friends, no ties to anything, it had been an easy decision for a lonely teenager. Why he, an American, lived in France, had never troubled her. It was a beautiful country. Why not live there?

And he'd been good on his promises. She never had to worry about food or clothing. Her education had not stopped. Christian had given her math and science and geometry books; the cook had tested her. And for extracurricular studies, Christian had educated her in the fine art of cat burglary.

When he'd first suggested the profession to Rachel, she had thought the idea of scaling buildings and infiltrating security exciting, mysterious, exotic and sexy—as Christian had intimated. She had excelled only because she had so wanted to please the charming man who gave her everything.

But the whole master/slave aspect of their relationship

could have never been anticipated. The process of getting there was so seamlessly eerie. She could have never predicted or seen it coming. Succumb she had to Christian's manipulation of her trust and heart. A cruel master, emotionless always, yet seductive in that he could wear a mask of emotion when needed.

The past few years at the compound had definitely been confinement.

Rachel thought now of racing across the courtyard, a packed bundle in hand, and that glance back to Christian, sprawled upon the muddy ground. Cruel of her to leave a human like that. (The cook and Garland should have returned within an hour; he had not been alone long.) She had done crueler things at Christian's beckon. Was it not fitting his end should come in such a manner?

He had given her everything. In trade, he took from her freedom, independence, her very sense of self.

Who was Rachel Blu Olson? It felt odd to use a last name he'd stripped from her. Was she the heartless, emotionless thug who'd often stood a pace behind Christian's left shoulder as he made a deal with a hotshot fence or buyer? The thug who had more than once exacted ruthless methods to lay flat a suspicious dealer. A kick to dislocate a jaw, the heel of a palm to break a nose.

You never killed anyone. Murder was unthinkable.

Was she the precise spider who climbed walls and scampered along ductwork, deftly avoiding security to steal the prize? A prize immediately turned over to Christian. Her reward? A night spent in her own room on the hard twin bed, instead of being kicked from Christian's luxury king to shiver on the scratchy sisal rug at the base of the bed.

Was Rachel Blu Olson the girl who now woke nightly, sometimes standing in odd places in her loft because she had actually gotten up, in her sleep, and walked about? And if she had not moved from her bed, then the strange dreams woke her. A girl, young, perhaps still in grade school, plucking a guitar and smiling up at a faceless woman. "I'm going to be a star, someday." Never an answer. But always that flaming wall would close over the woman's nondescript image and forever wipe her from Rachel's conscience.

Did it matter who she was? Christian had stripped her of dignity, and doled out little emotional respect, and yet, she'd known nothing else but to do as he commanded. To continue as she had been trained. Stealing and lurking in the shadows came so easily to her. It is what she knew. The danger did not bother her; it excited her. Challenge made her job interesting, made it worth doing over and over. It was her only reason for being.

You do want to change.

She had changed. She had started anew.

But are you worthy of such change? You are still just a glorified thief. You haven't escaped. You're walking right back into your past.

Rachel closed her eyes and clasped the contact book upon her knee. *You are not going to let that happen,* whispered up from her depths. Depths she'd not ever wanted to peer into. Depths that frightened her. But she sensed it was her true self, trapped within those depths. A self who wanted to be free and safe. And happy.

If she did not get the ruby back, she faced the stigma she had always feared. To be marked a criminal. For she had never once been caught in her career working for Christian. Now she had spoken to Posada. He could identify her. He would have no reason to suspect or believe another thief had shown up on the same night she had intended to survey the museum.

If that thief could only know how completely free and clear he was. He had won the prize and had successfully mastered her.

Mastered? In so many ways.

Rachel tilted her head upon the headrest and sunk into a woozy memory of early this morning in the hotel room. How quickly the tables had tilted against her. Intentions to seduce the thief and take off with the jewel had been toppled. With a few flicks of his fingers. A masterful manipulation of her safe dial.

A giddy flutter flapped in Rachel's belly. Her skin warm and her face flushed, she smiled at the sudden tingle that revisited her sexual encounter. There in her depths she felt herself grow hot. It was as if he touched her again.

Crossing one leg over the other, she slid her hands between her knees and sighed. A glance to the woman next to her confirmed she still slept.

Stealing a moment to dive into the sensation of bliss, Rachel let her dizzy head fall against the hard foam cushion. Right there, he had touched her. The man certainly knew his way around a woman. One orgasm would have been enough, a free fall into a denied pleasure. But three?

"Mmm…" Rachel murmured. Indulging this feeling felt more right than anything.

A wave of turbulence rocked the plane. She stiffened. The dream of bliss slipped away.

Turbulent. That about described her life to a T.

Stepping foot on French soil felt like coming home—to a dilapidated shack surrounded by starving wolfhounds. Mixed feelings of distrust, fear and anxiety rocketed Rachel's heartbeats to an overwhelming noise. As well, landings always resulted in her stomach staying thirty thousand feet up in the air, while her body descended. Making a beeline for the nearest bathroom was a must. She whispered "thanks" out loud to find an empty stall.

Minutes later she splashed water over her face, stuck her tongue out at her weary reflection and headed out into the fluorescent jungle of the terminal.

She barely recalled going through passport control and customs. She carried only her stuffed pack—and the search revealed clothing. No weapons. She'd learned to survive without them. Her body—woozy and exhausted as it was—remained the only weapon she needed.

Lot of good it had done her last night. Half of her felt the gnawing guilt at succumbing, allowing herself to be mastered so easily, the other half simply shouted *hallelujah!*

And while she should feel defeat, a well of power eddied within. It was a new and strange power. A very feminine-centric kind of bliss. One not entirely unwelcome.

Rachel had gotten what she rightly deserved last night. Pleasure that should have been hers all along. A pleasure she would not apologize for.

Not even when she was sitting in a jail cell.

Exiting the Charles de Gaulle with her head lifted to draw in the crisp summer air, Rachel strode to the c-taxi line, finding it relatively short. Tourists took the metro or bus shuttle because they were cheap. She hadn't the patience or the time. The périphérique freeway circling the city would be the quickest route to her destination.

Her cabbie arrived five minutes later in a stylish Peugeot 416 and she directed him to the Sixteenth arrondissement. If her guess was correct, the meet was in the old warehouse down the street from a tired old marketplace that sold Louis XVI antiques and tatty postcards; the Trocadéro—a monument that housed Napoleon's son's body—rose in the background.

Rachel knew of a little café that served delicious petite crème not far from the site. She could use the caffeine. Jet lag clung to her neck and shoulders. She'd have to eat something soon, or the drowsiness would only get worse.

Chapter 9

*Paris
Friday—9:15 p.m.*

The café had no official name and was simply known by regulars as *le Blanche,* for the whitewash that covered the entirety, including brick walls, tin ceilings, doors and even the sidewalk. It was situated a block away from the warehouse where the exchange was to take place.

Fighting another dizzy wave that warned she had better eat a nourishing meal soon, Rachel sat at an iron table nursing a cooled petite crème. The recessed table advertised Orangina Rouge beneath the circle of glass. Though a favorite, she'd avoided the drink for the caffeine might have tipped her woozy head over the edge. Hazelnut biscotti number three had been nibbled down to half. It settled her stomach a bit—she didn't want to overdo it with a full meal; slowly but surely to get back her strength—but she needed real sustenance, like spinach and apples and a thick piece of bread with warm honey on it.

The evening was quiet. The setting sun splashed gorgeous pink and orange across a Maxfield Parrish–blue sky. Christian owned an original Parrish; it hung in his bedroom, the one burst of lush color in the stark and natural-wood furnished house. It had been like a beacon to Rachel. Many times she'd stood before the painting, an eye to the nude bather perched at cliff's edge, soaking herself in the explosion of color. What would happen if the bather simply jumped from the rocky outcrop? Would she land in the sea? Would she fly? And, in certain lights, Rachel could spy the other bather, sitting lower in the shadows. Always there, but not so obvious. Like dreams lost.

Or dreams yet to come?

Now it was with reluctance that she drew her gaze from the color-splashed sky.

Not a lot of pedestrians this evening. Everyone was inside eating the evening meal or preparing their children for bed. Tourist season had yet to kick into high gear and so the streets were navigable, though the journey round the Trocadéro did take a bit of time. The city needed to implement a tourist lane, and a those-who-know-the-hell-what-they-are-doing lane.

Not that Rachel would use either. She was not a good driver. Christian had taught her to handle the Clio around the compound and during a few trips to the city. But she hadn't enough experience, and the whole ordeal, while accident free, had really put her off driving. The bus served just fine.

Two tables away, a young couple smooched over some chocolate concoction that made Rachel's mouth water. For her, decadence and food had never coexisted. She didn't consume what her body didn't need. If she didn't plan to burn if off, it wasn't needed.

But what would be the harm in an occasional chocolate bar? She often lingered in the grocery store as she waited in line, her fresh vegetables and fruits and nuts in an arm basket. Interesting how the sinful foods were lined up right there at the checkout, no way to avoid them.

Would a chocolate bar prove as blissful as a hot, bubble-laced bath? Maybe, but not nearly so delicious as an orgasm. Or another, or yet—

Where are you, Rachel? You're not paying attention.

The last time she lost track of attention she let a valuable ruby get away, and possibly, her freedom.

The museum had to know by now the ruby was missing. Had Posada tried to locate her? Were there storms of policemen invading her loft right now? By now the curator of the Lalique must be kicking himself for even trusting her. Likely he was on the phone to Finley, blaming him for the recommendation.

There must be a way to allay the curator's frustration. To buy herself time.

She could call him...convince him there had been an emergency, and that she would be back in town on Sunday. The dying sister, yes? Which would mean she must then confess to having the ruby, for why else would she call to convince him of her innocence? He'd never in a thousand years buy that another thief had robbed the Lalique on the very day she had planned. Sounded like a sorry attempt to cover her ass.

Sorry but true.

This sword Rachel balanced upon was sharp on both sides. She would take a cut, but she wasn't about to decapitate herself. No personal contact, like a phone conversation. Something more discreet.

Pressing her palms to the warm cup of petite crème, she closed her eyes and made a decision. If she had estimated times and guessed the meeting place correctly, the ruby would be in her hands in less than an hour. Then she would e-mail the Lalique and let the curator know the ruby was safe. Family emergency out of the country? Sounded good to her.

Blowing out a breath, Rachel nodded. That was the plan. It would work.

Slipping a finger down the side of the black shoe she wore, she eased the pinching leather away from her heel. It had been months since she'd worn dress shoes.

The dress fit her like a charm, and had served to place her as one of the crowd. But now she would employ a different use for the dress—distraction.

Unbuttoning the top two buttons, she slid a hand inside to skim the curve of her breast, to quell her beating heart. Her flesh felt sticky and warm. Jet lag? Likely. She needed time to rest and restore. An hour, if she could manage it.

Another biscotti was offered and she politely refused. The waitress went to check on the amorous couple.

A check of her watch—8:55. Rachel dug in her pack, and producing a compact, flipped it open and made to assess her nonexistent lipstick.

The view down the street behind her was clear save for a green Mini Cooper navigating a hairpin turn. The jagged line of water canons in the courtyard of the Trocadéro awaited sunset to produce a marvelous display. Across the street an elderly gentleman paused to allow his white poodle to do its business on the sidewalk. They both walked on. Clinks of porcelain and silverware echoed from inside the café.

Rachel swung a leg, impatient—that was a surprise. She was never impatient. So why now?

Because her life depended on retrieving that damn ruby!

So, back to nervous swinging. The subtle movement worked to counter her uneasy stomach.

She couldn't know if she would sight anyone from her position. But this was the quickest and easiest access to the warehouse. She would like to know who was buying the ruby from the Frenchman. Hell, she'd like to know who the Frenchman was.

On the other hand, lack of information would prove safest, if not wisest. The less she knew of the underworld, the less involved she became. If only forgetting all she'd done, known and seen could be so easy as walking away from Christian had been.

A silver Audi drove down the street, and then parked. A man dressed in a black peacoat and black skullcap stepped out and looked about. Not scanning, casually taking in the neighborhood.

Rachel turned to face the warehouse, then sighted the man walking toward the café. She watched him surreptitiously, never fully turning her face to him. Dark curls sifted out from under the tight cap. An awkward, violent bone structure pensively marked the surroundings. Her man. He hadn't gotten a glimpse of her face. Nor should he recognize her from behind. Hell, he but knew her in shadows and flesh.

Unless he had observed her this morning as she lay snoring in bed.

Rachel blew out an exasperated breath.

Another few strides and he'd be to the first tables set outside on the whitewashed sidewalk.

Rachel snapped her compact shut and stood, slipping a palm over her skirt and tipping a finger just under the hem. Holding her pack before her so he could not see it, she began to walk, swinging her hips more than usual.

Allure, it is a powerful device against the enemy, Christian had always said. "If he is male," she'd answered. *Either,* Christian had replied. *Even females will not be able to look away from your presence.*

Striding down the sidewalk, she sensed the thief closed in on her. Ahead, a narrow opening to an alley offered a dark slit between two four-story brick warehouses. If she timed things perfectly…

The man's footsteps paralleled hers. Boots—she'd gotten a look. The thick, clompy heel stole away his stealth.

She tilted her head up, feigning to study the carved plaster decorating the building fronts.

Five more strides and the alleyway.

"Bonjour, mademoiselle," a husky whisper said as he gained her side. Yes, his voice. The voice that had dripped over her body hours earlier, naming her a bitch, but then granting her heaven on earth.

"If you like good days," she said.

A spin of her hips torqued about her stance. Rachel reached for his coat lapels and swung him around and into the alley. His shoulders hit the brick wall.

Still using his surprise, she stabbed a heel into the top of his boot. The thick heel didn't penetrate the leather, but it didn't need to, the pressure forced a bark of pain from him.

"You?" he managed to say.

The compact opened and wielded in her palm, Rachel pressed the sharp plastic into the center of his throat. It sliced a gasp of air from him. It could cut flesh if need be.

"Mmm," he growled, acting completely aloof. In fact, a slimy grin curved his lips. No fear in his green eyes. His nostrils flared. "You reek of me."

"You smell like a thief."

Rachel felt along his torso. Flashes of last night blinked through her thoughts. Floating on bliss. Nothing in the front pockets. Firm muscles beneath the coat…and under her gliding hands. She'd held him in her fist. But he had been the one to master her.

Must be in his coat.

"Where is it? I haven't got all day. I haven't even got today."

A sweep of his hand sent the compact flying. Glass shattered against the wall behind her and slivered onto the ground. So similar to the pieces of her life that had been falling away since yesterday evening.

She fisted his lapels again and slammed him into the wall. "Damn you!"

Air whooshed from Rachel's lungs. His fist retracted from her diaphragm. She lifted a heel and raked the hard rubber edge down the inside of his shin, landing along the tender arc of his foot.

He swore and bent his head into her shoulder, driving her backward with a jarring connection against the wall.

Rachel slid her hands up the inside of his coat, lined in satin, and landed a pocket. Score. The ruby fit into her palm. But his fingers slapped about her fist and the ruby.

"Not yours, pretty one."

"Neither is it yours."

He lifted his head and when she thought he would deliver a skull-shattering head-butt he snorted blood and fell to her feet.

This time a knee to his testicles served its purpose.

Swooping low, Rachel retrieved her pack and then stepped out from the alley. Target hit. Vacate the premises.

Glancing back at the crumpled heap of black wool—only this morning they had shared excellent sex—she dismissed the thief with a tug of her skirt and skim of her palm over her hair.

A glance to the line of warehouses didn't sight anything, or anyone, in the windows. Whoever waited for the ruby either hadn't posted lookouts—unlikely—or the meeting was on the opposite side of the building.

Or, they had witnessed her debacle with the thief and had sent out thugs. Which is why she didn't slow her pace.

Slipping the ruby into her pack, she quickly strode down the street toward the silver Audi.

No keys dangling from the ignition. She wasn't keen on popping the hood to hotwire the car, had burnt herself once and had been admonished for her ineptness.

"I'll give you inept," she muttered. With one last sweep of the neighborhood, she hooked her bag over her shoulder and walked away, putting distance between herself and the only man in France who could pin any sort of crime on her. "America, here I come."

The Eiffel Tower receded in the rearview mirror as the cab neared the entrance ramp to the périphérique. Sitting in the back seat, Rachel sorted through her pack to ensure she had enough euros to pay the fare. Credit would buy a return flight. This cab did not take plastic. She kept a folded stack of bills secreted in an inner zipper pocket for such an emergency. Good. More than enough to see her home and back. But only a frozen hell would see her back in France any time soon.

Something was wrong. She had packed more than a T-shirt, her lucky bra and some pants. What was—

The contact book.

She patted the cracked vinyl cab seat, shuffling position to check the floor. It hadn't fallen out. Where could she have—damn! It must have been lost in her scuffle with the thief.

"Merde."

"Mademoiselle?" The cabbie's hopeful smile sought her out in the rearview mirror. The crystal dangling from the mirror bobbled in bright flashes.

"Stop right here," she said.

"We are minutes from *la périph*—"

"Just…let me think."

The cab stopped.

She had everything else, including passport and credit card. The contact book was valuable, but worth going back for? She'd dropped her pack in the scuffle. If anything had spilled onto the ground, the thief would notice it, then either take it or toss it. If he took a moment to page through the contents, he'd never toss it.

She checked her watch. Twenty minutes had passed. He was long gone.

"On to the airport," she said to the cabbie.

"You'll have a long wait."

"What?"

"The Charles de Gaulle is temporarily closed. The sanitation workers are striking."

"What? But—I just left there an hour earlier."

"Is true, *mademoiselle*. I just heard on the radio, and have been rerouting my fares to hotels to wait."

Over striking sanitation workers? Couldn't the flights continue while the garbage stacked up?

"Reports say no more than a twenty-four hour delay—no one likes to argue when the trash begins to pile up."

"Great." So she was stuck in Paris for a while.

"Would you like me to drive you to a hotel?"

Rachel sighed heavily and shook her head. "Take me to 1015 passage de Dantzig."

It was the one place she knew of in Paris where she might find an empty room and no questions. She needed a quiet space to rest and think.

Chapter 10

Friday—9:55 p.m.

After some thought, Rachel altered her course. The cab let her off beside the Seine. *Bateaux mouches* lit with strings of golden lights ferried tourists up and down the river. A boat announcer declared, "The Eiffel Tower on your immediate right" through a megaphone that carried his narrations to the street.

A small cybercafe, two stories high and lit with blue neon strips, perched across the street from the river. The city added another of the jacked-in cafés every week, or so Christian had once made the comment. The cafés stayed open until well past midnight, offering easy access to tourists to contact loved ones, traveling business people opportunity to connect with the home office, or lovesick cyber couples to simply get in touch.

The shop was quiet, save the hum of computer fans and the clink of a spoon swirling unconsciously about a teacup. Neon strips curled beneath a Plexiglas floor. Two computer stations were occupied, both of them by the window that overlooked the river.

Rachel offered a *bonjour* to the clerk behind the counter. Courtesy that. It was de rigueur to greet and thank when entering and leaving any Paris business. A slick white granite counter offered a rainbow of computers, all with various drives and an array of attached digital equipment. Rachel asked a clerk for a hook-up and he nodded toward the white iMac sitting at the end of the counter. Next to it, a digital camera was attached to the counter by a security chain.

"The whole setup, scanner, camera and DSL, *oui?*" the clerk said with a wink. Without waiting for her response he tilted his eyes back to the small Game Boy in his hands.

Positioning herself behind the computer, out of the clerk's view, Rachel slipped the ruby from her pack. The other customers were around the counter and across the room; they couldn't see what she was doing.

She placed the jewel on the white mouse pad gone gray around the edges from oily fingers and debris. A chunky little bit of steel, the digital camera fit into her palm. She snapped a picture and then quickly tucked away the ruby. When uploading the file to the computer, she made sure to erase the contents of the photo disk. No sense in leaving evidence.

Five minutes later she had typed an e-mail to Mr. Posada with apologies. A tragedy had occurred. She'd thought only to rush to her sister's side. She would be back in the States on Sunday. The ruby was safe in a vault at her home. The picture provided evidence.

Her finger poised over the send button, Rachel stared at the attachment file containing the picture of the ruby. It was early in the States, likely the museum was still open. This e-mail would be read soon. The origin of the e-mail could be easily traced. If the museum contacted the Paris police they would be on her trail within the hour.

But more troubling, if she sent this e-mail, she might never regain the self-reliance she had built up over the past eight months. All her hard work, gaining trust and respect, and establishing herself, could be obliterated with the push of a finger. She would never work in the city again. Probably, the state.

Maybe even the country?

"Everything working for you, *mademoiselle?*"

Startled at the clerk's voice, Rachel pulled her pack to her gut and checked the screen. The thumbprint of the ruby was smaller than her fingernail; he couldn't make out the picture.

"Er…yes."

"On vacation?"

"Hmm? Oh, yes. *Pardon,* it's been a long day."

She hit send, then asked the clerk if the computer received return e-mails.

"*Oui,* six euros."

She should have requested no reply. Certainly the museum would be discreet and not reply. Too late.

"Would you leave a number to reach you if a reply comes?" the clerk wondered.

She would be long gone. "No, *merci.*"

The sun had completely set as she stepped outside. Mature linden trees lined this wide street, walking distance from the city park named in honor of a famous Frenchman Rachel could not recall. Her chunky rubber-heeled shoes made little noise as she strode down the cobbled street toward the apartment building. The Parrish sky was now gray.

Rachel vaguely recalled, as a little girl, she had dreams of Paris after seeing a movie—couldn't recall the title—but the images had been burned into memory. The Eiffel Tower. The royal palace. The winding Seine that was green in the spring and brown in winter. Paris epitomized romance. Surely the little girl would find her prince across the ocean in the city of romance?

Right. She hated this city. For Paris had stolen her innocence. And ever since, it had been beating her down. Eight months ago she would have never dreamed to again set foot on French soil. And now, here she stood.

Funny, she remembered another movie. Her mother had rented it when she was young. It had featured a jewel thief who stole a priceless diamond. And—this part seemed odd to recall—a dancing pink cat had been inside the jewel. While vague, the memory was indelibly imprinted upon her soul. Had she once dreamed of becoming a cat burglar?

Weird how life worked itself out.

"Can I ever escape?" she murmured.

The three-story apartment complex featured a gorgeous multicolored tiled facade. Rachel dashed up the short stone stairs and entered the digicode into a security box.

The building was quiet, renting to artists and elderly women with poor hearing and too many cats. Perfect hideaway following a job, or even beforehand to plan mode of entry and exit. Dead or alive, the apartment had to still belong to Christian, for she was sure he owned it instead of renting.

What became of property owned by a dead man? How much time would pass before it was discovered no one lived here, and the property was resold? Rachel wondered now if Christian had a will, and if so, would she be in it? It was hard to guess.

She didn't want to think about it. She would take nothing that had once belonged to Christian Lazar. Except a few moments in this apartment. It would offer respite. Chance to catch her breath, make a plan and wait out the sanitation strike.

Grasping the door handle to the apartment, she steadied herself as a vicious wave of murk threatened to master her balance and topple her to the floor. *Have to eat soon.* Unrelenting this jet lag.

The slim steel handle didn't budge. Locked. To be expected. Not even registering on the nuisance scale.

A glance over her shoulder spied the ugly painting of the Eiffel Tower Rachel had never liked, for the artist had decided the tower should be pink. Sliding her forefinger along the cool black metal frame, she found what she was looking for tucked behind the upper left corner—a key. Thieves protected their property as well as the average home owner, but when it came to convenience they were all about the obvious overlooked.

A click released the lock and she twisted the knob.

Rachel peered inside and around the corner. Not a spot of furniture, as it had been when last she had visited. Plain hardwood floors advertised a coating of dust. No footprints in the dust.

Safe.

Locking the door behind her, she slipped off her shoes. Much better. From here on, she was all about comfort. The creepers she'd packed would serve.

Tiptoeing along the wall, she scanned the hazy main room. Six-foot-high windows were blocked by velvet drapes thick with dust. Connecting, a small kitchen with white appliances, and the same remarkable view.

A half wall separated the kitchen from the bedroom. Drawn shades emitted low levels of light from the street lamps below. A peek between the shades spied the Eiffel Tower, lit up like a Christmas tree. And then it blinked off. 10:10, she knew, for the tower was lighted for ten minutes at the top of every hour after sunset, and until 2:00 a.m.

Striding into the bedroom, Rachel dropped her pack at the

base of the bed. The king-size bed was stacked across the end with a folded counterpane. There would be sheets and a few towels in the closet. Just the basics. No armoires or rugs, very simple.

Around the corner, the bathroom door stood ajar. Rachel's heartbeat accelerated. She listened, tilting her head to open her ear. Glancing back to the front door, she eyed her shoes. The rubber heels were two inches high and as wide. Should have toted one along as a weapon.

Slowly she eased to the door and pushed it open. Not a creak. A press of the light switch did nothing. No electricity? Christian always paid the utilities because one never knew when the apartment would be needed. Which could only mean...

So he really was dead. Not that she had for one moment doubted he was. Proof had never been incontrovertible. But this strange little moment—lack of electricity—solidified he really was dead, like a funeral never could.

Who had gone to his funeral? The cook and Garland? Had Christian friends she had not known about? Family?

Why did she care?

But that didn't allay her immediate suspicions. Enough light beamed from the bedroom that she could see the plain white-tiled room—shower curtain pulled back and toilet seat down—was empty.

Alone.

Rachel pressed out a breath. She closed her eyes and nodded, satisfied.

He wasn't here. He would never be here. She was alone and safe.

Mentally, she was already miles high on a flight back to the States. But first, she had to determine if the States would be as welcoming the next round.

Padding back to her pack, tossed on the bed, she drew out

the ruby and for the first time had the leisure to measure its precious weight in the palm of her hand. As heavy as a petite plum, but smaller. The cuts were concise, sharp. Much more perfect compared to the two cuts in her palm gotten when dangling from the edge of the building. They'd closed up but wouldn't heal for weeks. She held up the ruby to allow the light from the dusted windows to play across the facets. Clear, bloodred, with the slightest tinge of purple, which made it even more valuable.

"You have played your last hand with me, crimson lady." She tossed it and caught it. "But can I bring you back?"

There was really no option. She had to return the ruby to avoid becoming a wanted criminal. It would be risky. She couldn't just stride up to Mr. Posada and plop the jewel in his hand. But—ruby returned—could she ever work the States again; that was the real question.

Tossing and catching the rock a few more times, her eyes moved to the bed. She had not managed a single wink during the flight. After eight hours packed into a tin can flying across the ocean—eight troubled hours at that—she wanted to rest.

Lifting the counterpane and giving it a good shake stirred up the dust. Rachel sneezed a couple times. Finally she spread the thick white down over the bed. She was about to jump on when she decided the ruby would leave her hands for a nap.

Never let down your guard, and if need be, secure the valuables first.

"I've got a safe place for you."

She strode into the bathroom and stepped into the bathtub. Reaching for the row of white tiles highest to the ceiling, she tapped a few, not recalling the exact one, until one rang hollow. A jiggle of the tile opened it into her palm. Stowing the ruby, she replaced the tile, used the toilet, then literally dived onto the down comforter.

* * *

"We have a problem. I just received a disturbing e-mail."

"Explain."

"The real thief doesn't have the Rousseau ruby."

"I don't understand."

"Your security expert has it."

A heavy sigh occupied the phone line for a few moments. "Does it matter? It's gone. You collect the insurance money."

"Not if she intends to return it."

"Oh."

"Yes. Oh."

Saturday—5:00 a.m.

Moments later Rachel woke. Had more than a few moments passed? She didn't feel refreshed. Rather groggy, actually.

The room was dark, but a line of moonlight traced across her leg. Immediately she sensed danger. A twitch of the muscles in her jaw. The scent of...something familiar. A tingle in her wrists...

No, that tingle—

Rachel jerked completely awake. She tugged her hand but it was fixed above her head. So was the other hand. Cold metal bound her to the chrome bed frame—handcuffs.

She tugged, but the steel dug into her flesh.

"How the hell—" Rachel stopped abruptly, knowing there was only one way this could have happened, and guessing whoever did this was still around.

A familiar scent crashed upon her senses. Masculine and edged with bay rum spice—toiletries imported from the United States.

Rachel turned her head slowly. There beside the bed, his eyes level with hers, squatted Christian Lazar.

Chapter 11

Saturday—5:05 a.m.

The drapes had been parted, a cold beam of light glowed in from the street.

Startled at the sight of a dead man's face, Rachel let out a shriek and jumped. The handcuffs kept her from scrambling away across the bed. She landed, arms stretched and head resting on her bicep, staring into impossible blue eyes.

Christian tilted his head, his lack of expression cruelly taunting. "That was quite an outburst. I've never seen you so animated. And jumpy. What has become of you, Rachel Blu?"

You're supposed to be dead, she wanted to spit at him. It wasn't every day she woke to a dead man's stare.

Rachel refrained from speaking until she could be sure he really wasn't a ghost. She could be in the throes of a nightmare. Lately, the hideous dreams had become more frequent.

But none had featured Christian; they had all been about that abandoned little girl.

"You're in quite the predicament," he said. A soft voice razored with an edge, an edge that sliced right through flesh and teased into her heart like tendrils of smoke from a toxic fire. "Nice of you to return to the city. I've been waiting for you."

She did not doubt that. But how had he known to find her, and at the very moment she was in Paris? And why—how—was he alive?

"You do know I've been waiting for you?" The sleeve of his charcoal linen suit brushed the thick comforter as he lifted a hand and placed it on the bed by her torso. Close, but not touching. Yet the heat of his body felt palpable. "Not a single day has passed without me thinking of my Rachel Blu. Eight months of hopeful days."

Not a nightmare—a very real, live man, speaking her name in that horrible, possessive tone that made her gut clench. And yet, a deep part inside her delighted at the sound of the familiar. Home. It was all she knew. All she needed to survive. With a few simple statements, he'd reopened the wound on her soul.

"I have waited for this moment." He stood. Rachel did not follow his gaze, instead focusing on the fine weave of his sleek gray suit pants. Armani, likely, nothing but the best for Christian Lazar. Precise, exact and clean. Just like his women?

"So many minutes I have spent imagining this reunion," he said. "Planning, anticipating, designing the best outcome—much like a heist. Would you come to me? Would I eventually have to seek you out? What were you doing in the States?"

How did he know she had returned to the States? In her next thought, Rachel knew it made for a likely guess. Besides France, the States was the only other home she had known.

"Well?"

He wanted an answer? She didn't have one. Should words exit her mouth, she expected them to gibber and plead. This wasn't supposed to happen. The last twenty-four hours should not have happened. Who screwed up the plan?

You did.

Right.

So what would she do about it?

"I devised the perfect scenario for this inevitable meet."

Of course he had. Christian planned everything to the second, oftentimes including steps, breaths and blinks.

"I planned to shove a blade up your sternum and commit hari-kari on you."

She heard his smirk. Hari-kari was officially suicide, but not the way Christian played it.

His hands crossed before him and clasped. He again bent to look into her eyes. Spice curled into her senses, seeping into her very being. "But it's different than I had anticipated. Seeing you."

Rachel closed her eyes. *Don't see me.*

"Smelling you..."

No.

"Fitting your outline back into my sight and knowing that it is a perfect fit. I don't want to hurt you, Rachel Blu." Fabric slithered as he straightened. "Yet."

There it was. *Yet.* The truth of Christian Lazar.

"If truth be confessed, I actually...missed you."

And she missed him like a tumor to the brain.

So, she had gotten herself into this situation. Time to start thinking on her feet. Or her back, matters as they were.

"Get these things off me," she muttered. Or did she plead? Her voice disconnected with her intentions.

She could not be here. Christian Lazar could not be here. He was dead!

Michele Hauf 111

"The cuffs are police issue. Not an easy pick, but possible. Though you're in no position to do so." He reached above her head and gave the chrome bed frame a firm rattle. "But if you work at it, I suspect you'll find your freedom."

Hadn't he the intention of freeing her? Of shuffling her back under his wing and once again into his mastery? Or would he sit and watch her squirm, waiting for her to display her escape skills, only to then commit the assisted hari-kari he had planned?

Best scenario would see him releasing her, and she taking him out with some physical moves. Worst scenario would see her still cuffed while he watched her squirm as the minutes ticked by and her future spiraled out of control.

The longer you stay here, hobbled and mastered by Christian, the less chance you have of making it out by yourself.

Christian tugged his coat lapels—an involuntary action due partly to his vanity, Rachel had long ago decided. Always, his appearance must be immaculate. "Surprised to see me?"

Hell yes! She nodded. And then she regretted that slip of her defenses. *Never let them see your weakness.*

"You know, I couldn't be sure if you would be surprised. That is one of many things I struggled with after the accident—the one mental fix that troubled me even beyond the exhausting physical rehab. Does she believe I'm dead, or does she know I survived?"

"I thought you could be dead."

"But you weren't sure."

Before she could coach her expression to an emotionless stare, the shrug escaped. Christian saw.

"As I concluded. So you used my incapacitation to flee. Because, surely, if you knew I was dead you would have stayed, yes?"

What sort of question was that? A Christian question. One that demanded compliance. An affirmative to show her respect.

No, she would not have stayed to help her wounded nemesis.

Nothing had changed. Save, that a dead man walked. And that made Rachel's world an instant nightmare.

"I didn't touch you with my blade," she said, trying to work the scenario in her brain. He'd collapsed when her arm had yet been retracted, still preparing for a defensive riposte. Yes, the rain had taxed her vision, but—no, she had not touched him with the weapon. "What...what happened?"

"Perhaps if you would have remained, you'd know?" He smoothed a hand along his jaw.

For a long time he preened along her body, taking her all in. She wasn't covered by the comforter and slid a bare foot along her ankle. Kneeling bedside as he was, she could kick him, manage a knee to his jaw. But that would have about as much effect as a lame fox in a trap biting at a hunter with a loaded rifle.

His breaths were light but noticeably fast. He was riled, she could tell from the volume of his breathing. Subtle clue to his temper.

"So...what happened to me," he said. "You really want to know? Isn't all that matters is I am alive?"

"I need to know—"

"If you caused it?"

She nodded. What if she *had* caused it? It didn't change things. Only that she had been inept.

"Very well, I stroked."

A stroke? But...he was young. Healthy!

"You look surprised."

He straightened, though, now that she really looked, it appeared he favored his right side, tilting slightly, as if his arm dragged him down. And his right hand dangled near his thigh—no; he flexed his wrist and shook out his fingers.

"Still rehabbing," he said at notice of her summation. "But

so close to maximum strength. Just a little twitch now and then that reminds me of your lack of compassion. The medication takes care of that. Didn't expect a visitor, did you?"

Had he been following her since her arrival in the city? The odds of him knowing she was in Paris were phenomenal. She traced her steps: she had taken a cab immediately from the airport, a stop at *le Blanche,* and then the cybercafe. She hadn't talked to anyone or suspected a tail. There was no one to clue him in that she was in Paris. Unless—

Could the thief be connected to Christian? She'd thought she recognized him on the roof. He and Christian had not been more than acquaintances then. But now?

In less than twenty-four hours she had been taken down by not one but two men. Rachel, the new woman set on a course to find happiness, perhaps even domesticity, the invincible, on the path to a new life, had suddenly been struck down.

How could he be standing over her with that damn smile and those condemning blue eyes?

"Take these off—" she rattled the cuffs "—then we'll talk." She winced. "Please?"

"You never did plead well. A good trait, if one were to worry about things like that. Pleading is so gauche."

He sat on the bed in front of her stomach.

Rachel thought to kick him off, but restrained herself. She was not to the advantage. The bed frame clanged as she straightened an elbow. The handcuffs, she could pick them, despite Christian's prediction her position would not prove a boon—*if* she had a pick.

He leaned over her. The heat of his presence, vile and intense, slipped into her being like a foul mist. All so familiar. Like returning home after being away, the smells, the sights, it was all so...welcoming.

"So the rogue thief comes home to reclaim her turf, is that

the way of it?" His left palm hovered over her hip, but he didn't touch. "In the city for a job?"

"No."

"I know otherwise."

"You know nothing!"

"Such feistiness! But to the wrong person." His voice took on a dry edge. "What have you been up to these past months, Rachel Blu? Want to know what I've been doing?"

"No."

"I'll tell you anyway. After you left— Do you know, I lay there in the mud with the rain pouring upon me, completely conscious? I was aware when you stood over me. What were you doing? Contemplating running me through with your rapier? You wanted to."

"No!"

"Hush, Rachel. I'm talking now. It's not polite to speak out of turn. You've developed quite the defiant streak." He tapped his knee with his right hand. A jerky motion. He had not complete strength on the right side, she sensed. "Cook and Garland arrived twenty minutes after your hasty exit and rushed me to the emergency room.

"I learned that a man has a three-hour window from the time he strokes before serious and irreversible damage sets in. I arrived at the hospital an hour and a half after the stroke. Totally paralyzed on my right side for a good week. But I came around." He lifted his right hand and turned it before him, then tightened his fingers to a fist. "I'm the picture of health, the doctor said. Attribute that to my clean living and exercise. Clean living." Christian's chuckle would never touch mirth. "If the doctor only knew my indulgences were so criminal, eh?"

"I still..." Despite her subconscious begging her to keep her mouth shut, Rachel had to know. "...don't understand."

"Those nasty headaches finally took their revenge on me."

The migraines the cook had told her about. But Christian had never let her in to see that part of him. It had been the chink in his armor, and that chink had been violated. Pity it hadn't taken him down for good.

"Yes, I know Cook told you about them." He smoothed a hand over his chin. Suave, cool, predatory. Still so frustratingly handsome.

That she could see his profile made Rachel suddenly notice the light—dull, yet white; not the muted moonlight. Was it morning? Had she slept so long? No, it was the streetlight, surely.

"You look tired, Rachel. Out of sorts. Jet lag? You never were good at flying."

"You're drooling."

He swiped at his chin with his left hand. "I need to medicate. I've a few more months of rehab. The physical therapist said I should regain ninety-five percent motor skills on the right. Pisses me off."

The force of his palm across her cheek took the breath from her. Her hands twisted and the cuffs bit at her wrists.

"The left side still works, though." He chuckled and stood to pace to the window.

Rachel stretched out her stinging jaw and followed his lopsided gait. He did favor his right side. It was a subtle fault, but a weakness all the same. For the first time Christian appeared weaker than she. And she was in no position to take advantage of such a coup.

She tilted back her head and eyed the chrome bed frame. The bar she was cuffed to fit up into the arc of chrome that designed the top border. It fit, but it wasn't welded. She clutched the bar and twisted. It moved a quarter turn.

"Much as I favor a reunion—and it will happen—I don't have time to chat now," Christian said. "Won't be long before the police arrive, eh?"

He was bluffing. "For what reason?"

"Well, you did e-mail the Lalique."

He knew? Impossible to have followed her trail. How was he doing it? *Nothing is impossible. You're just not looking at all the evidence.*

"I doubt the museum will be so kind as to take your word you'll bring the prize back to them. That is what you promised? So where is it?"

"What?"

"The ruby. You followed Rousseau to town and succeeded in taking it from him. You certainly could not have fenced it yet. Though I guess you've quite the arsenal to choose from. I do miss my contact book."

Rousseau? That was the name of the ruby. Did the stroke make Christian confuse things? If so, his lack of mental acuity may work to her advantage.

"The contact book was...misplaced."

"Right." Complete disbelief. "And the ruby?"

"It's not for sale."

"Why the hell would you steal it if you don't intend to fence it? I taught you to catch and release."

"None of your business."

"It is every bit of my business because something I created was involved!" He leaned over her and she stopped working at the chrome bar. Bay rum spice. He used the soap every day. Sweet, the scent. Heady with memories. *Stay back!* "My perfect machine has taken flight. It wanted to see if it could survive on its own. It cannot. It will learn soon enough."

How she hated it when he resorted to calling her "it." A response of anger.

And wasn't it time she let out a bit of anger, herself? "I don't need you."

"Really? How have you managed a living these past eight

months? You have no employable skills. I doubt you'd resort to flipping burgers. All you know is how to…"

He tilted his head, the hazy light ignoring any humanity in his eyes. What was he thinking? Had the stroke reduced his cognizance?

"I begin to understand," he said slowly. "I can't believe I hadn't figured this out earlier from the information I was—"

A hushed chuckle seeped into her senses, shimmering over her with a gloss of the familiar. His chuckles were the only piece of laughter she had known during her years of living with him. How she had craved his humor, a few moments of levity that had made the rest of the time bearable. No mirth, but just the sound of laughter—it was so different from his orders and anger.

"You're working for the police? That doesn't make sense. I've always taught you they were corrupt and—"

"The museum—" She stopped herself, but it was too late. Christian's smile grew.

"Ah? One of those thieves who go good? Like a security analyst? Someone who wears a suit and reads the labels on the underside of safes, then charges a ridiculous amount of money?"

She wouldn't justify his guesses with confirmation. Far too much had already been revealed.

"The hard way doesn't suit you, Rachel. You were made for the shadows, not the harsh fluorescent lights of the working class. You shine as a thief, creeping through the night, a literal shadow. To go legit? Look at you, your hair is dull, your arms are soft and lacking muscle—you've become less. You're not the woman I created."

Nor was she his machine.

She was so much more. No longer would she stand in the same shadows as Christian. But was he right? *Had* she been born to stalk the shadows? It seemed her entire life trajectory had been set on the course of meeting Christian.

"So you've stolen this jewel for a museum…in an attempt to…? Explain."

She remained silent. *Just tell me how you found me!* is what she wanted to shout. And then she wanted to manage a good position so she could kick Christian's immaculate face across the room.

Christian returned to the bedside and pressed his left fist—the good fist—to the bed beside her shoulder. The right hand drifted down her arm, the fingers tickling in small movements but not really touching. He'd used just such a touch to stir her longings when she had only wanted to drown in anger. Get them angry, then dredge up their emotions with promises of compassion—but never give it.

She had learned his game and knew how to play it.

The tickling sensations drifting down her arm ignited the lingering pleasure she had drowned in last night. Pleasure she hadn't realized could loiter for so long. It was still there, minute tingles, reminders of the uncontrollable ecstasy that had eddied through her veins.

Would Christian give her the one thing she had always desired of him? Dare she ask?

"Feels good, doesn't it, Rachel Blu?"

Closing her eyes and opening her mouth to whisper yes—she suddenly paused, the mutinous word still attached to her tongue.

He is the enemy. This is not pleasurable!

"I have to return the ruby," she blurted out, needing to silence the conflicting voices of pleasure and business in her skull. "It wasn't supposed to go down the way it did. I had no idea another thief would beat me to it. The ruby should have never left the museum, let alone the continent."

"Another thief? Now, that's interesting. And a pity. You used to be the best."

"I still am," she hissed.

He leaned closer. "Thanks to whom?"

Rachel now noticed the coffee on his breath. How early was it? Had morning actually come?

His lips moved closer to hers. Never—not once in the entire decade she had been with him—had he ever kissed her on the mouth. Too personal. *You don't deserve that connection with me.* No kisses. No orgasms. She had pleaded many a time—kiss me. He enjoyed it when she pleaded, but she had only ever been desperate for intimate contact. Some proof of love. Isn't that what a teenage girl wants?

You're not a teenager. Christian made you a woman.

Can you keep your independence? Not fall into the frightened girl who still seeks solace? Maybe…

Hell, she needed to eat. To restore her strength and bring back some sensibility. Her thoughts were not her own. When in Christian's presence she tended to react, and not defensively.

With a deft flick of Christian's wrist, the third button on her dress gave way, and then the fourth. He tucked his finger between her breasts and tilted a curious gaze upon her. The pale morning light slashed through his right eye. The sudden stroke of a finger over her nipple caused her to jerk. Yet a formidable opponent.

"So you would probably do anything to get that ruby back in hand, eh?"

"What makes you think it is out of my hands?"

"Ah." A smile to curdle her hopes twisted onto Christian's face. Leaning in to trace her hard nipple with his tongue, he then quickly retracted. He stood and walked toward the bathroom. "Let me see," he called as he entered the tiny room. "You wouldn't be so foolish as to…"

Rachel swore to herself as the dry scrape of tile across tile echoed from the bathroom.

Christian reappeared in the doorway, expertly tossing the

ruby in his left hand. "When did I ever teach you to be so foolish? I think it's the American air, no? All the pollution and chemicals in their food. Or have you poisoned your brain with all that media crap?"

Beyond pleading, Rachel focused her efforts on loosening the chrome bar. She was aware Christian paced the end of the bed. Let him gloat, she would pounce him in—a twist produced nothing but a creak—a few minutes. There was no reason she couldn't hold the upper hand against this crippled bastard.

"You could dislocate your thumb and slip out with ease," he noted. "Never taught you that one, did I? This is gorgeous. And worth, how much?" He held it high, moving to catch the burgeoning morning light in the depths of the red stone.

"Two million," she huffed and continued to work at the bar. Now it twisted easily within the connecting bar. But she wouldn't be able to pry it out unless she could bend the upper chrome bar.

"I assume the museum has all the information they need to locate you? And evidence you had promised to steal it?"

No address, no phone number—

Shit. The e-mail and attached photo. It had been an intuitive decision to stop at the cybercafe. Some strange moral part of her wanted to make things right. Would she fall because of her new morality?

"Like I said, I'd love to stick around, but it's too risky." Christian cupped a palm to his ear as if listening. "No sirens yet. Perhaps they didn't want to wake you from your nap?"

With that, he leaped onto the bed and landed over Rachel's body. Crouched, one leg to either side of her hips, he slid a hand inside his suit coat and drew out a dagger.

More curious than frightened, Rachel stopped struggling. He brandished a wavy kris dagger, his favorite, because the curved blade looked as imposing as it really was. The dagger tip slid through the houndstooth fabric, above the lowest button, and pierced her flesh, just below her rib cage on the left side. The entry point for hari-kari.

Could he do it?

Of course he could, but *would* he?

The entrance of the blade burned. Shock registered, but Rachel couldn't even squeak out a scream. Torture at the hands of this maniac was nothing new.

Christian shoved, but the blade stopped a few centimeters beneath her flesh. "What price for your life?"

Wincing at the pain, she focused on the fact she was not dead. Yet. "You already have the ruby."

"A pittance," he spat. "I want blood."

The blade moved subtly, beginning to twist. Rachel stiffened and gasped, "Do it."

Christian's laughter accompanied the exit of the blade. It cut through the bed just at her jaw. His fist brushed her chin as he let go of the handle. "And that is why I love you, Rachel Blu. You've still got that maniacal drive. It's all or nothing, yes?"

Put there by the only maniac in the room.

He slid off her body and yanked the dagger from the mattress. Rachel saw a glimpse of red as he tossed the ruby and caught it.

"I want...to play," he said. "I'm going to put this in a safe place for now. You'll know where to find it, of course. I expect you'll be out of those cuffs and on my trail in no time. But, will it be faster than the arrival of the police?"

With that, he gave the ruby a final toss then secreted it inside his jacket.

"Almost forgot." He held a finger high in exclamation, then slipped a hand inside his jacket to draw out—

"What the hell—"

He tore a strip of duct tape from the roll and approached

the head of the bed. She knew exactly what he had in mind. Bastard.

Wrapping the tape about her fingers, he did one hand, then the other, making sure each was tight with ends tucked. "Can't make this too easy for you. There. Now, I'm gone."

"Damn it!" She heard the door close.

In a fury of rage, she lifted her feet and swung them over her head. Her toes gripped the top chrome bar, and with her hands wrapped around the other bar, she pushed and pulled. The center bar bent. Exerting maximum pressure with her feet, she thought she felt the upper bar move. The center bar bent farther and gave free.

Momentum pulled her forward onto the bed. The handcuffs clipped her in the temple. An ungraceful face-flop landed on the bed.

Rolling to her back, she lifted the cuffs to eye them. Bound together by the sticky tape, her fingers were useless. No time to fashion a pick, and no means without digit dexterity. She needed that kris dagger.

Rachel rolled to the floor and raced into the living area. Rushing to the window, she looked down over the street. Christian slid into the back seat of a black Mercedes. It pulled away and she made a mental note of the license plate. Chase was not feasible.

Will it be faster than the arrival of the police?

By now the e-mail had been traced. So many hours had passed! If the museum chose not to trust her, they had likely contacted the Paris police. She had to move. But where to?

You'll know where to find it.

She hated Christian's games. No one ever won, save Christian. What was so fair about that?

Chapter 12

Saturday—5:45 a.m.

The cuffs were indeed police grade. One could pick them if they had a makeshift tool—a simple metal rim from a pair of eyeglasses—and time. And fingers.

Right now, Rachel couldn't manage either.

She pressed her forehead to the cool glass in the living room; the tip of the Eiffel Tower was shrouded in a heavy fog. Here and there, sun fought to burst up from the horizon. It had rained while she had been sleeping.

Staring down at her toes, Rachel closed her eyes and concentrated on the full, choking feeling in her breast. It hurt, right there, in her chest. Muscles tightened in her throat and neck, then relaxed, then tightened again. A loosening wash of an inexplicable *something* overwhelmed and then it all exploded.

Tears splat the window. Rachel could not stop the bellow

of frustration that followed in their wake. Shoulders shaking, she pressed her palms to the glass, the cuffs clinking. She could not recall a time when she had last cried, either out of pain or emotional frustration. This was both. A deep, unstoppable wave of emotion poured from her.

All of a sudden her life had gone completely wrong. She had only been trying to make it right, to dredge up a semblance of normalcy. Was she not allowed a fair chance?

Would she ever be free of Christian Lazar?

The glass clanked as she pounded it over and over. Her fists smeared through tears, blurring streaks across the dusty window.

He does not own you. You escaped! Will you surrender so easily?

She possessed such mettle that surrender was never an option. Put there by the very man she had tried to escape. *I did escape.*

And yet, he now held the ruby. Her very future rested in Christian's hands!

Let's play.

The bastard liked his games. Physical games with a mental edge, Christian had been fond of saying, for the brain must also be employed.

As Rachel figured it, there were two options. Succumb to Christian once again, fitting herself neatly back under his controlling hand and give up ever having a life of her own. Easy enough. It was a role she knew well, one she might even manage to feel comfortable in. She needn't worry about supporting herself, or blending in with society, or even missing a party given by a friend across the hall. Everything would be black and white.

Or she could choose to play in Christian's black-and-white world, seeking the prize—which meant fighting back. Fighting back would require getting the ruby back in the States in less than twenty-four hours.

You'll know where to find it.

She stopped the tears. With a decisive nod she chose the only possible option.

Staring hard at her taped fingers, she suddenly let out a snort. "I've lost all reasoning. He's not going to win this one."

She dashed into the kitchen and pulled open the drawer, in search of a knife. Nothing in any of the drawers. There had once been silverware. When had this apartment been cleaned out? For what reason would Christian do it? He could never have known she would arrive, months after his stroke, and plan to capture her.

Slamming the drawer shut with her hip, she leaned against the counter and studied her imprisoned fingers. It was just duct tape, not steel or razor wire.

Rachel pressed her fingers to her mouth, and worked to get a good tooth-hold on the edge of the tape. Christian had finished the ends and tucked them inside the twist of tape wrapping her fingers. She managed to get a corner of the foul-tasting tape with her teeth. A yank ripped a strand that frayed and pulled free. Saliva made another grip impossible.

"Damn it!"

Determined not to allow frustration to foil her, Rachel hooked up her pack, shoved her feet into her creepers and stomped out of the apartment.

Saturday—6:00 a.m.

Navigating the streets of Paris wearing a thigh-short dress torn at the shoulder, with a bloodstain just below her breasts, and handcuffed, was not easy. She'd thought to slip on the brown suede pants but hadn't wanted to waste time. Hell, furious as she was, and hobbled by a mere few strips of duct tape, Rachel had stormed from the apartment.

Not good. Keep calm. Find your center. You'll never win if you react. Pay attention.

Holding the pack before her kept the cuffs and tape from anyone's view. Keeping to the back streets and alleys, Rachel made her way across the Pont de Grenelle—where just last night she had heard the tour guide's narrations—to the Sixteenth arrondissement.

A small apartment with a view of the lush Bois de Boulogne housed the only person from whom she had ever earned the tiniest bit of trust—Jason Marland.

Rachel had not seen Jason in years. He would remember her. But it was unlikely he would welcome her.

The walk took a good hour. The neighborhood was upper-crust, pruned shrubbery and iron fences, waxed Mercedes and gardeners tending rare rosebushes—classy as it could get. Not a likely neighborhood for a safecracker to hide out in, but on the other hand, the perfect cover.

Counting the storefronts on the rue de la Pompe, Rachel neared a patisserie striped with pink and green paint. Hot, sweet scent filled the street, reminding her how little she had eaten.

She tilted back her head and scanned the facade of the marble building next to the shop. The windows on the third floor were blocked with blinds on the inside. Did he still live there? By nature, anyone making a living employing the criminal arts moved frequently. But she had always sensed that Jason was a bit of a homebody.

Clasping her cuffed hands beneath the pack, she made a silent prayer: *Please be there.*

There was a stairway around the back of the building, springing up from a tidy little garden that Rachel knew had— once, at least—been tended by a spindly old man with no hair and a toothless grin. No one used the back entrance unless Jason expected them—it was the business entrance. She would risk the faux pas. Besides, this wasn't a visit for tea and finger cakes.

The iron stair grating was firmly screwed to the plaster wall of the building and so made little noise with her footsteps. Her feet ached from the trek, her face ached from Christian's full-fisted slap, and her wrists were bruised. But most humbling remained the duct tape around her fingers.

"What a glamour girl you are," she muttered as she reached the top flight.

Just the fact that her appearance worried her suddenly troubled.

Rachel knocked three times on the knife-scarred door. She scanned the neighborhood below, noting two houses down in the courtyard, the woman who hung her laundry and the little bichon pup that playfully tugged a sheet.

She raised her fist to knock again but paused.

Behind the door Jason was likely getting his gun—

None of the surrounding windows showed interested observers.

—cock a bullet into the chamber.

One more knock.

The door swung wide and the barrel of a 9-millimeter pressed into Rachel's forehead.

Chapter 13

Saturday—7:13 a.m.

"Bloody hell. Rachel?"

The pistol remained pressed into her forehead. Threat level? High.

Rachel lifted her cuffed hands to placate, yet her stance remained firm, feet planted, shoulders squared—all business. Prepared to demand entrance, she decided on a softer approach. Just how forceful can one appear when one's fingers were duct-taped together?

"Can I come in?"

Jason looked over her shoulder, his fast gold eyes darting up and down the courtyard below. And back into her eyes. Suspicion could never be mistaken for anything but. And he was not sure of her. "Who sent you?"

"No one. This is not a job. I'm on my own."

'I—I must go and see if Emma is all right. I've been gone so long,' she said, her voice quavering.

'She'll cope.' Running the tip of his finger down her cheek, he felt it was warm and soft, like satin.

'William—I am extremely tired and would like to go to bed.'

'So would I. With you.'

'Please…'

'Are you going to get angry—to reject my advances?' Her eyes were dark, full of indecision. He smiled seductively. 'Come, Cassandra, you have been dubbed the Ice Maiden by every rake you've spurned. Prove them wrong. Shall we continue from where we left off earlier?'

'And I'm supposed to melt into your arms and sigh simply to prove I have blood in my veins and not ice? Please, William, my patience is wearing very thin.' Her words were definite, but her voice sounded unconvincing.

He laughed softly, his hooded eyes full of sardonic amusement as his arms went round her and pulled her close, moulding her body to his. 'I've certainly given you provocation.'

'I agree.' In his arms he was more attractive than ever, and despite her protestations the urgency to be even closer to him was more vivid than before. She watched him, anticipating, entranced, hardly breathing.

Bending his head and nuzzling her neck beneath her ear, hearing her gasp, in his sublime male arrogance, William knew her resistance was beginning to crumble. 'I'm difficult and impossible, I know, but that's because I'm attracted to you. I want you, Cassandra.'

'Want? There's nothing wrong with wanting, but it is a sin to take what is not offered.'

He laughed low in his throat, 'I have been sinning all my

life, so there is nothing new there. I'll do my penance later. I do want you. I have from the first moment I laid eyes on you.'

'And you're sure of that?'

'Absolutely,' he murmured, nibbling her ear. 'I am sincere.'

Feeling divine sensations shoot through her body, Cassandra closed her eyes. 'You haven't a sincere bone in your body.'

'But I have an overwhelming need for you.'

Feeling her legs tremble and the back of her knees ache, Cassandra leaned into him. He was as smooth as silk, an accomplished womaniser, but he was so appealing, and she was no longer a child. For the first time she felt the deep pull of physical desire, and here was the danger. She no longer feared a man's touch—instead she feared her own weakness.

When he raised his head she was unable to look at anything other than his lips hovering close to her own. She was shocked by how much she wanted to feel those lips on hers once more. She breathed out slowly as excitement and longing almost overwhelmed her. The touch of his hands inflamed her. Lowering his head, he kissed her gently, his mouth beginning a slow, unbelievably erotic seduction, and Cassandra felt the power of him, real and tremendous, in his restraint.

There was pleasure at the feel and taste of his lips. It was exhilarating, thrilling, agonising, all at the same time, and she was lost in a sea of sensation. Excitement gripped her and there was terror of the unknown. His arms went round her, drawing her close, his hand sliding slowly down her spine as he moulded her to his body. As his lips moved on hers, those lips and his touch unlocked something within her, releasing all the repressions and restraints she had imposed on herself for so long. Cassandra's breathing quickened and her body began to speak a language new to her, a language William understood perfectly.

When she melted against him, sliding her hands slowly up his chest and around his neck as she returned his kiss, William experienced a burgeoning pleasure and incredible joy that was almost past bearing. Minutes later he finally forced himself to lift his head and gaze down into her eyes, feeling them pulling him inexorably into their depths. He saw something there that reflected what he was feeling—desire. It was the way she stood—still, poised, willing him to kiss her again. Tenderness began to unfold within him—a sensation that had been as foreign to him as the voice of his conscience until he'd met this truly remarkable person and he asked himself how it was possible that this one woman could make him lose his mind.

'Have you any idea how lovely you are, Cassandra Greenwood—how incredibly desirable and how rare?'

Seduced by his mouth and caressing hands, the feel of his long legs pressed intimately to her own, Cassandra felt her body brought vibrantly to life. Drawing a shattered breath, she whispered, 'This is madness, utter madness.'

'I couldn't agree more,' he breathed, his mouth opening hungrily over hers once again.

As he continued to kiss her thoroughly, endlessly, producing a knot of pure sensation in the pit of Cassandra's stomach, the passion that ignited between them surpassed even William's imaginings—it surpassed anything he'd ever felt. Lust hit him with such unexpected force. His conscience stirred. Could this warm, incredibly beautiful and physically aroused creature be the Cassandra Greenwood the rakes of the *ton* had dubbed the 'Ice Maiden', and not a goddess by any means? But, by God, when she pressed herself against him and he felt her soft, ripe curves, she had the body of one. She was telling him silently, with her lips, her body, that she was definitely not made of ice.

When he finally released her lips he gazed down into her upturned face. Her eyes were liquid bright, and her lips, slightly parted, trembled and were moist from his kiss. 'So, the Ice Maiden melts. You want me. You can't deny it.'

'I suppose I am human after all. You've just proved that.'

'You're afraid.'

Disorientated and bewildered by what had just happened between them, Cassandra let her forehead fall against his chest. 'Yes.'

'You've nothing to fear from me.'

Raising her head, she looked at him, seeing no teasing light in his eyes. 'I hope not.'

'Cassandra, do you want to talk?'

She shook her head.

His lips quirked. 'I don't usually render a woman speechless when I kiss her.' He sighed, placing a gentle kiss on her lips. 'You are tired. Go to bed. We'll talk in the morning.'

Disengaging herself from his arms, she stepped back. 'Yes—I am tired. Please excuse me.'

Cassandra looked in on Emma before climbing into the bed in the room next door, but, as exhausted as she was and try as she might, she lay awake until the early hours, trying to understand the disturbing and consuming emotions William had aroused in her. How could she possibly understand this mindless, wicked weakness he seemed to inspire in her? Did skilled libertines make every woman feel that she was special? The wonderful memory of his kisses sent happiness spreading through her that was so intense she ached from it.

Was it possible to be so happy, to feel such joyous elation shimmering inside? At that moment she felt like the most beautiful woman in the world. She savoured again that feeling of exhilaration she had experienced in his arms, a sensation as heady and potent as good wine. She felt a melting sensation in her secret parts. Her thoughts began to travel beyond the kiss, and she felt the madness and the delight of secrecy at her forbidden thoughts. How she wished she could feel the strength of his arms around her now, loving her. She knew he was a man she could love, a man she could happily spend the rest of her life with.

She also knew William was a skilled rake and an accomplished flirt, but at that moment when she felt as if she was special to him, her heart rebelled against believing it. But she was no fool. Compared to him, she knew she was as naïve and unsophisticated as the proverbial newborn babe.

The following morning, William received Sir Charles Grisham in the library, his expression one of bland courtesy. 'What brings you to Carlow Park, Charles? Isn't it rather early in the day for a social call?'

'Dear Lord, William, have your wits become addled since you quit the army? Don't you listen? Why, only several days ago I told you I was to visit my aunt in Hertford.'

William's expression showed nothing more than mild surprise. Was it really only a few days since Lady Monkton's ball? It seemed a lifetime away. 'Yes, of course I remember. You told me Mark had invited you to call—something about a horse.'

'Two, actually, but that was before our wager concerning that paragon of virtue, the ravishing, sophisticated and highly desirable Miss Cassandra Greenwood.'

William's eyes narrowed, and there was no humour in his expression. 'Yes, isn't she.'

'Your interaction at the ball and the way you stalked off

and left her standing has become the talk of the *ton*. They're still trying to figure it out. London's abuzz with rumours.'

'And no doubt they'll put two and two together and make five,' William remarked drily. 'The rumours will soon be forgotten when some new scandal comes along to take their interest.'

'When I left Monkton House for White's, I had a mind to record our bet, but on second thoughts I decided against it, since a horse and no money is involved—except for the thousand guineas I shall have to part with if you win. I decided to keep the wager a private matter between ourselves.'

'I'm relieved to hear it.' This was one wager William wanted kept out of the exclusive gentleman's club White's famous betting book, in which its distinguished members recorded wagers on virtually everything, not only sporting events, but political and all manner of happenings whose outcome was unknown.

'Well, old man,' Charles said, sprawling, rather than sitting on the chaise before the fireplace, 'may your expectations be fulfilled—and my own—but if you're going to seduce the gently reared, unsuspecting Miss Greenwood before the Season ends, you're hardly going to carry it off buried in the country. The lady lives in town.'

'As if I need reminding.' On no account must Charles know Cassandra and her sister were residing at this very moment beneath his roof. Charles had many admirable traits, but discretion wasn't one of them.

'It's doubtful she's going to develop a *tendre* for you anyway in such a short time. Best get back to London, eh—otherwise that splendid beast you have in your stable will be mine. I think it will be anyway—so nothing to worry about there. You may have unscrupulously flayed the reputations of more pretentiously proud females than you can recall, but I told you when we made the wager that Miss Greenwood is made of different stuff.'

'Women fall for the most unlikely men, Charles,' William drawled, wearing a mask of genteel imperturbability, while becoming more irritated by Grisham's presence by the minute.

'There's no accounting for taste, I suppose, but in this instance you will fail—unless, of course, you have a strategy, Lampard. If so, be a good chap and pour me a brandy—and a cigar wouldn't go amiss—and I will listen with interest while you tell me all about it.'

Chapter Six

A wager! A horse!

Cassandra stood like a pillar of stone behind the slightly open door, her mind numb, unable to remember why she had been so eager to see William, to seek him out and look upon his handsome features once more, for him to confirm that she hadn't dreamt what had happened between them last night.

The conversation she had overheard hung in the air like a bad smell. No one had insulted her as much as this and it was more than her pride could bear. Dazed and unable to form any coherent thought, she backed away from the library door, and turning walked towards the stairs, wanting nothing more than to seek the refuge of her room. As the full realisation of what she had heard sank in and renewed life began to surge through her, her magnificent eyes shone with humiliation and wrath. She was appalled and outraged; there was no excuse, no possible way to deny the awful truth.

The unspeakable cad! The lecherous libertine! The man would seduce a nun in a nunnery if he had a mind. And just when she was beginning to trust him, to respect him and believe he had been unfairly maligned, to think that there was little truth in all the disgusting and immoral things she had heard about him—all her tender feelings were demolished.

William Lampard was a heartless beast and she could not believe that she, sensible and intelligent Cassandra Greenwood, had let him kiss her—and shame on shame, that she had wantonly kissed him back. What a fool she had been, a gullible, stupid, naïve fool.

Her mistake was that from the moment they had been thrust together, his easy banter and relaxed charm had completely disarmed her. She knew that men took advantage of foolish, innocent girls, so how had she allowed herself to fall into that trap? She had enjoyed his company, had melted into his arms like some besotted idiot, and had felt gratitude for his immense generosity in bringing them to his home, when all the time he had been playing a game with her. She was his prey, and he was intent on seducing her, dishonouring her, and to win his bet nothing was going to deter him from trying.

He had made a wager with Sir Charles Grisham to seduce her before the Season ended; should he fail, Sir Charles would be so much richer by a horse.

A horse, for heaven's sake! It was more than her lacerated pride could withstand. Her face blazed with fury. Oh, the humiliation of it. And if he succeeded, what would her life be like, following a tainted liaison with a renowned rake? The discovery of his treachery had destroyed all her illusions. She'd never trust him again, ever. How could she? He would never redeem himself from this.

As she went back upstairs, all these thoughts marched through her tormented and rage-filled mind. She would never forget what she had heard—ever—nor did she want to. She wanted to remember it so that never again would she be taken in by the likes of William Lampard. Of course, if she wanted to avenge herself, she could play him at his own game and he would have no idea of it—but, no, she wasn't like that and she had no time to waste on such foolishness.

By the time she reached her room an icy numbness had taken over and she was surprised to find she was no longer in the throes of heartwrenching pain. Stiffening her spine, she decided not to let him know what she had overheard, but this had given her an advantage and she was determined that she would outmanoeuvre him. Immediately she began planning a way to thwart and foil and exasperate the plans of this infuriating lord. She was strong and resilient and would get over this. They would leave Carlow Park just as soon as Clem arrived.

Back in the library, William poured a couple of brandies and handed one to Charles. Raising his own, he proposed a toast to Monarch.

'The horse is yours.'

Charles was incredulous, and then a slow, disbelieving smile broke across his face. 'But the wager? Good Lord! Have I heard right? Have you lost all reason?'

'I have never been more sane in my life.'

'So I am to assume you've had a change of heart and no longer wish to seduce Miss Greenwood? That you're folding—as easy as that?'

'Absolutely.'

'Then you're the most peculiar player I've ever had the pleasure of opposing,' Charles remarked, sensing something crucial was going on here that he knew nothing about. 'Unfortunately, I enjoy a challenge and the pleasure is somewhat muted by the wager's outcome.'

'Then I am sorry to disappoint you. I have developed a deep regard for Miss Greenwood. I will not dishonour her.

However, I have no intention of reneging on our wager. You can take the horse with you today if you wish, Monarch—I refuse to part with Franciscan. He was my brother's horse, so I'm sure you will understand my reluctance to part with him.'

When Cassandra went in to Emma, she found her up and dressed and sitting on the window seat, her knees drawn up to her chest. She was staring bleakly out over the gardens, her eyes, soft as velvet, looking at nothing. She looked pale and fragile, but, when she saw Cassandra, she managed a weak smile.

'How do you feel?' Cassandra asked, sitting beside her, facing her.

'I have felt better.'

Cassandra squeezed her hand affectionately. 'We're going home shortly. Clem will soon be here with the carriage. You'll start to feel stronger when you're home with Mama to take care of you.'

'Is she very angry with me, Cassy?'

'Mama has been extremely concerned, Emma. She loves you very much and is sorry you're ill.'

'But is she angry,' Emma persisted, 'because I eloped with Edward?'

'Naturally she is upset by the whole dreadful event. She wasn't best pleased when she found out—and poor Aunt Elizabeth blamed herself most wretchedly.'

'Where is Edward?'

'He went to Woolwich with Will. Lord Lampard.'

Emma looked stricken. 'He's—he's gone to the academy—to be a soldier?' Cassandra nodded. 'Oh, I see.' She bent her head. 'It isn't fair. I wanted to be his wife so much. I shall be lost without him. How can I possibly carry on?'

'You are stronger than you know. In two or three years this

will seem a small thing when you look back. Don't let it hurt so much, Emma.'

'But it does and this is now.'

'If you truly love Edward, it will endure.'

'You would, Cassy, I know. I have not your endurance. I—I won't give him up. I know you think I'm young and silly and that I don't know my own mind, but I do love him.'

Emma's face had taken on such a look of agony and despair that Cassandra softened involuntarily. 'I know you do,' she said gently and sighed. 'I know you're grown up, Emma, but do you really think you're ready to be married?'

'Yes, of course. Eloping was all my idea. I persuaded Edward. You mustn't think badly of him.'

'I was wrong about Edward, I realise that now. I misjudged him completely and I apologise for ever doubting him. You are right. He is a fine young man.'

Emma lifted her head, relief and hope lighting her eyes. 'You do? Oh, Cassy, I can't tell you what it means to me to hear you say that.'

'He loves you—genuinely loves you. Despite this foolish indiscretion, I believe him to be a good person—destined to be wounded by those harder, more selfish and less sensitive than he. I'll tell you what I said to him—give it time. Leave it for a while. I am of the opinion that things should be temporarily held in abeyance. Only until after you have come out, you understand, and this unfortunate business is behind us. Perhaps then, if you both still feel the same, then Mama will have no objections.'

Cassandra wished she didn't have to face William before she left. She remained with Emma for the rest of the morning. When it was time to leave, with her head held high and her delicate chin stubbornly set, she accompanied her sister downstairs. William was waiting for her in the hall. Outwardly she was composed and very calm, but inside she was seething.

William came towards her, curious as to why she had not come down earlier to see him. He ached for her—to touch her, to gaze on her lovely face, to hear the sweet, soft sound of her voice. When he had held her, she had touched a tenderness and protectiveness within him he hadn't known existed. After she favoured one of the footmen with her broadest smile, William was taken aback by the courteous and impersonal smile she gave him.

He wasn't to know how all her senses were crying out for him, how she was slowly dying inside. He had callously set out to dishonour her, and yet it was all Cassandra could do not to humble herself at his feet. With tremendous will she knew she would have to be strong to withstand a man of his character. William Lampard had no claim to being a gentleman in her interpretation of the word, but she knew him to be a proud man, and she intended to trample his pride to pieces.

'Did you sleep well?'

'Like a babe,' she quipped, trying to sound cool and amused. 'Indeed, I slept so well I failed to wake until a couple of hours ago.' She was surprised that her voice didn't shake.

Her tone, her very posture, were cool and aloof. William peered down at her, trying to read her expression. He wasn't sure what he had expected. An acknowledgement of what had passed between them, he supposed. His gaze went to Emma, who was hovering several paces behind, unsure how to approach Edward's imperious cousin who must be furious at their elopement. He took pity on her and softened his expression. 'Your sister looks pale. I told you I would be delighted to have you stay a while longer until she is fully recovered. I would not have said it if I did not mean it.'

'I know—and thank you,' Cassandra answered, her manner brusque, causing a flicker of consternation to cross William's face, 'but I am anxious to get home.' Only once did her composure slip a notch, and that was when Mark Lampard and a woman emerged from the study and came to stand behind William. Her bright smile faded uncertainly.

William turned to acknowledge them. 'Mark, you have met Miss Greenwood.'

'I have had that pleasure,' he replied, his eyes never leaving hers.

His hard, direct gaze told Cassandra their encounter had given him as little pleasure as it had her. 'It's good to see you again, sir,' she said politely.

He turned to the dark-haired woman standing beside him. 'Allow me to present my wife, Lydia.'

'I'm pleased to meet you, Lady Lampard,' Cassandra responded.

'Likewise,' Lydia replied smoothly.

Cassandra could read no expression in the woman's clear, attractive features, and as she regarded her closely, she felt her thoughts probed by careful fingers. She suppressed a shudder. Tall and slender, her nose aquiline and her hair perfectly coiffed, Lydia was quite beautiful, as a statue is beautiful—remote and cool. Her features were finely moulded and her lips showed a bitter twist. There was an indefinable poise about her, a certainty, and she had power. One thing Cassandra ascertained when she met her cold grey eyes—the coldest she had ever seen—was that this woman did not like her.

'Please excuse us. My sister and I are just leaving. We hope to make London before dark.'

'Then I wish you a safe journey.'

'Thank you. I'm sure it will be. Please excuse us.'

Taking Emma's arm, she led her outside to the waiting coach. William held out his hand to assist her down the steps, but she turned away. He was certain she had seen his hand, and he frowned in puzzlement as he watched her walk away. After a moment he realised she had an obligation to attend her sister, who still looked poorly, and he felt slightly easier. When Emma was inside the coach and it looked as if Cassandra was about to climb in without saying anything more to him, his face darkened and he took her arm.

'Cassandra, a moment, please.' He drew her aside out of earshot. 'Why are you doing this? Why are you angry with me?'

Her wide-eyed look was one of complete innocence. 'Angry? I am not angry,' she replied with a brittle gaiety, trying to harden herself against him, to forget his kiss and the way he had held her.

'I thought after last night—'

'Last night should never have happened. It was a mistake. We both lost control.' She looked up at him, looked away and back again. 'I should have known better than to submit to the charms of a philanderer.'

'I'm sorry you feel that way, because I think you are the loveliest, most courageous young woman I have ever met.'

Cassandra felt as if her heart was breaking. His gaze was one of consuming intensity, his mouth all wilful sensuality. 'Please stop it. Your compliments smack of insincerity. What happened was nothing more than an amusing diversion. It was just a sophisticated flirtation—the rule being the one you, a skilled libertine, usually play by—that no one takes anything seriously.'

He frowned. 'Are you afraid of what happened between

us?' he asked in a voice of taut calm, wondering why she was behaving like this.

'Afraid? No, of course not. Why should I be? It's just that I do not want you to be courtly or romantic. It's not you. Why—before I know where I am I might start falling for it and believe you truly care.'

'You cannot mean that.'

'Why not?' she said, struggling valiantly to sound flippant.

'It meant nothing to you?'

'Shall we leave out the dramatics?'

William's face hardened into an expressionless mask, but his eyes were probing hers like daggers, looking for answers, as if he couldn't really believe this was the same woman who had melted in his arms with such sweet, innocent passion and yielded her lips to his. His disappointment made him carelessly cruel. 'You would do well to remember how you responded to my kiss—willingly—and how you enjoyed kissing me.'

'That was last night. This is now—and I didn't enjoy kissing you,' she lied primly, doing her utmost to avoid his eyes as a change came over him. In all her life she had never encountered such controlled purposeful anger.

William stared at her. 'Forgive me if I appear dense, but you gave a fair imitation of it last night.'

She smiled. 'And no doubt after all your conquests, you're surprised to discover there's a female who finds you resistible.'

Reaching out, William gripped her upper arms and jerked her against him. When he spoke his voice was dangerously low. 'I would like to convince you that you can overcome that problem—to persuade you.'

'Try as hard as you like, but you will not succeed. I will not allow it.'

She'd always thought she was the only one. Skilled. Superior. Unique. A selfish thought. A proud thought. And for what purpose? Well, it was her life, wasn't it? It was all she knew. The machine had done what it was told, and she did it well.

And now to learn she was not the only one? Not unique, no matter the meaning?

"Tell me about them. No." To learn so much would take time, and a disposition to be open to take it all in. She was in no mood. Such information could prove a can of worms too deep to wade through for the hook.

Jason hadn't kissed the girls? He'd considered it? How many girls had he trained? Kept handcuffed to his bed? "I...don't want to know. There's no time. I've got to find Christian."

"You're going to eat first. Or you'll pass out. And probably a change of clothes, eh? Won't do to scamper about Paris flashing your tits."

Rachel tugged the houndstooth. "I'm not flashing."

"You most certainly are." He winked and strolled out, tossing the cream in the air.

Taking his exit to look over her unbuttoned dress, Rachel realized that indeed she did reveal a good bit of cleavage. Open to just above her naval where the last button had been bloodied by Christian's blade. If she bent way over, something would fall out. Christ, she was so off her game.

"I've some fresh strawberries and blackberries," Jason said. Returning to the kitchen, he opened the fridge door. "You like cream on them?"

"Sounds delicious." Rachel sat back down before the table and slid the cuffs in a circle, with her finger as the axle.

His back to her, Jason shuffled berries into a bowl. A throaty hum accompanied his busywork. A tune not unfamiliar to Rachel. She'd always known she'd picked up the wordless song from Jason, but the connection of how and when just now hit. He hummed whenever he cooked!

He turned and placed a bowl of berries and cream before her. A swing around, a few more bars hummed—what was that tune? Oftentimes she found herself humming the same song when she sat before a safe manipulating the dial.

Bakery paper crinkled and he cut her a thick slice of chewy rye bread. With a turn and a few finishing notes hummed, he landed it on her plate and sat across from her. An inspection of his chai decided the cooled liquid was still fine enough to drink.

Dodging looks at her from over the rim of his cup, he set it down and grinned. "Now what did I cock up, sweet?"

"Nothing." She spooned a mouthful of berries and pressed them against the roof of her mouth. The seeds burst and spurt juice down her throat. "You just...you still do it. Hum."

"Yeah?" He shrugged, touched his tongue to his lip. "I don't notice really. I suppose it's something I do when you're around."

"I've heard you whistle that song before. What's the tune?"

"An Elvis oldie. You do know who Elvis is? I know Lazar never let you do media."

"Of course." Though she could only recall that her mother had adored the singer and that she had waxed on and on about his handsome looks. Hard to imagine her mother happy and mooning over a musician when now all memories of her were blurred with fire.

"He's an American singer," Jason added.

"I know. I *am* an American."

"Yeah, and so is Lazar. Why the bloody hell did he pick this continent to torment?"

"I don't know. I never asked." She dipped a spoon into the bowl of berries.

Easier to entice a teenage girl to the exotic country of

France, maybe? She suspected Christian had lived here longer than she, for he had been trained here. But he was an expatriate, she knew, because his passport was American. "You don't think he torments anyone *new,* do you?"

"Only you, sweet. A man like him doesn't know a good thing even when it's stealing millions of dollars in rocks for him."

She shrugged, finding it difficult to agree when he used words like *thing* and *it.* So easily the facade of machine threatened. *It* had worked for Christian.

It no longer existed.

At least, *it* was trying to fade away. Just lately, everyone wanted to keep *it* alive.

"So why is a British safecracker holed up in a ritzy Paris neighborhood? Maybe the same reason Christian is in this country."

"I'm here because that's where the rocks are. And French pussy is a delicacy I admire."

She lifted a brow at that statement.

"So, you look good," Jason offered.

Smiling with a full mouth of food, she nodded. He was lying, but she didn't mind. The last spoonful of berries slid past her lips. Food, glorious food. The bread followed in big bites. The woozy cloud that had muddied her brain was beginning to recede.

"If not bloody ravenous. When was the last time you ate?"

"Probably yesterday morning. Is there more bread?"

He stood and cut her another slice. This time he placed the remainder of the loaf on the table, the knife stabbed in the heel. "Didn't you eat on the plane?"

"Please. It's a struggle just to keep an empty stomach down during a flight. I wouldn't dream of introducing food into the equation."

"Gotcha." He leaned back and watched her go at the bread.

Avoiding his gaze, Rachel scanned the room.

Bare of homey touches, the kitchen was sleek, with steel fixtures and appliances. Funny, how the men she had known, and who followed the criminal mien, never flaunted their riches with excessive material luxury. While Christian's home was immense, he'd furnished it sparely, with fine but simple items. Jason's home offered little decoration, as well, just the basic furniture, but finely crafted. The upscale neighborhood was the only real clue to his apparent wealth.

A guess decided it was not the money that kept them stealing—it was the thrill. An adrenaline fix that likely compared to a drug addict's craving for the needle. The same thrill that kept her doing something she loved. What luck she had found a way to do it without risking jail.

On the other hand, that luck had run out. And here she sat, doing absolutely nothing to change the outcome.

Just a few more bites. Build up your strength.

A small television sat next to the sink with a black box and a large green *X* on it.

"What's that?" Not about to let the bread crust go to waste, she tore the heel in half and dipped it in the fruit-sweetened cream at the bottom of her bowl.

"By the telly? Xbox. Video games. It keeps my fingers nimble."

"Ah." She tilted the bowl, wiping out the last drops of cream with the bread. "I don't do screen."

"That's right. Ultraconditioned and constantly training. No need for leisure activities. Like some kind of robot," he commented as he stood and wandered out of the kitchen.

Like some kind of robot? *Not anymore.*

She had been reading lately. Lots of books: mysteries, romances and nonfiction. She devoured the words like a hungry child. Some even made her cry or laugh out loud. Not like a robot. Robots didn't feel.

I do.

Sometimes. More times than she cared to admit. Most times, really. It was as if her emotions had been closed off for so long that now, once they began to leak out, they just flooded. And the flood threatened to bring her down if she didn't dam back the waters.

Jason reappeared with a soft blue sweater in hand, and toed the pack she'd tossed at the base of the wall.

"I've got pants in there," she said. "Bulletproof. Always comes in handy."

"Brilliant, 'cause I don't think any of my trousers would fit your skinny hips. This sweater shrunk last time I washed it." He feigned innocence. Difficult for a man with a face like a mug shot. "I don't think you're supposed to wash cashmere."

"I wouldn't know. I send my laundry out." She accepted the sweater and impulsively rubbed it aside her cheek. The fabric was soft as a kitten. Her fingers stuck to the weave. "I've got to scrub this sticky stuff off. Can I use your bathroom?"

"Sure." Jason bent over her pack and upended it. The invasion of privacy didn't bother her; he had every right to check for weapons.

"Hand me the pants," she said as she strode toward the bathroom. "And the bra."

"Ducks?"

She turned to find him dangling her bra before him. Bright yellow ducks on white satin. If she didn't know better, that might be a blush shading his neck. Likely it was stubble.

"You got a problem with ducks?"

"Nope. In fact, I think I'm growing fonder of them by the minute. Just ducky, eh?"

She tugged the bra from him and pressed her face into the sweater to conceal the warmth she felt flush there.

"Hey, what's this?"

She heard plastic crumple as she stepped into the bathroom

and closed the door only partway so she could keep up the conversation while she dressed. He must have found her emergency stash. "Gummi Bears, the finest sweet in the world. You can have some."

She slid into the suede pants and snapped up the fly.

"That's all right, I wouldn't want you to run out. If I can't identify the ingredients I don't eat it. For all I know, this stuff is made from rubber. So you've quit the carbs and protein that Christian fed you?"

"No. But I'm slowly allowing myself to try new things. One of the luxuries of freedom, you know." She bent over the sink and splashed her face with warm water. Pressing her fingertips to the bar of soap on the vanity, she worked them to get off the sticky residue.

"Ducks and Gummi Bears." She could hear the smile in Jason's tone. "That's a bit of all right."

Looking up, she startled at her reflection. Strawlike from the harried day, her hair shot this way and that on her scalp. A bruise darkened a curve high on her right cheek, not dark, but it could deepen before the day was over. She looked like crap.

And she was bleeding. The cut on her chest was shallow, but still seeping. With no Band-Aids in the medicine cabinet, she pressed a folded square of toilet paper to the wound.

Snapping on her bra, she smiled as the ducks then disappeared beneath her camisole shirt.

"How old were you when…"

She strode out from the bathroom, tugging the sweater over her head. "When what?"

"Well, you know." Jason stepped over and smoothed out the sweater's twisted collar. One hand remained on her right shoulder. "When you and Lazar…"

"When he seduced me into his clutches and then molded me into some kind of machine?"

"Sweet, I didn't mean—"

"I was fourteen. Just escaped from my fifth foster home."

He smirked and shrugged. "That explains the ducks."

"It does?"

With a shrug he skated a hand down her arm. But the touch didn't end, and instead he clasped her fingers loosely.

Rachel didn't pull away.

"Fourteen is like puberty and parties and boys and all that coming-into-age sort of stuff, right?"

Concentration vacillated between his voice and the touch. He held her hand. No man had ever just Held Her Hand. So casual. This was…exciting.

As for knowledge of puberty, she wasn't sure what normal was. She had never had a first date, or a party. Tampons and cramps had been explained to her by the cook. She'd frequently missed her periods because she'd kept her weight down.

"So," Jason said, "you're a girl on the verge, and along comes this power-freak monster of a criminal who takes you away from all that and turns you into a, well…a literal machine."

"No emotion, no hesitation, just do the job," she repeated an oft-spoken mantra. Her shoulders straightened at mere mention of the rigid rules.

"Exactly. And now, here you are, away from Lazar's influence, and for the first time in your life you can do whatever you bloody well please. Grocery shopping and libraries. Ducks and Gummi Bears. It's like the girl wants her chance now. Yeah?"

"I never thought of it that way. I suppose I did miss some things."

But if you hadn't the experience, then how could you know to miss it?

"Keep it up," Jason said, "and the next thing you know, you'll be dancing and partying and crushing, just like a teenager."

"Crushing?"

"You know, crushing on a boy, er, well, a man. I think teens still call it that. Making eyes at him and watching his every move. Oh, isn't he dreamy?" he mocked in a higher tone.

She reluctantly pulled her fingers from his and made to ease her wrist with her other hand. "I've already crushed."

"Christian?"

She had to admit she admired Christian physically. Had she any choice? But there had been another. "You were my first crush."

Jason pressed his fingers to his chest and mocked a "me" look.

"You're a smart man, Marland. You know you were."

"I suppose I do recall you were always gazing at me."

"No one else to look at while I was here."

"But you never called me dreamy."

"Dreamy sounds juvenile."

"True."

"I worked very hard for that kiss."

Could I have another? So difficult to hope, to let down her guard. It wouldn't be wise.

"I would have kissed you the moment you walked through my door had you not been attached to the master of control, you know that."

"No, I didn't. Do you mean to say you were...crushing on me?"

"Big-time."

"Hmm." She rubbed both arms, snuggling into the soft sweater. His sweater. She wore a man's sweater. A man who had once— "Are you still crushing?"

"How can I resist a woman who wears a ducky bra?"

Letting her arms fall loose at her sides, Rachel hooked her thumb in the back pocket of her pants. Open. But not really sure how to take the first step. Inside, a piece of her shattered and began to disperse. In its wake a hollowness pulsed. That missing part of her craved Jason's touch. A part that just wanted to surrender. And this time the surrender must come at her bidding.

He stepped forward, tentatively, then cruised his palm along her left arm. The touch skimmed shivers across her skin. It was everything she had hoped for.

And when had she hoped for anything but freedom? How her teenage mind danced at this close connection.

He touched his lip with his tongue, then said, "I'm crushing pretty heavily on you right now."

She looked into his gold eyes and saw her own feelings. A little soft and unsure, yet tense, there in the pulse of his jaw.

Crushing? Rachel toyed with the idea of crushing her mouth to his. A real kiss.

Instead of wishing it—it happened.

Jason leaned in and kissed her. Lightly. Tentatively.

Rachel didn't move to react, she merely took on the powerful force of the kiss. It was as though he had read her mind. The man kissing the crushing schoolgirl. He'd been right to guess those years stolen from her were now demanding their release. She wanted to kiss. She wanted a boyfriend. She wanted a relationship.

She wanted to belong to no man.

Sliding a hand up his hard bicep, Rachel broke the kiss.

"I know," he whispered. "It's not wise for this to happen right now."

"Oh? Oh, yes." Back to action. Had she just been thinking silly thoughts about the man? Boyfriends and relationships? Right. You don't want to be controlled by him. Keep it business.

"You've got a lot to do in so little time," he said.

"I know. I'm acting silly."

He tilted up her chin. A mix of gold and green and some indefinable color, his eyes glinted like a rare jewel. Worth a cool million, easily. "Girls are supposed to act silly."

"Not when Christian Lazar is toying with their lives. And I'm not a little girl."

"Definitely a woman."

A moment of indecisiveness stilled her. Still caught in his eyes. Kiss him again?

And lose her edge.

"I'd better get back to business."

He caught her by the shoulders. Jason's eyes weren't about to release hers. "I hope when this is over, and you're left standing—because you will survive, I know that—that you get everything you desire, sweet."

"And what if I am still standing, but behind bars?"

"You won't be. You'll get that rock back. Hey, why don't we just pull a fake?"

"It's not that easy. This rock is huge and has been carefully documented. The Rousseau ruby—"

"Rousseau ruby? You didn't tell me it was the Rousseau ruby." His tone changed, but she ignored it for the sudden warmth that fell over her. A dragging call to...sleep?

"I just did."

"But...that means—"

Rachel yawned and surrendered to a wobble.

"Hey, are you all right? You don't look so good."

"Must still be a bit of jet lag."

"You need to lie down."

"Haven't got time. I've already slept."

"Obviously not enough. An hour. Just to let the food settle and realign your center. You won't get anything done right unless your head is straight. You can sleep on my bed."

"But—"

"No buts. Do I have to handcuff you to the bed?"

She smiled and, led by Jason's guiding hands, sauntered into the bedroom. Collapse came easily. "Wake me in an hour?"

"Gotcha. You sure it's the Rousseau ruby?"

Rachel nodded. She thought she heard Jason swear, but sleep attacked with expert aim.

Saturday—9:45 a.m.

Rachel rolled over on the thick goose-down coverlet to face the door. Someone was knocking? But not at the back door opposite the bed, the one down the hall. The front door, which opened to a hallway with an elevator and stairway.

Dragging herself upright, she came to her senses with a shrug of her hand over her face. There was another noise. Water droplets.

So Jason was showering and someone was knocking at the door. The shower stopped. Another knock.

"Jason?"

"You awake? Yeah, it's been almost an hour, time to rise, sleepyhead."

"There's someone at the door."

"I called delivery, there's a pastry shop below. Got some great little petite cream puffs. Will you get that?" He peeked his head out the bathroom door. Water dripped from his face and bare chest. Steam scented with minty coolness poured into the bedroom.

"Sure." Rachel slid from the bed, tugged down the soft cashmere sweater and turned her head to hide her smile as Jason winked at her.

She strode out to the front door. Bright sunlight sparkled on the marble floor. Delighting at the cold stone beneath her bare feet, Rachel took a moment to shuffle her fingers through her hair, then grasped the doorknob.

Suddenly aware, she slid her back to the wall beside the door. "Who is it?"

"Who are you?" answered back.

Not the reply a friendly delivery boy would make. Opening the door, Rachel grabbed for the neck below a very familiar face. "You?"

Working a deft move on her, the man grabbed her elbow, which released her hold on his neck. Rachel got in a right hook to his shoulder but, just as quickly, an angry fist of five knocked out her lights.

Chapter 15

Saturday—9:55 a.m.

"Why did you chin me so hard? *Merde!*"

"You don't punch a woman."

"That woman—" Vincent worked his jaw with his fingers and then jabbed the air before him "—is very punchable."

Conversation segued into her muzzy thoughts. Rachel realized she lay prone on the hard marble floor. Voices of two men volleyed nearby. Men? Where was she? Did she know them? Her jaw burned. What had she run into?

"Hands off, Rousseau."

Jason's voice.

"What is *she* doing here? Of all the— Are you working with her? Making plans against me? *Merde!*"

And who was the other—

"The *salope!*"

Now she remembered.

"You bastard!" Rachel shot upright and lunged for the Frenchman squatting at the nearby wall and tapping his jaw.

They landed on the floor in a sprawl of limbs. Skull bone clacked the hard surface. Blood squirted from the Frenchman's nose. Rachel jumped up, crouched, and pulled back her arm. Before she could get a fist into his face, she was being restrained. Hands pulled back at her hips, a foot dipped around in front of her ankle to shake her balance.

The Frenchman leaped to his feet. "Keep your wench at bay!" He snarled as Jason held Rachel away from the throat she wanted to crush. The thief touched his bloody lip and sneered at her.

Tugging out of Jason's hold, she straightened and resumed calm. Every muscle in her body screamed for justice.

The thief made a silent but indignant gesture to his bloody nose and mouth. She hadn't touched him! How was he bleeding?

Jason's fingers bit into her shoulders. She jerked him away. "Don't touch me."

"You gonna stay in your corner?" he asked in a soft but obvious command.

"The bastard punched me."

"Yeah, well, don't get your knickers in a twist, I got him for you."

That's where the blood had come from. Rachel smiled. So he'd been looking out for her?

Now she noticed Jason wore but a pair of blue jeans. No shirt. Fresh from the shower, not a single shred of fabric over the hard rolls of muscle fit to his chest and abs. Man, but the guy worked out.

Then she remembered how the whole debacle had begun. "I thought you said it was pastries?"

"It should have been."

"What is he doing here? He stole the ruby."

"Then you took it from me!"

"Children," Jason cautioned. "Let's agree to a bloodless discussion, shall we?"

"How is he here?" she wondered. "Do you know this man?"

"Vincent and I are old friends." With a deft move, Jason forced her to the wall backing the kitchen. He stood before her, blocking her from a lunge to attack. No touching this time. But Rachel wasn't riled anymore. Just stunned.

"I didn't realize he was the thief you'd had a row with until you mentioned the Rousseau," Jason offered.

"Where is it?" hissed over Jason's shoulder. The Frenchman leered. Fitting, for the devil he was.

"Back off, Vincent." Jason angled his shoulder so she could see the Frenchman.

She had just walked into a trap, a nest of thieves. Nothing smelled right about it either. "You two are in this together?"

Jason made a pained face. "It's a bit more complicated, sweet."

"Salope!" Vincent made an angry gesture at her, but Rachel felt sure it was also directed at Jason.

"A right gentleman he is," Jason said of his...friend? "Rachel, meet Vincent Rousseau, sixth-generation Rousseau in line to inherit the famed Rousseau ruby."

Ah, so Christian hadn't confused his information.

"So you see it is mine," Vincent snapped. He held out a hand and flicked up a four-fingered "gimmee" gesture. "Cough it up."

"Fuck you."

"Rachel," Jason warned.

"You are protecting my enemy?" Vincent asked Jason.

"Sweet here doesn't need protection. And since when did she become the enemy?"

"Sweet?" The Frenchman rolled his eyes and lifted his arms to the heavens. "I should have guessed!"

"What?" Jason snarled. "We aren't working together."

"But you two are?" Rachel tossed out.

"I thought we were," Vincent spat. "I call anyone who takes what is mine enemy. Where is it?"

Maintaining a defensive splay of hands between the two opponents, Jason said, "She doesn't have the ruby, so just take it down a notch, all right?"

"How do you know, if you are not working with her? Have you frisked her? Checked out—" Rousseau dragged a lecherous preen down her torso "—all cavities?"

"Christian Lazar has it." Rachel pushed away from Jason's blockade. She strode past the Frenchman and to the window, wishing she could just keep walking, lose herself in the lush wilds of the park below. The beginning of a headache pulsed at her temple.

It should have been a simple heist. *Simulated* heist. In little over a day, she had been worked over by another thief, survived a flight to Paris, learned Christian Lazar still lived, faced down Marland's gun, taken a sucker punch from the same irritating thief—and still the ruby eluded her.

How much more convoluted could this get?

Vincent Rousseau? Jean-Jacques Rousseau was an 18th-century Swiss philosopher and writer. And the thief claimed to be a direct descendant. Just because he had the name did not grant him ownership. There must be thousands with that same surname in France. If it even was his real name. False names were common amongst her ilk.

Your ilk? Christ. She wasn't about to reduce herself to their level. Not when she'd almost pulled her chin above water. Standing here with these two men was so wrong on so many levels.

Another knock at the door sparked a rousing reaction. All three turned, fists at the ready.

"It's the pastries," Jason decided. He strode to the door and opened it to reveal, indeed, a delivery boy holding a waxed white Paul's box prettied up with a pink moiré ribbon.

Rachel turned back to the window. Fisting her hands akimbo she glared at the sky. Not an airplane in sight.

She should be home soaking in a tub right now. That she had ever allowed Rousseau to leave the States with the ruby had been her most critical mistake.

Vincent and Jason were working together? Had she picked the wrong place to come for help.

Or maybe it was exactly where she needed to be. If both were involved, she needed to know exactly what plans they had to find the lost ruby. And…to keep them far from the prize. An enemy close at hand was easier to manipulate than one allowed free rein.

"Lazar?" Rousseau said. "This *salope* works for Christian?"

Much as she knew a calm head was required—if he called her a bitch one more time…

The thief dug around in the pastry box, produced a small fruit tart and popped it in his mouth. Noticing her observance, he stuck out his tongue, coated with half-chewed pastry, and waggled it at her. Pig.

Rachel couldn't make herself speak with any calmness, so she spun to face the window and remained silent. As long as that man stood in this room she could only think to attack.

"Is she one of the network?"

That got her attention. Rachel turned her head so quickly her equilibrium dizzied.

There was that name again—the network. Or was it a title? How was it she had been with Christian for so long and had never heard the term? And in the period of one morning she had heard it from two men.

"No longer," Jason said. He tugged the pastry box across

the table and scanned the contents. Disinterested, he let it be. "She's Lazar's thief. Or was. She was there when Christian stroked. Made her escape that same day, and hasn't looked back. Until now."

"A freelancer now?" Vincent asked in nasal mockery.

"I was working for the Lalique museum," she said sharply.

"Ah. *Oui.*" Vincent's demeanor changed so quickly Rachel could have sworn she heard him giggle, though he merely exchanged a glance with Jason.

Something was going on between the two of them. Hell, *something* had already gathered fuel.

Stiffening her spine, she assumed the calm, emotionless facade required. This game was not even going to begin. She had already discarded this chump once, he wasn't about to mess up her plans now.

"I was hired to check the security. That ruby was never to leave the States. It should have never left the museum."

Vincent's laughter hit that just-kill-the-asshole button inside Rachel, and she rushed him—

—only to be caught around the waist by Jason.

"Let me at him!" Arms flailing and fists fierce, she beat at the air before her. "Just let me kick the jackass in the balls!"

"The name is Vincent," he said.

"I don't care what his name is—"

"Do you always avoid getting the names of the men you fuck?"

Chapter 16

That comment stopped Rachel in Jason's arms. He set her down and she twisted to look at him. Their proximity pressed her hip to his hard stomach. She could see the change in Jason's expression. His soft eyes hardened. His jaw pulsed. The grip on her waist loosened.

"No." She stepped to the center of the room and crossed her arms—both men stood an equal distance to either side. Drawing the cold mask of indifference across her face, she had to struggle to match her voice to the expression. "Why bother with names when the event was so forgettable?"

"Forgettable?" Vincent tipped back his head and let out a chirp of laughter. "How could you forget three orgasms, baby? You were begging for more. *Merde,* you passed out on the last one."

Passed out? No, she had fallen asleep. Fast.

Had she passed out? The notion was unbelievable. Idiotic.

Yes? Because the orgasms were so powerful. Far from forgettable. No, she couldn't have fainted.

"I was tired." An explanation wasn't necessary!

Rachel turned from Jason, unable to look at him, nor did she want to feel his condemning look upon her. Or was it pity?

"I rocked you, baby."

"That's enough, Rousseau." Jason, fingers to his jaw in thought and head down, walked to the fridge, leaving Rachel and Vincent glaring at one another. "We don't have time for this rot. Lazar has the ruby and Rachel has to get it back to the States."

"You're going to let her have *my* ruby? When did you change the fucking plan, Marland?"

"It's not yours," Rachel snapped. Control, she coached inwardly. If she punched him, she'd only draw back a hand sticky with the white powder that sprinkled his cheek. Relaxing her shoulders, she continued. "You stole it, then I stole it. Fair is fair. And what, if I may ask, *is* the plan?"

"Actually." Jason returned with two Mexican beers—the latest rage in Paris—and held one out to Vincent. "It really is his ruby. Been in the family for years."

"I am Vincent Gerard Rousseau," the surly Frenchman said. "Direct descendant of Jean-Jacques Rousseau."

"He's dead." Rachel hadn't the time or the patience for this crap. "Besides, explain the fact that the ruby was to be displayed by a museum. If it had been yours, you wouldn't have *stolen* it back, you would have simply waited until after the showing to have it returned."

She caught Jason's smiling lift of brow, a silent challenge to Vincent. Yeah, so explain that one.

"The ruby has been out of the family for over a decade," Vincent said. "It was stolen from the Fouquet in the early 1990s and just resurfaced last year. This is the first public display since then."

"Why didn't you just announce your claim to the rock? If it really is yours."

He dismissed her with a narrow green sneer and a gulp of beer. "The paperwork was lost."

"Ah. Of course. The missing paperwork. An obvious glitch. The ruby is mine." She intercepted Jason's beer as he tottered it in the air between two fingers and swigged back a swallow. "Get the hell out of my face, Rousseau."

"Tell her what she has fucked up for the two of us," Vincent hissed.

Yeah, tell her the plan. Rachel turned to Jason, defying him to explain.

Two idiots trying to nab a two-million-dollar sparkler? She didn't believe Rousseau's story for a moment. On the other hand, Jason was no idiot.

"So?" she prompted Jason.

Drawing his palm over his face, he let out a heavy sigh. "It was an insurance job, sweet."

Cold shimmied over Rachel's scalp and prickled at the base of her skull. She tilted her head against the tightening muscles in her neck. Please, do not let it be what she was thinking.

"The curator for the Lalique put out feelers for a thief. Sidney Posada?"

No, do not know so much, she thought. Jason had merely done his research. A requirement for any heist.

"The museum is teetering on the verge of bankruptcy and needed some quick cash."

Christ, no.

"The museum 'hires' a thief to steal an item and they collect the insurance money. The thief's pay? The rock."

But that didn't explain why the curator would have hired her to check security. It didn't make sense. Unless it was just a safety net, to prove to the insurance company that the museum should have been secure.

No. Not right.

A smart man would have never hired an inspection and the theft in so close a time period.

She looked to Jason. Clearly he was caught between a boulder and a speeding truck. Or was he? He and Rousseau were obviously allies.

Eyeing the door, Rachel counted the strides. Her pack sat in the bedroom at the base of the bed. She could make the back door. But could she do it without taking a bullet to her back? No heat had been introduced to this quaint little chat, but Jason's Beretta was close, on the kitchen table.

"Posada contacted me," Jason offered. "I was ready to refuse—you know, I don't like to leave the country—"

Right, because America pissed him off. Too much materialism, he'd once told her. Everyone trying to improve their neighbors, without first looking to their own faults. A bunch of self-righteous prigs.

"—but when Posada said it was the Rousseau, I knew Vincent would want in on the action."

"I still don't understand," she said. Keeping a keen eye on Rousseau—to her left and four paces behind—Rachel focused on Jason. Trust had just flown out the window, but he was the closest thing to an ally in this room. "The museum had hired me to check security. They knew my methods, that I would simulate a break-in. I'd suggested it wasn't necessary to remove anything, but the curator said it would be better if I did. So why..."

Suddenly it hit her. But of course. She always gave a window of four days in which she would do the job—and then beat that window by one day. They had expected Vincent to hit the night *before* she should have approached the place. No way would she know that there had been activity before she stepped into the cat's seat. Why hadn't she seen through that idiot plot right away?

Vincent spoke. "No thief in his right mind would have taken that score, unless he was guaranteed an alibi."

"Me," she muttered. Dread curdled her blood. She'd been set up. By Posada and these two.

"I should have walked away with that rock," Vincent said, "but you had to go and muck it all up."

Yes, because, had she not shown the night of his heist, he would have walked, free and clear, while the only suspect would have been her.

She eyed Jason. "You knew it was me the Lalique had in mind?"

"Hadn't a clue, sweet. No names were used, you should know that."

She nodded. But that didn't allay her suspicions.

"Lazar really has it? *Merde!*"

"So even if I do bring it back," she started, frantically figuring all sorts of schemes in her brain and not liking any of them, "I'll still be arrested."

"They'll be waiting for you with the cuffs dangling, sweet."

Eyes scanning Jason's face, not really seeing, Rachel ran the impossible through her brain. So this was how it was all going to play out? To be arrested for a crime she did not commit? Her years of theft while serving Christian would finally, and wrongly, be punished by another thief's scam.

"I have to bring the rock back."

Vincent spat beer. "What?"

"I won't take the fall for him. For the two of you! I'm leaving."

"Where the hell are you going?" Jason followed as she strode to the bedroom.

"To find Christian. He wants to play? I'm in for the count." She dived for her pack settled at the base of the bed and toed the plastic bag of Gummi Bears inside. A wide arc slung it over her shoulder. "There are a few places I know to look."

"Like?" Jason held out his arms in wait of her revelation.

"Why the hell should I tell you? We're both in this for the same prize. Damn, I can't believe I came here."

"You had no idea, Rachel. You made the right decision. Now we all know what we're dealing with."

"Why are you working with him? What part of this job is for you? Are you taking half?"

"It's my rock!" Vincent spat from around the corner.

"I got the call," Jason explained. "I take a commission. The usual thirty percent."

"But if it's an heirloom he's not going to sell it. Who were you meeting last night?" she shouted to Vincent.

The Frenchman popped his head around the corner and tipped his beer bottle to the two of them. "My partner."

"Partner?"

A tilt of Jason's head affirmed her suspicion. "I was going to keep the ruby on ice until we found a buyer."

"A buyer," she stated. "For a fucking heirloom. My ass!"

"A man's gotta pay the rent," Vincent tossed out.

Jason approached her. She allowed him to get close, for the fact that it kept their conversation semiprivate from Vincent. But she wasn't kidding herself; Vincent heard their every word, and so she kept her back stiff and her intuition on alert. "I don't want to hurt you, sweet. I'm not going to hurt you."

"Then step back."

"Fine." One step placed him about four feet from her. A quick flash of his palms wasn't long enough for her. She wanted him cuffed and incapacitated, as well as Vincent.

The distraction of Jason's bare chest toyed with the machine's ability to focus. Rachel switched her gaze between his biceps and the wall just beyond his shoulder.

"Do you think he'll go to the X first?" Jason wondered.

She reacted to the name of the club with a tight jaw. Stupid. Vincent saw.

The X was a techno-dance club that rocked 24/7. Intrigued by the atmosphere of stainless steel and dancing bodies that never stopped, Christian had invested in it years ago. After the suspicious death of the X's owner, Christian had taken on the management himself. A hobby, he'd once claimed. A different avenue for his bountiful energy.

The upper-level office overlooked the dance floor and was walled with two-way glass that allowed those in the office to observe without being seen themselves. It was equipped with two safes. Christian used it for storage between laydowns or before transferring rocks to be fenced.

Rachel had been there once, and had vowed never to return, for reasons that Christian well knew—the music blared nonstop.

Now that the club had been mentioned, it was the first place Rachel could think to look. It made sense, because the other locations that immediately sprang to mind—an empty warehouse at the edge of the Marais and a private office overlooking the Jardin des Plantes—were too subtle. If Christian wanted to play, the X would offer the perfect challenge. A challenge that, even to think of it, made Rachel's brain spin. She'd take a day-long flight to Australia over a raucous dance club any day.

The phone rang. Jason turned around to pick up the cell phone from the dresser by the bed. He eyed Vincent and walked farther into the bedroom. Rachel pricked her ears. Hell, she'd do more than that. She followed him across the room. The back door was but a stride away.

"I've heard," Jason said. He turned and seemed startled to see her right behind him. She tilted her head, querying. No way was she going to give him the privacy his pained expression pleaded for. "Yes. That's...right. Yes. No, not a problem. I'll see to it. Today. Yes, I've got your number."

He hung up. All blood had drained from his face, marking

the absence of his five o'clock shadow more distinct. He clasped the phone like a weapon but made no move.

It had not been a good call, Rachel sensed. Likely it had something to do with the fouled snatch and—*I'll see what I can do*—her?

A headlock and some extreme force to the back of his spine might make him spill. But she had already guessed there were no allies standing within shouting distance.

"I'm leaving." She spun to hook up her pack and stalked to the door.

"I'm coming with you."

It was not Jason who had volunteered that unwanted accompaniment.

Rachel stopped abruptly at the front door, catching Vincent's broad frame squarely against her body. A snort of cinnamon breath preceded his sneer. He tapped his beer bottle against the door frame and didn't smile.

"You're not invited."

"Then I'll beat you there." He jammed the beer bottle into her palm and took off.

So stunned at that exit, Rachel could but stand there staring at the half-empty bottle. She was aware Jason came up and embraced her.

"You okay?"

Startled more by the embrace than Vincent's exit, she swiveled in Jason's arms and pushed against his chest. How long she stared at her fingers, pressed to the hard-muscled pecs, she couldn't guess. He was so solid. There. A definite part of her life. And…confused the hell out of herself thinking that.

It was so, so wrong. He was the one involved in a heist that relied upon her to take the heat.

"What do you think you're doing, Marland? Nicing up to me? I get it. The old good-thief, bad-thief scenario, eh?"

"I thought you didn't watch television?"

She shrugged from the embrace and downed the last of Vincent's beer. Nasty stuff. Grimacing, she handed the empty bottle to Jason. "I'm out of here."

Kicking the door wide open, Rachel strode out and, aware Jason followed, she made for the stairs three apartment doors down the hall, picking up speed with each stride. The stairway was narrow and the stairs were short; the entire twist verged on medieval. Top speed was not possible. Landing the first floor, Rachel reached for the steel door pull. Jason hurried up behind her and slammed a palm against the painted metal to keep the door from opening.

She bent and spun, catching him in the gut with a fist. Solid muscle. Her punch did little more than make him wince. In the next instant, she slipped her fingers about his wrist. A deft yank turned his arm behind his back and she jammed his face into the door frame where it met the wall. A torque to his arm ratcheted a yelp from him.

Pressing her body to Jason's backside, she shoved her hips, hard, moving him snug to the door. "That call was about me, wasn't it?"

"Listen, sweet—*yei-iih!*"

With him in this position, she held all the cards. He was strong, but stretching his elbow taut kept him from moving. Muscles he could use against her were incapacitated. "Tell me!"

"It was Posada. He knows you're in Paris. He doesn't believe for one minute you've got the ruby stashed in the States. They wouldn't have known things are so fucked, but you did e-mail them."

That statement hit her like a bomb. *They wouldn't have known...*

And for all her reluctance to send the e-mail, why hadn't she listened to her intuition then?

Either way, the Lalique still intended to use her as the dupe.

"What do they want you to do? Follow me?"

"Posada has no clue I know where you are."

Made sense. But did she trust Marland?

"But they know I am in Paris and so are you."

"Right."

"You need to get the rock from me."

"Posada wants me to find you, yes."

"God forbid I should return and they don't collect the insurance check."

"Exactly. Christ! Let up, woman. I won't make a move."

With a satisfying slam of his head into the door, she released him. The violence felt good. It fed her like a log to the flame. Rachel stepped back, her arms loose and her fingers ready for fists. The stairway stretched another flight down—escape. But Jason made no move, save to touch the corner of his mouth where it bled.

A twinge in her forearm tempted her to lift her hand and touch his lip. She fought the mutinous desire.

For the first time she was actually reluctant to make a move. Take him out or take him on as an ally? The air between them was definitely gray. No black and white. Not that simple. He called her sweet—and meant it. At least, it felt as if he meant it.

Get over it, woman! Allying herself with him wasn't an option.

"Are you going to keep me from the ruby?"

Lifting his head, he looked down at her. "Not sure."

"But you're going to follow me? Hell, you have to. You don't get paid for the job unless you turn me in."

"That's not the way I see it."

"Oh? Enlighten me."

"The jewel has been stolen. That's all the museum asked for. Posada just doesn't want the jewel showing up when he's going to claim it missing."

"I see. So, knowing I want to return it, you want to keep it from my hands?"

"I haven't decided yet."

"I'm gone."

Pressing his body against the door to keep her from exiting, he warned, "You're not going anywhere without me."

"Just watch me."

"I'll offer you a ride."

"You think I don't know how to hail a cab?"

"With what? You don't have any cash."

"Yes, I—" She clutched her pack. There was no reason to look. "You took my money?"

"I'm a thief, what do you want from me?"

When had he been sorting through her things? She'd watched him dump her stuff before she had changed. When she had been sleeping? But he'd been showering. He must have done it *after* the call. Which meant he wasn't any more on her side than Vincent was. Whether or not he wanted to acknowledge it, he'd already decided which side he was on.

"Let me drive you, sweet. I'll get us to the X fast. Which is a lot more than your driving will do. And that is *if* you can jack a car."

How did he know she was a crappy driver? Rachel fisted the wall over Jason's shoulder. It hurt. She didn't care.

"You're Vincent's partner?"

He didn't reply with a yes or no. "Vincent and I go back a few years. I taught him—"

"All he knows?"

"Of course."

"Just like me." She leaned against the wall, lowering her head. "And Christian."

Jason had his hands in it all. Anyone who Rachel had ever had to deal with on a personal basis had either known Jason or had been trained by him. It occurred to her now that she couldn't figure why the man would be so generous with his abilities. Why did he want to train his competition? Or maybe, he charged a fortune. Maybe Jason's real money scheme was in the training, not in the actual fieldwork.

It made sense. He called the shots but kept to home base, while someone else did all the legwork. Tidy up with thirty percent commission? A dream job.

And a blunt reminder that while they had been soft on each other earlier, it couldn't have been anything more than a tease. On both their parts.

"How did you and Christian ever…? And you *not* being a part of the network?" She met his eyes, both but a breath from one another. "Did you know the man who—" *Made Christian the monster he is.* "You know…"

"I did." Crossing his arms over his chest, he relaxed his defenses. "Julien de Toire was the first to give me a break in the field."

Julien de Toire? A new name. Another Frenchman. Yet, the name stirred her curiosity.

"De Toire mentored me for about a year, then along comes this ultraobsessed teenager with a penchant for power. I stepped back before he could cock things up for me. Pretty thankful now that I did. I think you know me, I'm too laid-back, like to stay in the background."

Rachel nodded. She wanted to ask more, to know about the man who had created Christian, but what did it matter? De Toire no longer existed. Christian had confessed to killing him. Obviously Jason had distanced himself from the maniacal morals that fed Christian's very soul. Jason was a good bad guy—if there were such a thing. He lived by a code of his own making, and that code made him exemplary amongst his peers.

That code also said every man for himself—even if the man was a woman.

He toed her shoe. "We gonna motor? Vincent drives a mean pace."

"I can't ask you to divide your alliances."

"Sweet." He made to touch her chin, but at the last second, retracted. "I'm only offering a ride. I didn't say I'd take the guy out for you. You can either accept the ride, that'll likely see you there before Vincent, or walk."

Or, she could nab his keys and her money. But the challenge of keeping him close compelled her.

Wisdom said deal with only one of the two. If Vincent was on his way to the X, she'd have a handful to deal with. Her heart—and Jason's sexy grin—said, give this guy a chance.

An even harder part of her said, you can't risk losing him now. Keep the enemy close. He knows things.

"I still don't know if you're in with Lazar," he offered.

This was a risk for him, too. Why was he taking it? Clearly, Vincent would be the only of the two to benefit, should they find the ruby. He'd never fence the rock for two million. He'd be lucky to take seven or eight hundred thousand. Thirty percent of that was a pittance.

"Will you promise to give me a head start after I've got the ruby?"

"Lady, I've never promised a thing in my life."

"And I've never trusted a promise, so that squares us." Rachel drew in a breath and exhaled. "At least I know where I stand with you. Should I turn my head, you'll swipe my feet out from under me."

He didn't have a comeback for that one.

"On to the X?" he asked.

She nodded. "Guess that's my only option."

Chapter 17

Saturday—11:10 a.m.

Jason parked his car in a garage down the street from his apartment building. Rachel strode alongside him, pack slung over her back. The cashmere sweater fit snugly but it might prove too warm later in the afternoon. Suede pants and her creepers finished the look. The need for a rubber binder to pull back her hair from her face was fore—wearing it down just felt too free—but she could use the look to conceal her features if need be.

Jason, having donned a thin long-sleeved blue sweater, waved to an elderly woman done up in diamonds and pink maribou, and who stood behind an iron gate. She blushed and waved back.

"Girlfriend?"

"Like I said, these Frenchwomen…"

As they walked, a black commercial-model Hummer 2 cruised by. Rachel nudged Jason but kept her head down, hair splayed across her cheek. Feigning another wave to an old woman that wasn't there, he spun a scanning look behind them.

"What's up?" he said in a low voice.

"You don't think it odd to see a Hummer in this neighborhood?"

"No more odd than my car. Hummers mean money, and this street definitely reeks of it. 'Course, it is a bit big to navigate this neighborhood."

"What about the dark sunglasses on the driver, and the fact that they pulled a U-turn and are now but a shout behind us? Where's the garage?"

"To the right. I got your vibe now, sweet. Let's leave the street."

"We leading them in with us?"

"Probably wiser than a confrontation on the street. That sussy old broad will have the police on us in minutes. And you know what that means? No more friendly waves for me." He swung a look over his shoulder. "I count three, but I can't see any weapons. You take two, I'll take one?"

"Such a gentleman you are. I knew those muscles were just for show."

"There was a reason Lazar kept you at his side. But let me do the talking."

"Fine. Talking is not my thing."

They strode into the cool shadows of the parking garage. Gas fumes dallied with the suggestion of all the Cordova leather sealed behind polished Mercedes and BMWs. Sure enough the Hummer followed. Jason kept walking toward the back of the garage where the covered car sat.

Jason owned an ancient red Fuego that was no longer red, but pink from fading. Rachel suspected the car might be held together by the rust in places.

The tail parked, and two doors opened and closed.

Following Jason's lead, Rachel turned at the sound of approaching shoes. There were two sets; the driver remained behind the wheel. She kept an eye to the interior, while summing up the standing guns. Classic thug. Black suits, sunglasses, outline of guns very obvious beneath the cheap linen.

"Gentlemen," Jason said as the men stopped four paces from them.

Rachel positioned herself at Jason's shoulder, just slightly in front of him. She caught his look—let-me-handle-the-talk—and stepped back a pace to parallel him.

"Mr. Marland," one of the thugs said.

They knew each other? Yet, Rachel didn't get the sense Jason recognized the man who had addressed him.

"Who wants to know?"

"Knight's the name." The man eased his shoulder forward in order to cross his hands before him. Thick with muscles. But had he brains to operate the brawn? "I wonder if you might offer me some assistance?"

"Likely not," Jason offered. "I don't care tuppence for charity."

Rachel could feel the tension mist off Jason. He was winding up, not relaxed at all. For every notch his adrenaline raised, she felt calm overwhelm. Muscles loose and alert, she was ready.

"I'm looking for Vincent Rousseau." All serious now, the one who spoke slid a hand along his coat, readying to grip a gun, but he did not. Just warning, they all knew that.

Rachel kept a keen eye on the silent one. Hands clasped before him, dark sunglasses concealed his eyes. Brute force, she judged from his meaty hands. This one would be slow, but even minimal contact would be exact and possibly even deadly.

"Haven't heard that name," Jason said. He looked to Rachel. Nothing to read in his expression, just a tension she wanted to obliterate. Center yourself, she wanted to say. Didn't Jason deal with muscle? He really was a homebody. "Have you, honey?"

What was this? She was just muscle. Muscle didn't join the conversation!

Not sure how to react, Rachel spread her hands to exclaim lack of knowledge, but then the signal came. Jason shouted, "Now!"

That was a simple command machines like Rachel could respond to.

Swinging a high roundhouse, she smashed the silent thug's jaw with a heel. He fell straight back. Out cold. Nice. Being a woman did have its advantages. Like limberness and speed all in one sleek package.

Jason dived for the speaker, the twosome landing on the concrete floor. The obvious clunk of a gun hitting the concrete prompted Rachel to search for the weapon. Must still be inside the man's jacket. Jason was on top, delivering punches. He didn't need her help.

Gunfire forced her to a crouch. She scrambled along the floor up to the passenger side of the Hummer. The driver had fired. But she hadn't remarked his position. Easing up to the front of the vehicle, she bent and searched underneath. No feet on the ground. He was still in the vehicle. If she moved to look she'd offer a target.

A Glock skidded across the concrete, stopping but a lunge from Rachel's feet. The girthy black weapon spun once before stopping, the barrel aimed for her. Jason was still engaged in hand-to-hand. Somehow he'd managed to toss the gun.

She didn't use weapons, didn't need a gun to take out bullies. If it had been closer, she'd grab it and stash it in the waistband of her pants. But it wasn't, so she couldn't summon concern.

Crawling on her knees to the left side of the car, Rachel did a quick peek around the corner. The driver's door was open. The driver stood on the sidebar, but was aiming over the hood.

Must be looking for her. She doubted he'd miss a second time. She wasn't about to give him the opportunity to think, let alone get a laser bead on her.

Scrambling around the side of the Hummer and standing, she reached over the top of the door and tapped the driver's back. The wall of black gabardine turned. A semiautomatic sought her as target.

Rachel slammed her body against the driver's door. The gun fell and clattered onto the floor behind her. She tugged open the door. An entire body fell on top of her.

Fell wasn't the right word—the body jumped.

Her spine and skull connected with concrete. Unable to roll into the fall, Rachel saw stars. Before she could shake the stun, a fist squashed into her gut. She spat involuntarily, but managed to target the driver's face. Which only made the bull angrier.

A kick resulted in a hard stub of her toe into the undercarriage of the car. Vicious growls preceded every punch the driver delivered to her gut. But now that she'd taken a few blows, the rest were just nuisance. Waiting for the next punch to fall, she flipped up her hip and rolled, breaking his hand free from the concrete. Bringing up an elbow, it found its target in an eye socket.

Springing up, Rachel delivered a kick to his head. Sunglasses flying, the bull ceased to move. Rachel surveyed the garage. No one was moving.

A hand gripped her ankle. She started to topple.

Her shoulders fell into waiting hands.

"Need some help?"

The Glock had a silencer. But the driver's yelp woke the dead. Jason had shot his wrist.

Suddenly free, Rachel bent and delivered a hook up under the man's jaw, this time silencing him for good.

"He's out," she said.

"Not for long."

"When I put a man down, I lay him down," she said, emphasizing the words to make a point.

"I got it, sweet. Still, I'd be overjoyed if we just got out of here."

"Right behind you," Rachel called as she followed Jason to the Fuego. "You know these guys?"

They climbed into the little pink car. Jason gunned the engine and they spun out into the daylight.

"They're Vincent's buyers," he said. "You think they're pissed?"

"Just a tad."

Saturday—12:00 p.m.

But for its age, the Fuego ran smoothly and quietly. With a pat to the dashboard, Jason commented on *her* reliability. Leave it to a man to name a car a woman, the one constant in his life he must rely on to get him places. And yet, did they ever acknowledge the real women in their lives with such affection and upkeep?

The X was nestled at the edge of the Fourteenth arrondissement in a row of rehabbed factories that backed up to the périphérique. A good position, should the volume rise during the day or night. Though the club tended to keep the volume to a reasonable level during the day, Rachel knew that the best level was silence.

But not so uneasy as the silence she'd been stuck in since getting in the Fuego.

Jason had been closemouthed since they'd left the garage.

Fine. There was nothing to discuss about the thugs. Vincent's buyers? Delay them was all anyone could do. Why bother? They wouldn't give up. Obviously Vincent had made a deal to sell the ruby. Family heirloom, her ass. Likely *Rousseau* was one of the bastard's many false names.

Her gut ached, but besides that, she hadn't taken any hits to the jaw. She was fine. Jason showed no signs of suffering. Not a drop of blood on either of them. Such a team.

A quiet team.

Drawing in a few deep breaths, Rachel tried to keep her focus. Ruby. Club X. Must find. Freedom.

But the silence insisted. As if it needed an explanation, a vise to draw close the divide Vincent's stark confession had wedged between her and Jason. That had been when Jason had changed. He'd snapped back his head at Vincent's announcement about them sleeping together; his eyes had changed. Even with the few endearments he'd offered in the stairway before they left, Rachel could again feel his distance sitting an arm's length away.

"It meant nothing," she said suddenly. "Me and Rousseau."

Jason looked to her, wrinkled a brow and focused back on the road. The strain in his jaw made his disgust more apparent, even from her side view.

Okay, so she hadn't planned to just toss it out there like that. Lately her emotions had been reacting more swiftly than her logic. As though the gray just wanted to swallow her up. But it was out there. And, despite her inner freakiness over the gray areas of life, she wanted to talk about it. "You know...what he said about us."

"Him fucking you?"

"Yes, but it was more me..." Fucking him—in the sense that she wanted to fuck him over, not fuck him as in making love. She'd never liked that word. But it fit perfectly the emotionless manipulative acts she had performed with men only to then steal from them. Early Friday morning she had failed horribly at it. Yet, failure had resulted in her getting the ride of her lifetime. And she'd take that as a success, small and strange as it was. "You know how I work. Sometimes the machine has to do *things* to get what it wants."

"So you got what you wanted?" He stopped at an intersection and sent a questioning golden gaze her way.

Swallowing, Rachel turned away. "No. He took the ruby." And yes.

She closed her eyes. Only when the window suddenly rolled down did she realize what a clamp she'd had on the door handle.

"Initially," she added, thinking to clarify. "Before I stole the ruby back."

"Doesn't bother me," Jason offered in a breezy tone. He shifted the car into gear and took a left turn. The Fuego rolled past the massive front lawn of Les Invalides, the military hospital. "No need to explain the sordid details. I don't care tuppence."

"I want you to care!" Oops.

Jason shot her another wonky look.

"Did I just say that out loud?" She sank a little in the seat.

Still, the bizarre expression on Jason's face. As if she'd slapped him!

"Yes, you did." He turned his attention back to the road. A police officer wearing a yellow sash directed tourist traffic in and around the hospital. After darting the Fuego out from a tangle of confused vehicles, Jason put them on a quieter road. "I get it. You're...dangling at the end of a rope. Don't know what you're talking about. It's like female hormones and stuff, right?"

"Hormones?" Oh, she could give him hormones in another few days. Then, watch out, because if he thought she was dangling now... "Would you pay attention to the road?"

Jason slammed his mouth shut and turned just in time to swerve away from an oncoming van. In the opposite lane.

Adjusting her position to sit higher in the seat, Rachel made a point of tightening the plastic clasp on her pack. She sensed Jason's looks, the twist of his head to eye her, back to the road, another glance, and back again.

Oh so gray.

"Sorry, this is so...not me. Hell, I'm acting like some teenage girl trying to get my way, to make everyone agree with me. You're right. We all do what we must to survive. Turn here."

Only the side of Jason's face was visible, but she noted his lifted brow and subtle nod. He was thinking he should have never offered the ride. He and Vincent, whether or not friends, were partners on this heist. And one of the unwritten rules was never screw your partner. Why had she thought to trust him?

Because this was just an excuse to keep the opposition close to hand.

Right. *You know it's really because you do want this man to care.* No one else had ever simply touched her without then expecting more. And Jason's silence hurt. What was he thinking? Did he ever want to kiss her again? Why did she care more about a silly kiss than the real emergency—the world of grown-up problems and danger?

Talk about dizzying up the girl. Jason didn't need to give her anything; just sitting next to him thoroughly scrambled her better judgment. She felt out of her world. Not able to grasp anything solid, for it was such new, unfamiliar territory.

Back to reality, Rachel! She drew in a breath and pressed the window button. The X came into view as Jason steered from a cobbled street into the parking lot.

The music emanating from the X permeated the closed windows of the car. Rachel could already sense the bass vibrations shiver up her spine as they pulled in to a half-full parking lot behind the club. The sensation—a techno-beat pounding in her heart—stirred the bile in her throat.

Shifting into park, Jason remained facing forward, his eyes on the club. He tapped a few beats on the steering wheel with his thumbs.

"You don't need to come in," she said, fingering the door handle. "I'm cool from here."

"I'll be right here. You'll need a getaway."

All business; as it should be. Yet not about to let her off so easily. "Fine."

Should he attempt to take the ruby from her, she'd deal with him when the time came.

Rachel exited the car and blew out a breath filled with apprehension and all the confusing remnants of desire and want and need that had suddenly crept up on her. Sorry time for her emotions to decide to be heard. Couldn't she ditch them until the ruby was in hand?

And then what?

Getaway, right. She would need a ride out of here. And a place to collapse following. If she could survive walking through the cacophony.

Striding around the hood of the car, she paused outside Jason's door and took in the club. The back of the four-story brick building was nondescript; the only sign it was a club being the painted red X one-story high, and the green-and-white striped awning over the door. A line always formed, day or night, no matter the day of the week. The front of the building, Rachel knew, welcomed people through the bottom cross of a huge brushed-steel X. But that entrance was reserved for the elite, those with PR people who called in advance to announce their client's arrival.

This location was the worst of all evils, so far as Rachel was concerned. Always rule out the worst first, because everything that followed would seem like a piece of cake.

Rachel slid a palm across her thigh and tugged at the sweater. The sun made her grimace. Sure, it was the sun.

She wasn't positive Christian would be here. He'd never visited more frequently than once a month, and only when he had reason, like stashing rocks or a preliminary stop before going on to a laydown. Of course, he did have a rock to stash.

She scanned the parking lot, thinking to spy Vincent's silver Audi, but decided it might have been a rental. He could be driving anything. He could be here already. Might even have found what he wanted and made a fast escape. Another trip in her path to getting the hell out of Dodge.

The driver's window rolled down. "You going in?"

She nodded. "Don't you see my feet moving?"

"Rachel." Jason gripped her hand.

The touch reassured. But it was a false assurance, she knew.

"You scared? 'Cause I can come in."

"Scared?" Try petrified. "No, I don't want you involved. Besides, you're my wheelman. Promise me if you see Rousseau leave first you won't pick him up and drive off into the sunset?"

"Sun's not going to set for more than half a day, sweet. And I don't make promises, remember?"

"I know. I just—" Feel like a promise right about now. *It's every man for himself.* "I don't know what I'm saying. I don't normally..."

"Feel?"

She chuffed out a breath that neither disagreed nor agreed.

"Don't worry, sweet. You can do this. Scope the place out. If you see Vincent, don't start a row, it'll only attract attention. Just follow him out."

"I *have* done this kind of thing before."

"Yeah, well, if you see Lazar, maybe you should call for backup."

She shook her head. "I'm cool now."

As cool as a fever victim shaking from the sweats.

Don't look back, she coached herself. That's not what you do. You stride right in there, take out any security surrounding Christian and force him to hand over the jewel. If luck was with her, Rousseau hadn't even arrived.

"Rachel?"

She turned back to Jason. He never used her real name. "What?"

"I do care."

Mouth falling open, not a single word formed. Rachel turned away.

"I got your back, sweet," Jason said as she strode across the parking lot.

Chapter 18

While she looked less than sexy wearing Jason's oversize cashmere sweater and her snug brown suede pants—and don't forget the bruise curving across her cheek—a flip of her hair and a lower of her head to look up through her lashes was an automatic action. Detrimental to a man's sensibilities, Christian had once described her subtle seductions. Slink up to them and rub them to a frenzy with your purr. Those thick red lips and green eyes will get them every time.

At the bouncer's invitation, Rachel strode past the line, head held high, and slipped onto the grated-metal catwalk. She'd not seen the bouncer before, and so guessed he would not recognize her either.

The back door opened to emit such a blast of sound that Rachel actually cringed. But she forced herself forward and into the dark back hallway lined with shuffling bodies and clinking glasses. The office was located on the south side of the building—she had merely to walk this hallway, turn left avoiding the dance floor, and walk down another hall to the stairs.

Shrugging her hands over the soft cashmere sleeves of her sweater, she induced some warmth. Smoke infused her lungs. The piped-in scent of myrrh sickened her. Music snaked through her pores and rattled in her belly.

She reached out in the mire of noise to steady herself. The music was loud. Too loud. Concentration darted elusively.

Feminine giggles segued to squeals. No delight in that piercing noise.

Rachel stumbled and caught herself against a brick wall painted black. A hive of insects buzzed against her palm. Vibrations shivered up from the floor and through her bones. Beyond, the flashing red and violet lights from the dance floor pulsed in time to the music. Or so she could only guess. Too quickly her senses were decimated.

Her equilibrium teetered. Drawing in heaving breaths, Rachel struggled to maintain control. Her brow grew hot. The scent of smoke, alcohol and cheap perfume overwhelmed her.

Too much noise. It annihilated, literally raping her senses.
Make it stop.

You've done wrong, Rachel Blu. When will you learn to follow directions? You cannot change the plan halfway through the execution. Sit there until you learn. It's not noise, it's music.

"*Demoiselle?* You all right?"

"She must have had too much to drink."

Laughter segued into the mire. Rachel pressed a palm to a wall; it felt like a wall, but the wall moved.

"Ah, there you are, *salope*. Back off, she's mine! Likes to tip the vodka back like a sailor, eh?" Feeling her body being directed, Rachel realized the wall was a man. "What is wrong with you? You act as if you are drunk."

Someone was talking to her? No. Just more noise. Evil sound.

"Rachel? Are you drunk? What is wrong?"

...wrong? Did she just hear her name?

"Chérie?"

Her mind processed a voice: Vincent. Enemy.

But right now, her only ally.

"Noise," she managed in a gasp. "Get me...from here..."

"Can you walk? I'm taking you outside. There's a side door."

"Always locked," she murmured.

"Not today. Let's go. There are no people out this way."

Her legs were moving. She sensed the motion. Her torso, supported by someone—she didn't care who—she could only be moving to freedom. And then she was hit by a smack of silence and fresh air.

Feeling the hands supporting her under the arms slip away, Rachel collapsed upon a concrete slab. The door slammed behind her, muffling the music.

Still her insides were assaulted by the remnants of technobeat. Her ears rang. Heartbeats worked a beastly march. She saw her fingers curling into the loose sand collected at the dented wheel of an industrial garbage container. And a shoe—the toe tapped. The someone who had helped her?

Catch your breath. Bring yourself back up. Surface, Rachel!

She felt an arm lift her at the waist and press her spine against the garbage bin. Her shoulder bones thunked the hard steel.

Scan of the surroundings. Everything wobbled. They sat in a narrow alley. The opposite building sported a fringe of tall weeds about its brick base. French graffiti prettied the plain facade.

She'd known of this exit. It was always locked, never used, save for emergencies. The back parking lot was not in view. Did Jason sit in his car awaiting her exit? Or had he pulled away as soon as she was out of sight?

I do care.

Thieves, by nature, used words only to their advantage.

"Was it the noise?"

Oh, but music devastated.

"Please." Wearied so easily by the tumult of sound, she lifted a hand and laid it on the man's leg. Yes, her Frenchman. Her enemy. Her incredible lover.

Rachel let out a moan, long and cleansing—not unlike the soft sigh that follows orgasm.

She couldn't summon the effort to kick him. But her subconscious had already laid him flat and broken his nose. "Just a few moments…to…catch…"

"What happened? You collapsed. Did you drink something? You have to be careful. There are assholes who will drug your drink then rape you."

She wasn't going to offer this particular asshole any information. When he bent to her face, sniffing, she shoved him back.

"No booze on your breath. Ah." He tilted up her face with a finger to her chin. Too exhausted, Rachel allowed the touch. Curious green eyes held laughter, ready to burst. "Lazar's little pet. I know his methods. Let me guess."

And how could that be? They'd only met once before, less than fifteen minutes, if she recalled correctly, for the entire deal to go down.

"The loud music. Your utter lack of ability. He tortured you with sound, *oui?*"

Closing her eyes, she nodded minutely.

Surrender to my will, Rachel Blu. You have no choice. Don't be so stubborn. I will break you. I can *break you.*

"How long?"

"W-what?"

"How long did you have to endure?"

"I don't know." Was he asking about the noise torture?

"You try your place, Rachel Blu. Don't ever challenge me like that again."

"But the combination—"

She'd communicated that the digital safe they'd expected during the heist was actually digital *and* biometric. They had not planned for such a surprise. Common sense said to abort, but Rachel had felt sure she could overcome.

"I said to abort!"

"I figured it out!"

"You disobeyed a direct order."

And Christian had locked her in the little gray room with the padded walls. The lights never went out. The music never ceased. And her tears always flowed.

The gray...how she feared it.

Once she had thought it Christian's way of making her experience his migraines. Share the pain. If he must suffer then so would she.

Really, it was just another method of control. An exploitation of his power.

Man, did it work.

"The longest...I went in the morning and when I came out it was dark." Rubbing her thumb over the elbow of her sweater, she pressed, hard. A small technique to redirect the pain by coaxing it elsewhere. "What are you doing out here? Why not make off with the ruby—"

"The office is down an unguarded hallway, turn left up a stairs—"

"And five paces to the right," she finished, gaining the better portion of her senses with a huge intake of oxygen.

"I can't access the office. The lock is biometric. I don't know if it requires a retinal scan or—"

"Thumbprint."

"Yeah? And can I guess Lazar has given his pet access?"

"None of your business."

"Of course he did. Otherwise you wouldn't have risked entering the club knowing the challenge that waited."

An easy guess. Why did the man have to best her every time they met? He was not physically superior. Just…trickier. Cocky. For once she wanted to knock him so hard he would turn tail and run.

And she thought Christian her nemesis.

"You want to find the ruby?"

She nodded.

"You crack the lock, I'll stand guard."

"I can't go back in there."

"You have to!"

"Don't touch me!"

He splayed placating hands before him. The mocking *tcht*-ing sound he made riled her.

"Even if I could go back in there, I wouldn't invite you along."

"Is there even a safe on the premises?"

"Two."

"Fine, then you take one, I'll take one." He bent to catch her gaze. "Admit it, you need me. I can carry you in there if I have to."

Rachel thought about it. With two safes she had a fifty-fifty chance of winning the prize. That is, if said prize was indeed inside the office. It seemed unlikely Christian would let the thing out of his sight. However, he knew she hadn't a chance at making off with the thing if her senses were obliterated by a mere dance tune.

Of course, he could be sitting in the shadows of the dark office, waiting, anticipating.

"Did you check the entire place?" she wondered. "Maybe he's sitting out on the second level, nursing a vodka?"

"I looked."

"You even know what he looks like—" Yes, he did. That one deal—if only she could recall the details.

She was about to mention Jason sitting out in the parking lot, but thought better. No reason to clue him in that a getaway waited. Nor would she tell him about the thugs. If there was a tail on Rousseau, then lack of information on his part sounded all the better.

"Fine. But I don't know how—"

"Just wait here." He stood and tried the door again. It was a Medico lock; a difficult pick unless one used specialized tools. Vincent sorted inside his coat and produced two picks. Minutes later the door was open.

So the man carried all the right tools, as well as besting her.

"Give me a minute or two. Don't go anywhere."

Go anywhere? On her shaky legs? The effects of the noise still eddied through her veins like an army of ants marching in time. She felt unsure and shaky. Not her favorite feeling. The only cure was silence.

Pressing her hands to the sides of her head, Rachel closed her eyes and mined the solace within that was her touchstone. Meditation always preceded a job. It centered and focused her. She should not have thought to rush into the club without meditating beforehand.

You're not at the top of your game. You're too worried about your own ass to protect it!

Yeah, and what's with that idiotic conversation about wanting Jason to care for you?

The little girl threatened to take all she had been denied. How to put her off?

Focus.

True to his word, minutes later Vincent emerged. He dangled a string of tiny white earplugs before her. "Bought them off an idiot for fifty euros."

"Sounds like you're the idiot."

"Will they help?"

She stuffed one plug into her right ear. A cottony muffled sound cushed inside her ear. "Not sure."

"They'll reduce the noise."

Right. But she'd heard him say that perfectly clear.

"They'll do." She wasn't about to accede to weakness when enemy number two stood over her. But she had to admit, a lookout could not be disregarded. Especially when her senses would not be to full capacity. "You know exactly where the office is?"

"Don't you?"

"I do. But I'll have my eyes closed, and you'll be leading me. The more senses I can close off from the sound assault the better off I'll be. I can't believe I'm going to trust you."

"You don't have to trust me, you just need to work with me. Big difference. Take my hand, baby, let me rock your world. Again."

Chapter 19

Saturday—12:20 p.m.

This time Rachel made it twenty paces down the painted black hallway before she felt her muscles begin to protest. The earplugs barely dimmed the noise, but it wasn't so much the sound touching her ears as the beat pulsing inside. Her heart felt ready to shatter.

Thinking sure it would explode and the entire room would be splattered with her blood, she clutched Vincent's arm. He wore a long-sleeved silk shirt. Concentrating on the dry smoothness of the fabric focused one of her senses and stole it away from the pounding beat.

Walking blindly, she felt Vincent lift her arm, and so she stepped up. The stairway up to the second-floor office. It would be dark unless Christian occupied the mirrored-glass office. She clung to Vincent, trusting him.

What else could she do? If he tried to double-cross her later, she'd do her best to allay such, but she'd chosen to walk into a perilous situation knowing she was not at her peak. Now, to let come what may.

Making slow steps at Vincent's direction, his thick palm stretched along her right side to push her gently and guide. Her foot misstepped. She stumbled. Strong hands caught her around the waist.

She felt his breath against her cheek. Likely whispering something like, *Watch out,* salope, but she couldn't hear beyond the insanity in her skull.

She was strong; and she wasn't about to let a little music fell her.

Still held upright by Vincent, Rachel focused. Was that his heartbeats thumping against her rib cage or some crazed dance beat? She thought to seek his scent, occupying yet another of her senses, but could not pinpoint cinnamon or male heat at all. She knew his scent, it was blazoned across her soul, embedded three times over.

Keep thinking. For it kept her mind busy and seemed to lessen the threat of another collapse. Collapse could only come with a complete surrender to the sound.

She sensed they now traveled the hallway to the office. When he placed her hand on a cool bar of metal, Rachel opened her eyes. It took a moment to adjust to the darkness, but soon she could make out the trace of the circular silver lock, set low near the floor, and there was another at eye level. Two different key locks to dissuade a quick entry.

Vincent pressed some tools against her palm—lock picks. He nodded, encouraging.

She gave him a shove and pointed to the end of the hall, where he took up guard.

Using the door for stability, Rachel tilted her body to lean against her left shoulder and hip. She pressed her palms over her ears and pushed the plugs deeper. So much noise. Music? Not this erratic stuff.

But it hadn't killed her yet. This machine took her knocks and kept on standing.

The door required first a key or pick entry, and following, confirmation by pressing a thumbprint to the biometric scanner.

Jason had taught her to work this sort of lock blindfolded. She stretched shoulder height for the top lock and inserted a raking pick with her right hand. Tension was added with a torque wrench in her left hand. This sort of lock took patience and extreme touch sensitivity. It was difficult to feel anything with her heart pounding in her ears and behind her eyeballs.

Pressing her forehead to the door, Rachel gritted her teeth. Everything was just too loud. She did not want to be here. It had already unearthed memories of a time she wanted to erase.

Yet, they were *her* memories, and they were all she had. Christian was all she had.

You need me, Rachel Blu.

Truly?

Pausing, she closed her eyes. It had been so easy once, life with Christian. Could she go back?

Her hand was lifted and placed to the lock. She had forgotten Vincent's presence. The contact made her gasp. But at the same time it obliterated her idiotic thoughts.

Now he held her around the waist, his chest to her back. She could feel Vincent's breath on her neck. He spoke to her, saying something indistinguishable from all the noise. But his touch remained gentle. His fingers held hers over the lock, patient but directing.

It was odd, but Rachel noticed the beat of his pulse against her shoulder blade. That she could pick out a single moment like that amongst the drowning rage of sound... But then again, it was similar to detecting a single number in a combination of dozens.

The warmth of Vincent's nose nuzzled her hair to her neck. Rachel closed her eyes. *Slide your hand down my thigh, she thought. Make me come again.*

His hand remained on her fingers. A tap upon her knuckles seemed impatient.

Just crack the lock!

Yes. Heartbeats pounding and breaths huffing, Rachel cursed her sway from the task. Had she wanted him to make her come? Yes. And why the hell not? She had every right to seek her own pleasure.

But not now.

You can do this. Just pick out the pulse of the lock.

An elbow to Vincent's ribs hissed a chuff of hot breath across her neck.

Rubbing his ribs, he watched her. In the darkness his eyes glittered. Fingers of his left hand thrust in wonder. Coy challenge?

She nodded, and he went back to stand guard.

Yes, feel the pulse. She teased the lock with the picks, wondering should the vibrations from the music even allow a pick; it seemed the very walls moved with sound. The pins surely rattled about inside the lock like packed bodies on a dance floor.

The easy twist of the tension wrench slipped in her hand. Success.

Rachel sank to the floor and used her elation to dissuade the outside distractions. Not bad, considering the obstacles. Immediately, she went to work again. The second lock opened after a few minutes.

Now the real test. Rachel stood. Pressing her thumb to the biometric pad, she held her breath until the screen lighted green. He hadn't deleted her record. Because he had known she would return?

I've thought of you every day for eight months.

Stroke or not, Christian never forgot a thing. This was all part of the game.

Turning the knob she pushed the door inside. No lasers to worry about. Christian had not bothered to enhance the security because to get past the biometric scan was a feat.

Stretching her head inside, she searched the darkness. The north wall was a huge double-way window that overlooked the dance floor. Observers could see out, but no one could see in, not even backlit shadows moving across the window. Mirrors lined the remaining three walls, distorting depth. The room was sparsely furnished with a thick gray leather couch and a short steel table stretched before it. Christian's desk sat just to the left of the door, and to the right, a marble-fronted fireplace. Grooving shadows from the dance floor gyrated across the Maxfield Parrish lithograph hung over the fireplace.

Vincent forced her body completely inside with his and closed the door. There were no proprietary boundaries between them. He treated her as if she were a piece of property he could touch and move about at will. And she allowed it only because it was too difficult to focus and not worth the effort of an argument. If he got too pushy, she'd knock him cold the next time.

Cotton pounded in her ears. She tugged out the plugs. Here in the office the music was deafened considerably thanks to the acoustic walls.

"I was worried about you for a minute," Vincent said as he walked the room, scanning the walls, seeing things normal people did not see, for he estimated everything a potential hiding spot. But he didn't bother with discovery. "Where are they?"

"Right here." Rachel lifted a signed lithograph from the wall above the fireplace. "This is the largest, a Goliath IV.

Should take about six or seven minutes. The other is a small fire safe above the towel warmer in the bathroom. I'll take this one."

"Maybe I will take this one."

"Beggars can't be choosers. I got us in here, it's my crack."

"Fine." He tugged the earplugs from her hand. "I'll hold on to these."

Shit. That ruled out a fast escape with the prize. But she let him go; he wasn't a threat to her—unless they were naked. And she wasn't about to remove so much as a single shoe in front of this man.

Her safe would take longer, but she figured it the first place Christian would hide something he might want her to find, for it was a four-digit combination as opposed to the simpler three-digit dial in the bathroom. Cracking it would take time. Best get to the task.

With a keen ear concentrated on the hallway outside, she stepped onto the marble hearth and twisted the combination lock. Christian did not use obvious combinations, such as birthdays or social-security numbers.

On the other hand, he never wrote anything down, unless it was a contact.

She wondered. If not a combination of numbers that held meaning, then perhaps... Would he make it so easy?

Scanning through a mental list of combinations, Rachel tried a set of four numbers.

No deal.

Another set was tried.

Nope.

The third try—12-11-32-7—cracked the box.

The man had kept the original combination! There were dozens of factory-issue try-out numbers that opened any safe. As part of her training, she had memorized them all. Fifty percent of the time, safes could be cracked with a simple test number because the owner was too lazy to change the combination.

Interesting. That Christian was so particular about every single breath, and yet, his own security was so lax. Guess he thought highly of his biometric lock.

She cranked the safe handle and the interior light flickered on to reveal the two-foot-square interior. Empty, save a few documents and a necklace.

That left the other safe. If Vincent found the ruby he would not leave the X with it.

So long as the music remained a muted background nuisance, Rachel was up for a fight.

Rachel stretched her neck to peer at the slender black string sitting on top of a folded document. Strange. It wasn't sparkly like most of Christian's finds. It didn't look of value. She took the necklace and held it in her palm, using the light from inside the safe to look it over. Tiny shells strung together on a waxy black string. It was as if a child's—

"Oh my God." Rachel pressed the necklace to her breast and closed her eyes.

Visions of a little girl, swinging in the playground... So carefree...

"My mommy let me wear her necklace today."
"So!"
The little girl stuck out her tongue at the teasing boy.
And then the police car pulled up. Escorted to a huge white station teaming with uniforms, the little girl had been told her parents were killed in an accident. They're in heaven now, the officer explained. There were no close relatives. She'd be sent to foster care that night.
A strand of tiny shells was the only evidence she had ever been loved.

How quickly life altered. Tracing the thin curve of one of the shells, she couldn't decide whether to marvel at it or simply toss it aside. She'd thought she had misplaced this after arriving at the compound. Christian had promised to replace it.

He stole it from me.

"Find it?"

Rachel bent over her hand, clasped tight to her chest. How precious life, like a tiny shell. "Nothing in this one."

"What's that?"

"This? A stupid necklace. You find the ruby?"

"Not in there."

"Did you even crack the box?"

"Yes, I opened the safe."

And nothing inside? That was strange. Though maybe her guess that Christian would abandon his best leverage over her was even more strange. Allow her to sashay in, pocket the rock and skip away? Not likely.

"You plan to keep that pitiful thing?"

Rachel felt the tiny edges of the shells dig into her palm. Until this very moment, she had forgotten that horrible day— it had been pushed into her depths by the will to survive. That was the day her life changed. The day she lost love. Forever. The day her soul had began to pray for love.

"No." The string of shells dangled from her fingers.

"Each tiny piece holds a little scoop of love." Her mother's voice.

"No." She dropped it beside the marble hearth. "Let's get out of here. Hand me those earplugs." She caught the string Vincent tossed.

As they approached the door, it opened. A blast of sound was overwhelmed by the visual danger. Christian stood there, flanked by two hunks of muscle that towered and stretched well beyond even Vincent's size. She didn't recognize either of them. New muscle, then.

Rachel had suspected the game couldn't be that easy.

Chapter 20

"Thought I'd give you a few minutes' head start," Christian said. "Those manufacturer's numbers came in handy, I see." He stepped inside the office, forcing Rachel and Vincent back a few steps.

Rachel felt the shell necklace crunch under her thin rubber sole and quickly lifted her shoe. The lights flicked on. She blinked at the brightness and looked to the discarded necklace.

Christian noticed her dismay. "Ah, yes. I thought it a trinket worth keeping. Priceless, wouldn't you say? It is perhaps my most valuable piece—or rather, was."

Rachel merely shook her head. She could get out of this situation if she remained calm and alert. Behind her the door still stood open; escape, yet it also allowed in the noise.

"Close the door, Theo," Christian commanded. One of the thugs kicked the door shut. Christian winced at the lack of decorum. But he quickly got down to business. "Now, who's got it?"

"Got what?" Vincent snarled.

Clad in soft charcoal Armani and with his hair slicked back to enhance his sculpted jaw, Christian still cut an imposing figure. He lifted a brow, summing up the man. The two had dealt with each other before. Did either remember?

"You know we don't have it," Rachel said. "It wasn't in either safe."

"Oh yes it was."

Behind Christian, thug number two took out a dagger and flashed it for effect. The gesture worked. Rachel knew either would kill with but a nod from Christian. He'd never mastered her that way, had never been capable of commanding she kill someone. Though, he'd never pressed, either.

And the nod came.

The blade plunged into Vincent's gut. Vincent let out a groan. Blood scent touched Rachel's rattled senses. Her partner in crime toppled at her feet, covering the broken shell necklace.

"Search him."

Rachel stiffened as one of the thugs bent to search Vincent's body. The thought to retaliate stalled—she needed to play this one out. Should she react, a fight would only weaken her already waning physicality. To match Christian she must remain on his level. And he wasn't looking at all lopsided at the moment.

Vincent had landed on his back, so shuffling through his pockets was easy. The thief groaned and splayed out a bloody hand, gasping at the thug's rough intrusion. His fingers brushed Rachel's shoe. Still alive. But for how long? Sprawled in an awkward position that concealed the wound, she could not determine if the cut would prove fatal.

"Got it."

The flash of red caught her attention. The Rousseau ruby.

Vincent had been going to lead her out from here then take off with it. Or maybe just leave her behind to succumb? Bastard. She didn't care if he died.

Christian picked up the phone receiver from his desk and spoke to someone, "Hey, it's the office. Could you crank up the music? Can't hear it in here."

The game had played out. Time to move.

Rachel kicked high, landing the thug's hand and sending the ruby flying. The mirrored walls flickered with the jewel's flight, distorting its trajectory. Unfortunately it did not fall anywhere near her. Taking a fist to her gut, she chuffed out a hard breath. Two fingers to the thug's eyeballs reduced him to a yelping heap.

The sting of a blade cut across her shoulder. Bending, Rachel spun at the waist and cannonballed into thug number two, pinning him to the hearth wall. A hard fist to his solar plexus flattened him.

The music in the background was still low. The ruby had landed on the steel coffee table stretched before the gray velvet couch. She twisted to lunge but stopped at the sound of a very precise click.

The barrel of an imposing Desert Eagle pressed to her temple.

A gun? And a big one. This was new. Christian never used heat. Not around her...

"Try me," he said.

"I just want the stone."

With a bend of one knee, he angled to pick up the ruby.

"You can have it."

Rachel eyed the glittering red stone held between Christian's forefinger and thumb. It paralleled the barrel of the gun. "What's the catch?" She could guess—

"My contact book for your ruby."

Heart sinking to her gut, Rachel maintained a calm facade. Where was the damn contact book? Either swept up by a street sweeper or—taken by the bleeding body at her feet. Would Christian really make the trade? Didn't seem likely.

He'd waited for her for eight months. There was more to this, had to be.

She hadn't time for this game.

"I don't have it."

Christian tilted his head. He tucked the ruby into an inner suit pocket. "You want the ruby, I'm sure you'll bring the book to hand. Now, you've got about five seconds to run before all of heaven comes crashing down upon your shoulders."

He meant the music. Rachel straightened, hands splayed at her shoulders, and eyed Christian's devilish blue gaze. It was difficult to read in the hazy light. But the black mouth of the gun's barrel said more than enough.

"Game's not over yet," he said with a smirk.

The sudden explosion of music set Rachel to a run. She remarked the *ching* of a bullet hitting the doorjamb as she sped out of the office. He'd fired at her? Just playing? Or dead serious?

Not taking the time to look back to see if Christian stood in the doorway, she scrambled down the stairs. She needed Vincent to find the book. Too risky to go back for him. She should have bargained right then and there. *Just don't let him die before I get the book.*

Each step thundered with the raucous clamber of techno-rock. Halfway down, Rachel clutched at the black walls, directing her way, and straining just to make it to the bottom step.

Another bullet took a bite out of the wall under her left hand. She didn't feel that she'd been hit. Tumbling forward, Rachel took the last few steps in a roll. She landed at someone's shoes. Shudders racked her body so that she couldn't find hold on anything solid.

"Oh Christ—" a male voice "—what did he do to you?"

What did he— Was someone talking to her?

"I had a nasty feeling and figured I'd better come for you. Did you take a bullet?"

"N-noise."

"Let's get you out of here." Lifted from her crouch, Rachel threaded her arms about the man's neck. Brilliant sunlight blasted the fuzzy mirage that blurred her vision. Numb, yet her entire body shaking, she clung, and tucked her head to his chest.

"Did he shoot you? I smell blood. Where are you hurt? Sweet, talk to me!"

Sweet? Jason had come for her?

He set her in the passenger side of the car and slammed the door. Vaguely aware that he rolled over the hood of the Fuego and got into the driver's side, Rachel pressed a palm to the window and saw the image of a man standing outside the back door. His arm was outstretched, holding…a gun.

Jason tugged at her opposite arm. Rachel merely sat there, a rag doll rescued from the clutches of a monster.

I'll take you to Paris. I'll be your family. You'll have everything you could ever wish for, Rachel Blu.

A bullet ricocheted off the Fuego's hood.

"Bugger!"

Rachel's head clacked the window as they spun out of the parking lot.

Chapter 21

Saturday—12:50 p.m.

The Fuego pulled to an abrupt stop. Chain-link fencing lined the opposite side of the street, and a small dirt yard littered with rusted pipes sat behind the blockade. No recognizable buildings for as far as she could see. Must still be in the factory district.

Smelling a bit like a drunk—and feeling it too—Rachel pulled herself straight in the seat. She must have leaned against something wet, because her sweater sleeve was sticky. She couldn't remember—but she didn't expect that she should. Club X, and what went on inside, blurred, then snapped to focus, then muzzied out again.

Slanting a look at Jason, she managed a lackluster smile. It was meant as a thank-you, a silent expression of something she just wasn't ready to deal with.

"Where'd he get you? Let's be having it," Jason insisted. He twisted in the seat and leaned over her. Prodding her shoulder, he wanted her to lean forward, but she sat still. "The wound looks shallow. A knife?"

She nodded. "I'm not hurt."

"You staggered down those stairs like you were."

"It was the noise."

"What?"

She sighed. "I don't do loud noises."

He made the classic, you-sound-like-an-idiot expression, his face filled with uncertainty. His nose almost looked as if it had never been broken when he did that.

"Music. It messes me up. I didn't get the ruby. Christian still has it, and he won't give it up until I trade the contact book for it."

"What the hell is a contact book?"

"It's a...none of your business."

Jason sat back in his seat. He gave the steering wheel a tap with his thumb. "Did you see Rousseau? Where is he?"

"He's..." Rachel clutched the door handle, easing her palm along the cool vinyl. "I think he's still alive."

"You think? He was in there and we left him behind with that nasty piece of work Lazar?"

"One of Christian's thugs knifed him. And after, they found the ruby on him." She gave Jason the full-on evil eye. "He was going to walk out, by my side, with the rock in his pocket!"

"Yeah?" He turned to look out the window. His jaw pulsed. Thinking? Then he said, "It takes a thief to know one."

No sympathy in that statement. She didn't deserve any.

Jason had drawn his side. She knew exactly what to expect from him.

You did what you had to do. The music would have had her kneeling before Christian like a sinner begging for mercy.

"Turn the car around. I've got to go back."

"And just how to you propose you'll go about nabbing the ruby if you can't endure the noise? What, did he torture you, or something?"

"I need to get to Vincent."

"But you just left him. Who's screwing who, Rachel? Are you and Vincent shuffling the rock behind my back?"

"Give me a break. I despise that French bastard. He's got the contact book."

"Yeah. Which means nothing to me."

"It's Christian's book of contacts. You know, everyone he's ever dealt with, from thief to buyer to cleaner. I stole it when I escaped last winter. It fell from my pack when I struggled with Rousseau after first arriving. He's got to have it."

"Well, if he's got what Lazar wants for trade—and if Vincent is still alive and is with Christian…"

Jason didn't finish. Rachel could figure out his thoughts. Vincent could make the trade and walk away. Neither needed to involve her.

But would Christian trade for *just* the contact book? She suspected—hell, she hoped—that the unspoken deal breaker was that he wanted *her* in trade as well.

"Christian won't hand the rock over to Vincent."

"But if he's got what Lazar wants?"

"I'm what he wants. You're not going to win this one, Marland, so give it up."

She opened the car door, just needing to feel the air on her face, and swung out her legs. The blast of warm air readjusted her breathing, calming her, bringing her to focus.

"I don't—" Jason's cell phone rang.

Rachel turned to look at him. He stared at her for two rings, then, frustrated, dug the phone out from his jeans pocket and snapped it open with a violent shake of the wrist. "Bugger it. What?"

As he listened, Rachel studied his eyes. Soft gold, frazzled with worry. A tilt of his head focused his attention entirely on her. As if he was reading a script in her eyes. Already his five o'clock shadow had begun to form. A sudden resolute calm softened his tight jaw. He nodded and handed her the phone. "Lazar."

How had he known to call Jason?

Christian had seen Jason pick her up from the bottom of the stairway. Likely, he'd recognized the Fuego as it had spun out of the parking lot. Damn, that man had such a tight grip on her. How was he always able to locate her? She had removed the trackers.

And if he had called, that meant he knew Jason's number. Hmm...

Rachel pressed the phone to her ear. Christian spoke immediately. "We need to talk."

"I was just there. You didn't like the mood? Outfit not pretty enough for you?"

"I'm impressed you made it out of the building. I suppose those knights in shining armor come in handy once in a while. When did you join with Marland?"

"You tell me. You seem to know my every move."

"This morning. You arrived at his apartment after dawn." There was a pause, a smirking breath, and then, "Sends a shiver right up your spine, doesn't it?"

It did. Rachel eyed Jason. He wasn't looking at her. One wrist was propped on the steering wheel, and an intense gaze burned a hole through the windshield.

"I'm not in the mood for any of your games. Let's meet."

"You're one step ahead of me, Rachel Blu."

"You'll bring the ruby?"

"You'll bring the book?"

"You haven't searched Rousseau?"

"Don't tell me you gave it to that fool."

"I'm not telling anything." She twisted to face outside, hooking her free hand on the opened window. "Let's meet."

"Ah, a date. How novel. Hang up. Wait for my call."

"No! I don't have time."

"I know you don't. Fun, isn't it?"

"Chris—"

The phone clicked off. Rachel stared at the tiny silver device as if it were going to bite her.

"What did he want?"

"To meet."

"For the ruby?"

"Yes."

"Well, let's go." Jason tugged the phone but she held firm.

"He said he'd call back."

Stepping outside, she went around to the front of the car and sat on the hood. Jason's door closed behind his exit. Coving the small phone between her palms, she cursed Christian's hold over her. But did he really have a hold?

Rachel went through all the locations he could possibly be—that is, if he had left the X. There were a few office spots on the island center of the city. An old mansion in the Marais. Two other locations, only one was a warehouse, a likely spot for an exchange meeting.

Dare she simply go there and wait?

Jason paced before her, arms crossed high over his chest. "Bloody Lazar, he's just stalling."

"Toying with me, trying to knock me off balance. But I'm not going to let it work."

She would use this time to center herself. Come to a grounded position. It was the only thing that would see her a formidable opponent to Christian.

Rachel drew in a breath and exhaled, closing her eyes. Meditating next to an abandoned junkyard? It was difficult to quiet her mind. And if noise torture and double-crossing

Frenchmen weren't enough to dizzy her brain, the presence of a box-man with a calming voice and charisma that oozed from his pores pacing before her only pushed concentration further from her grasp.

But she managed a series of deep, cleansing breaths. Filling her lungs, Rachel slowly exhaled, imagining the bad floating out with her breaths. So much bad of late. Another inhale, and a long, cleansing exhale. Tension slipped out through her toes. Her muscles relaxed.

Opening one eye, she saw Jason stood, his back to her, surveying the length of chain link that stretched about the junkyard. Why did he stay with her? It was so obvious that he simply wanted a chance at the ruby. Thirty percent was no small bit of change.

"You could just drive away, leave me standing here."

He turned to her. "For what gain? I'd only mark one of the toughest women I know against me. Bugger, but I'd hate to have you as my enemy. Maybe you already are?"

"I don't have enemies, Marland. Just...obstacles."

"Am I an obstacle?"

"Not sure."

He nodded, accepting her indecision. "Vincent Rousseau an obstacle?"

"You know he is."

"You want to go look for him?"

She shrugged. "I thought to just relax for a bit. Tried to meditate, but I need a while longer. I've got to settle my insides before meeting with Christian. Prepare. You know."

"You want me to sit in the car, leave you alone?"

"No," came out quickly. "I like having you...here."

He tilted a smile at her. A genuinely surprised bit of mirth. Wincing at the sun beaming in his face, he shaded his eyes with a flat hand to his brow. "So if I asked, would you tell me what it was like?"

"What?"

"Living with Lazar. Him training you. I gotta wonder, as a teenager, what it was like to be taken from all your friends and family."

"There were no friends or family. Explains it all, doesn't it?"

"Sorry, sweet."

"You don't have to be sorry, and I know you're not. I followed Christian. He didn't kidnap me. I didn't struggle. He did seduce me…"

She stared off to the horizon, blurred by the consistent crossed wire of the chain-link fence. Christian had not fenced her in with wires and high security. It had taken but an admission to love and a few tender touches. Because all a teenage girl really wants is to be cared for and loved. *She just needed a string of seashells.* Christian had stepped into the space ripped out by her parents' deaths. What a masterful man.

You're the only one I kissed. Had the others been seduced and stolen from empty lives with such ease? The discovery that there were other women, possibly like her, would not be put from her thoughts.

Rachel looked up to find Jason stood close, his thighs touching her knees. To look into another man's eyes for more than a few seconds either meant a promise of sex or danger. But she persisted, and he did not look away.

And there in the depths of Jason's gold eyes she saw his gentleness, a kind heart and a promise never to make promises. And fear. He was an obstacle, but one so unique she wasn't sure how to overcome it.

"You don't think I can win," she stated.

"Why ask something like that?"

"I've never looked into a man's eyes for so long. I saw your fear."

He shrugged. "Worry, maybe. Concern. Look again."

She did, and he moved closer, but stopped when they could have kissed.

"Christian never kissed me," she whispered. "Not once."

"Really. I don't understand how denying you something so vital could have kept you under his command."

Vital indeed. "It was the promise of a kiss, the longing that kept me faithful. I've never kissed another man on the mouth. Maybe a peck to the corner of the lips. Or a smear from a drunken mark. You're the only one who has ever really kissed me, Jason, and not expected something in return."

That confession was followed with a gasp of breath. Whew, this gray stuff was getting easier.

"I didn't know that." Stuffing his hands into his pants pockets, he touched her at the waist and looked to the sky, but he wasn't seeing, even though he feigned to be looking for something.

"Real kisses are more powerful than sex," she said. "Don't you think?"

"Depends on who you're kissing."

That was so true.

"Kiss me," Rachel said in a falter. Already her better judgment fought to wrangle the machine back to tether. But her heart pushed even harder. "Please?"

As he drew close again, she watched Jason's eyes flick back and forth between hers. His breath hushed over her lips, sweet with traces of minty toothpaste. And he kissed her. A simple kiss. And then another. And with each following kiss they grew slower, more intense and delving.

Wrapping her legs about Jason's thighs, Rachel didn't so much pull him to her as melt into him. The quiet she had sought earlier ascended and filled her. This kiss felt so right. And even better than—

"Oh." She pushed him back gently, but clung to his shoulders and did not uncross her legs. "That's kinda overwhelming," she breathed.

"It was bloody brilliant, sweet. Another?"

He nuzzled against her mouth. Strong arms wrapped across her back and lifted her slightly from the car hood. Everything segued away from her until she felt but one entity, this man and herself, alone in the world, two shells on a string.

"I like kissing you," she murmured against his mouth. "Might be better than sex."

"You think?"

"Better than any sex I've had." Including the night with Vincent. Because this pleasure was mutual, and it wasn't meant to win, manipulate or conquer.

"If you think this is good—" he kissed the corner of her mouth, another to the other side of her lips "—I wonder what sex will be for us."

Us? A word loaded with promise. But she knew better; this man didn't make promises. Nor did she expect them.

"Doesn't matter. Everything is perfect right now. I wouldn't change a thing. I wouldn't take another step further if forced."

His eyes sparkled with sunlight. Rachel smoothed a hand over his head, jittering her palm back and forth over the short bristles on his scalp. "You're sexy, Marland."

Rachel giggled, and halfway through the giggle she realized she sounded like a silly teenager. And then she didn't care because Jason swept her up into his arms and spun her around before the car hood.

"Feeling pretty ducky, eh, sweet?" He spun to a stop and kissed her jaw.

"Ducky is good, yes?" Landing on the ground, she wavered and caught herself by leaning her entire body into Jason's. Woozy from that kiss. And loving it.

"Ducky is brilliant."

The sudden rattle of the cell phone, vibrating across the Fuego hood, cut a blade through their light mood.

Rachel dodged for the phone. "Yes?"

"Be at the warehouse behind the Jardin des Plantes in one hour. You know the one. Come alone."

Jerked back to reality, Rachel squared her shoulders and tossed her hair over her shoulder. "You'll offer the same deal by sending your thugs hiking?"

"I always favor a fair playing ground."

Truth. The man craved an equal match—difficult to find with his skills. Another reason he'd trained a sparring partner. "I'll be there."

"Excellent. Winner take all."

The urge to throw the phone through the windshield worked the action halfway. Rachel clutched the cold silver cell phone and, first giving it a fierce shake, then handed it to Jason.

"What's his deal?"

"He wants to meet in an hour, about a twenty-minute drive from here. Winner take all."

"I'll drive you there."

Still thinking he could muscle his way between her and the ruby? But he'd kissed her as if he cared.

And how on earth would you ever know the difference?

"Fine. But then you'll drive off and leave me to handle this my way."

"Deal."

She blinked at him.

"Someone's got to find Rousseau."

"And the contact book?"

"As you've already guessed, I suspect—book or no—Lazar wants only to deal with you."

"You're very perceptive, Marland."

"Comes in handy for a man in my profession."

She smiled. Couldn't help it. Charm oozed from the man, trust him or not.

"Thank you."

"Just keeping my end of the stick upright."

"Thanks mostly for the rescue. I was out of it in the X. Wasn't sure who was carrying me, only that it was moving me away from bullet fire. It's been said…a knight in shining armor rescued me."

"Hmmph. Well, the Fuego is getting a touch of rust under her bonnet, so I don't know how shiny her armor is. Bullet holes, too."

"Sorry about that."

"What for? Just adds a touch of charm."

All this gray talk wasn't improving her chances to defeat Christian.

"I understand now," Jason said. She didn't turn to him, toeing a discarded cigarette butt on the ground. "About the noise? Sorry, sweet, I knew that some of the network used torture to break down the tough ones."

The tough ones? She smirked.

"About these girls…"

"They're like you." He sighed heavily. She sensed him relaxing and felt the brush of his finger over her arm, but she didn't turn to him. Because if she did it would end in another kiss. And the phone call had cooled their ardor. "About half a dozen girls. Plucked off the street when they were young, and trained to perform a highly specialized skill. Together the network forms a team of thieves, grifters, drivers, assassins, art experts and hackers. Their combined financial worth, well, it must be bloody staggering."

"How do you know so much about this network?" She swung around to catch his look, but the sun forced her to shield her eyes with a hand. "Are you one of them?"

He smirked. "Not for all the gold bullion in Bangkok. But I've trained a few of the girls, as I mentioned to you before."

"Right. No kissing?"

"Absolutely not. Promise."

"You don't do promises."

"Then take it as a truth."

It shouldn't matter if he had, or had not, kissed any of the nameless, faceless girls. But it did.

"None like you though, sweet. None like you."

"If Christian never told me a thing about the network, then why would he tell you so much?"

"He didn't." Pause. Wondering how much to reveal? "Rousseau is one of them."

That statement wasn't so much a surprise as she thought it should be. Though, still incredible. Christian and Vincent had ties. Did that buy Vincent his life? And if so, was he sitting back right now, toasting his and Christian's success over her?

No, Christian would not count his successes until she was back under his control.

"So who did Vincent train? What kind of machine did he create?"

"I'm not saying."

Just when she slid close to trust, Jason slapped up a wall. A reminder that this game was still every man for himself.

"Hey, we're not bloody princes or priests. We. Are. Criminals," he said, emphasizing each word with a stab of his finger in the air between them. "And that *we* includes you, sweet. You can try all you like to get back the ruby, to clear your name, but once a thief…"

No need to finish the obvious. Rachel eyed the fading pink hood. She poked a finger into the bullet hole. Crossing her arms, she looked up to the sun and squinted tightly when tears formed.

Michele Hauf

Once a thief…always a thief. Bluntly put.

Had she been fooling herself for eight months? Playing at her quest for domesticity? For a normal life? She was no better than a cat burglar who steals in the night. Only thing different is she gave the jewels back and justified her profits by donating half to charity. It was like some kind of movie script that only a little girl could imagine.

The car lowered as Jason sat on the hood and clasped his hands between his knees. "I'm sorry."

"No," she said. "You've got me pegged. Not that difficult. I *am* a thief. I'll never be domestic, probably never have a house with a little garden in the window box. Hell, I'm not big on family. Normal for me is scaling buildings and spinning dials. Cracking boxes. Taking down thugs. It's what I do."

"It's what you *did*. You've got a great start on a new life."

"What do you care?"

"I do. Don't ever forget that. I think what you've been doing, this security-specialist thing, is brilliant."

"It was a stupid idea. Like you said, once a thief…" She sighed. "Christian's machine is good for but one thing."

"If you want to give up so easily."

"Easy?" She chuckled. If he only knew. But maybe he did. "Christian, he…took things from me. He took away my world bringing me to France. He took away my fear. My safety. So many little things a person never thinks about but relies on—like the media, friendships, parties—and crushes! Even music. I can't listen to any of it. I hate that, because I think I once wanted to be a musician."

"Really?"

She shrugged. "I remember I played the guitar. Might have wanted to be a rock 'n' roll guitar player. Something silly like that. A teenager's dream."

"You could be still."

"Music is gone from me. So are a lot of simple pleasures."
"Such as?"
She shrugged. "Sex, for one. I don't know what to think of it. It's a tool, a weapon. It defeated me quite thoroughly the other night."

"You and Rousseau?"

"I thought I knew what I was doing. I've been trained to seduce the guy to get the jewels. But...hell, Christian always denied me an orgasm. To keep me strong, you know?"

"Uh-huh. So...Vincent took you out with but a few strokes?"

"It sounds pitiful." She sighed. "But it was good. And now I'm beating on myself, 'cause it shouldn't have been good. It should have never happened. And then you kiss me and change the rules again."

"I can't say that I understand."

"There's nothing to understand."

He clasped her hand, drew it to his mouth. "I can guess that your whole sexual-priority scale is dangerously out of whack."

"Sex is not a priority."

"It should be."

"I can't believe I'm discussing this with you."

"Why? You're not embarrassed?"

"No, I just..."

"Want to know what it feels like to have another orgasm?" He kissed her knuckles, then drew his tongue along one bent finger. "If the whole sexual-pleasure thing is your chink, why don't you just do it for yourself? Then no man can master you, because you've already taken care of the problem."

"You mean?"

"Jill off."

Masturbate? "I've never heard it called that."

"No shit? I guess there's a lot you don't know about sex.

Even though you're like this incredible Amazon powerhouse of a woman. Lazar really did mess you up. Pity."

She tugged her hand from his grip and tucked it between her knees. "Don't feel sorry for me. I can handle myself."

"Really?" A sneaky grin intimated another meaning to her statement. "I'd like to watch."

"I think we're going too far here, Marland."

They both grinned.

The rumble of a semitruck passed by on their right, stirring up a plume of dust. Rachel shaded her eyes and nose from the dust while Jason flipped off the back end of the truck.

"Wanker," he commented, then with a clap of his hands together announced, "So, your love for music is trashed. There must be other things you could try."

"I'm sure there is. Christian gave me things, too. He gave me confidence and strength. A cognizance that is almost scary. I've many skills. You must admit I don't fear anything."

"Sweet, you escaped. So I gotta believe that you wanted freedom. You don't have that yet. And you won't have it until you can condemn Christian Lazar."

"I do hate him."

"Yeah, but you still love him."

He knew her well. Could he read it in her external actions, her face? Or had the man a deeper connection that tapped her secreted soul?

"How do you stop loving someone?"

"It'll be a snap when you realize it's not love." Jason leaped from the hood and spread his arms before her. He made a gesture like he wanted to hug her. "Can I?"

Faced with a plunge into the gray, Rachel nodded. Falling into Jason's arms, she felt like a child coming home.

"I do care, sweet."

And that was good enough for her.

"Why do you call me sweet?"

"Just a name. Might be because you're the one piece of sweetness in my life. Might not be."

No promises, just straightforward Jason Marland. The way she liked him to be. They had developed a distinct respect and understanding for one another.

But he didn't know the whole of her.

"A thief. A little lost child. A machine. Like I said, you have pegged me, Marland," she said. "But not completely."

"I'm usually fair to excellent at the like. What did I miss?"

"The fact that I never go down without a fight."

"Yeah? I knew that. I was just waiting to see how long it took you to remember it." He jogged a few steps before her and swung his fists in a mock challenge. "You ready for a fight?"

She tugged off the sweater and tossed it to him. The thin camisole shirt welcomed a shiver from the cool air. A stretch of her neck, and easing her legs in a hamstring stretch was about all the preparation she could muster. There would be time to meditate in the car on the way to the warehouse. "I'm ready for a fight."

Chapter 22

Saturday—1:50 p.m.

Again with the humming. But it made Rachel smile, and she slipped easily from the soft rhythm of Jason's hums into a meditative state as the Fuego sped toward destiny.

"I don't know how you do it."

The Brit's voice lured Rachel out of her meditation. She exhaled and uncrossed her legs and set them on the floor of the car. They'd stopped. She hadn't noticed until now.

"Do what?"

"That meditation stuff. Especially in a moving car."

"Not that difficult once you find your core. Time—" She checked her watch.

"We're early. You going to wait?"

"For a few minutes."

She glanced up the facade of the warehouse. Tall, narrow

windows sectioned by many panes. Dirty, broken and streaked. Hadn't changed since she'd last seen it, must have been two years earlier. The riverboat laydown. She'd lifted half a million small diamonds from a floating mansion while the owners partied on deck with fifty of their friends. The buyer— "It was here."

"Hmm?"

"Here. The meeting. We—Christian and I. I knew I remembered Vincent from somewhere."

"You had a laydown here with Rousseau?"

"Yes, but I didn't know his name at the time. I just remember him as impudent. And I recall that it seemed he knew Christian just from subtle eye contact, and a nod here and there. But of course they had known one another if they are both part of the network." Tapping the dashboard with her forefinger, she looked directly to Jason. "If he's alive…is there anything you need to warn me about?"

"About Rousseau?" Jason shrugged. "The wanker is definitely out there, but a woman like you has got nothing to fear from him."

She lifted a brow.

"Well, unless you're naked. Obviously." A teasing smile tugged his rugged face into the picture of charm. Then it slipped to serious business. "This is what I know. He doesn't talk a lot about his connections, his dealings. And I don't ask. Rousseau's smart, but not socially smart, you know? He's doing a lot less lately, but I do know he's been after the ruby for years. Since Lazar's stroke, Vincent has not had communication with him. I don't think any of the network has."

"I can only hope he isn't up there with Christian."

"I'll go up with you, sweet."

"No. Christian promised no others. He'll keep his word. The game wouldn't be fair otherwise, and he does like a fair playing ground. You'd better take off."

"Are you sure?"

That question, soft, almost whispered, tickled up Rachel's arm and landed on her neck in a prickle of sensation. Sure? She wanted to ask him to stay. Stand behind her and offer support. To be the one grounding force that she so desperately needed right now.

"I'm sure. This is my battle." She opened the car door. "Don't watch for me to drive away."

She swung a stern look at him. Now was no time to change the plan.

"I'll sit here until I'm sure you're where you should be. And I'm going to roll down the window and keep a keen ear for gunfire."

"He's not going to take me out that way. Too easy." Also, too quick for Christian's preferences. Though, she would have never expected him to fire on her at the club. It had been a tease, a test to see if she panicked. And she had, hadn't she? "Just drive away, Marland. Go find Vincent and make sure he survived."

"You care?"

She nodded. It was a simple admission. "He's likely got a valuable book of information. You think I want him dying in an alley somewhere?"

For her tough facade she did care more and more about the good and the bad, and the separation between the two. Vincent toed the line; but he was good at heart, she sensed, else he would not be friends with Jason. Like attracted like.

"Thanks," she murmured, "for everything." And exited the car.

She wasn't about to look back. He'd watch her every step.
I do care.

And just knowing as much made her lift her chin and stride forward with a new purpose.

Saturday—2:00 p.m.

Rachel stood in the center of a warehouse, upper floor, twice as large as her loft. Half a dozen steel support beams spiked down the center of the huge room. Overhead, thick round vents, frosted with woolly dust traced worm trails across the open ceiling. To her left a huge hook hung from a dusty chain, sporting links the size of her fist. It resembled something a cow carcass might hang from in a butcher's shop.

Across the vast stretch of pocked wood floor stood Christian Lazar. Feet square beneath his shoulders and arms loose at his sides. He nodded acknowledgment.

"You said just the two of us," she called. A peripheral scan sighted in the two thugs standing at the door behind her.

"I did." He nodded toward the men.

Rachel listened as the sound of their thick-soled shoes echoed down the hallway. An outer door creaked open. They wouldn't go farther than the building perimeter, she knew, but at least Christian was honoring their agreement. Vincent was not here. Which either boded well, or deadly, depending on how one wished the outcome to be.

For Jason's sake, he had better be long gone. The thugs would certainly check out any cars on the empty street.

Christian turned and walked away from her. Rachel observed as he pulled a crisp linen shirt from his arms and tossed it to the far wall. Just tossed it to the dirty floor. Remarkable! What had become of his anal perfection? Had the stroke relaxed his attitude?

He flexed and moved his muscles in his usual stretching exercise. A broad back, well defined by years and consistent attention to his body offered proof he'd not overlooked his workouts as she had. Impressive, that the stroke had affected his physical appearance so little—save the weakness on his right side she had noticed previously.

Lunging out, he stepped and stretched his quads. A slash of an arm through the air, the movement, graceful and silent, highlighted his exquisite form. Lean, and wrapped neck to ankle with steel-hard muscle, is what she remembered from the many times she'd stolen glimpses of his sleeping naked form. And the frequent times he'd join her in the shower to simply watch as she slicked her body clean.

He had mastered his body as easily as he'd mastered her. Control oozed from his being. Iron will pulsed in the flex of his pecs.

Rachel drew in a breath. She stood before her equal, very likely her superior. This man had taught her everything she knew. How to think like a thief—attitude is everything. How to protect and defend—again, attitude beat a muscle-bound idiot any day. Mastery of the mind, body and soul had been her reward for taking the hand of a stranger and following him away from her horrible life—to a new nightmare that had only begun to reveal its nasty truths.

The one awful truth being that she would never be free.

Ever? Hope had not completely vacated her soul.

Hell, it was strong, still alive, and ready for some fight.

Turning in a precise circle, Christian tilted a devious smile on her. Even across the room his blue eyes twinkled. *I will give you everything.* "You ready for this?"

"Where's the ruby?"

He dug into his pants pocket, and while doing so, kicked off his shoes to the far wall. So they would fight bared. Rachel toed off her creepers. The wood floor was cool and minutely dusted.

The glint of ruby held between Christian's fingers fascinated more than any jewel had ever teased. This single chunk of red stone could either make her a fugitive or a free woman. It all depended on who held the rock.

Stepping forward, he bent and placed the ruby on the floor then stepped back. The prize glinted but ten paces between them. Rachel had no desire to lunge for it and run. The call to fight tensed her muscles. Instinctively she loosened her arms by shaking them at her sides and limbered up with some squats and flexes. She wasn't leaving this building without proving once and for all to this man that she would never again be controlled.

"Where's the contact book?"

"Rousseau has it," she said. "You didn't search the body before dumping it? I did tell you to check him."

A brief flicker clouded Christian's gaze. He believed her. And he hadn't checked Rousseau. Score one point for Rachel Anderson—Security Expert.

"How much did you sell it for?"

Her very life? The freedom to walk anywhere she wished in the States? "Not nearly enough. But you don't really care about some damn book."

"I do, but present company is of more immediate concern."

At Christian's silent instruction, he raised his hands, palms toward one another, and spread them wide, a sun-worship meditative pose. Rachel did the same. It was a routine they had shared before their morning workouts. Stretch out the muscles, open the body to its potential, calm the inner and focus.

With an exhale, she looked to Christian, who bowed. She returned the obligatory bow, a call to arms, a twisted genuflection to past chivalries. Honor among thieves. There would be no such high ground to claim a win this day.

Sweeping her arms out before her, Rachel formed a fight-ready posture, hands stiffening to play a blow, but she yet remained grounded, positioned loose and ready. An intake of breath filled her lungs. Centered, she pushed back all mind traffic.

Christian was the first to approach, on guard. A high kick. Rachel dodged the attack with a deft bend at the waist and a turn to riposte with a kick that skimmed Christian's thigh.

It was a dance, really. A match of skill, muscle and determination. Discipline reduced Rachel's focus to the form, the connection of might to muscle. She scored the first hit. The side of her foot to Christian's solar plexus. He huffed out breath and stumbled off balance.

Would his chink keep him from a win? Not a migraine; he had developed a new chink. The stroke must have weakened him.

A cocky grin interrupted their spar. "Nice. But I don't think you've been keeping up with your workouts. You're slower than usual."

He swung out a leg, slashing a high roundhouse that she easily dodged. The kick swung his head and shoulders low. He grabbed her ankle and brought her down. Springing up and bouncing at the ready, he chuckled. "I've been waiting for this a long time. You don't think I'm not physically and mentally stronger than you?"

"You might be," she said, rolling to her stomach and pushing upright. "But I've got more at stake. Which dog has more to lose? Isn't that what you always taught me? The hungry dog gets the prize."

"Or the soused dog." With that, Christian's body made a fascinating change. Every limb loosened. He swayed, and appeared to wobble off balance, his shoulders lifting and dodging.

Impossible to judge his next move when he fought like a drunk. Be not there, he called it. A skill Rachel had never quite been able to master, for she'd never had the experience of being drunk. She followed his elusive gyrations, thinking to pull a punch. But his movements were designed to rob her of her balance and redirect her momentum. He swayed back, almost hitting the ground, then recovered with a snicker and a quick fighting skip of his feet.

"We can go at this all day," he said. "I'm not going to get tired."

"Nor I."

"Hell, you can knock me out and run, but I'll always know where you are, Rachel Blu. Always."

"If you've spies following me, they can only track me so long. Sooner or later, I'll give them the slip."

"Spies?" He smiled and delivered a direct punch to her nose.

Rachel swallowed blood and knocked the sting from the blow with a shake of her head. She spat to the side.

"You think I've loosed spies on your trail? Ha!" He bent and ducked a punch toward her, but he was too far to connect. Just playing. Keeping his body moving. He was all there now, having dropped the drunken tactic. "You know I couldn't stomach any man constantly watching you. You're mine to watch."

"Give it up, Christian. It's over. I gave you a lot of good years. Stole some incredible jewels for you. Isn't that enough? I don't want to be with you. I want my own life."

"You don't know what you want, Rachel Blu."

"Yes, I do! I want the ruby. You don't need it. You only want it because it's something that'll give me more satisfaction than you were ever capable of giving me."

He silenced her with a kick to her ribs. Air forced from her lungs, Rachel landed against the wall. Blood swirled across her tongue and dribbled over her lower lip.

Christian pinned her to the cinderblock wall. "I have always been capable, just not willing, to relinquish the control. It's what kept you strong."

Strong, yes. But a match to any? For her caper with Vincent only proved otherwise. Sexual release, the chink in her armor. While teaching her control, Christian had inadvertently given her a grave fault.

But it wasn't a fault that would challenge physical combat. Fighting required no seduction.

They stood at the wall, both tense with adrenaline.

Blood ran over Rachel's lips and dripped from her chin. Christian's closeness filled her with a confusing mix of hate and disgust and desire. Chest bare, and muscles thick with sweat and steel-hard control, his every movement challenged in distinctly different ways. He smelled primal, hot with feral strength. He vibrated an intensity of spirit and command that mastered her innate female needs. He had protected and taught. He had punished and stolen her innocence.

Ramming her head into Christian's throat, Rachel brought him to the ground. He sprawled onto his back. She delivered a hard drive of palm into his sternum. His feet caught her at the waist and shoved her back against the wall, where she hit with a blood-spattering chuff.

"Time to change the rules," he said as he jumped up and strolled toward the center of the warehouse where the ruby glinted. "Theo!"

The door behind her opened. Without even looking, Rachel knew the thugs had entered. Swinging in a tight circle, she stood down the approaching threat. She managed a fist to one jaw before both of her arms were wrenched before her. Iron clanked. Anticipating the worst, she let out a guttural cry and leaped to kick both feet, each landing on one of the thugs' knees. As a threesome they went down. Wrists still not free, Rachel twisted and kicked. A fist to her spine dropped her to the floor. Her body was rolled. The heavy weight of iron manacles snapped about her wrists.

"Over here, gentlemen!" Christian called.

Dragged forward to the center of the warehouse where the hook hung, she spied Christian pressing the control on one of the steel beams. The hook lowered and her wrists were strung up. Electricity humming, the hook rose until her toes just lifted from the floor. She had to stand on tiptoe to keep from dangling. If she kept her head at a slight tilt back, it prevented the muscles in her back from maxing out too quickly.

Christian paced a few leaps away. His thugs left the room. Curious.

Had Rousseau sold her out? To his own detriment. Likely the thugs had gone to clean up their mess at the X. No, Christian must have called in a cleaner. Safer and neater when one kept their hands from the mess.

"You forced me to change tactics. No complaints?" he asked.

Of course not. One should never fight fair; it was the next thing Christian had taught her after attitude.

Allowing her head to fall completely back, Rachel studied the situation high above. The hook was suspended on a length of rusted chain—about thirty feet long—that stretched to the ceiling. The mechanism was secure. But the hook wasn't closed. The chain on her manacles had merely been slipped over the thick half-moon iron hook. About a sixteen-inch stretch to get herself down. That is, if she could make a leap. Or inch her way up by gripping the chain—an insurmountable feat, even for one physically superior like Christian. If she just had a boost...

"I knew that eventually you would return to me."

Christian's pace swung him about and blue eyes fixed to hers. He thought he knew so much. On the other hand, how had he found her so easily? It was almost as if he was tracking her, and yet, she bore the scars on her arm to prove that impossibility.

"Not much for conversation?" He approached, his bare feet making no sound on the wood floor. A flex of his left arm bulged his chest muscles. "Or maybe you are stepping into your role again, Rachel Blu? Silence shows respect."

Conserve your energy, she thought. He wants to break you down by engaging you in conversation. That's how it works.

Start chatting and soon you find yourself agreeing to everything and making promises to behave.

Anything for freedom.

The electricity of his hand moving up her thigh and cupping into the curve of her waist sent a mix of confusing signals to her tightened determination.

Christian's had been the first sensual touch she had experienced. Albeit, a touch doled out sparely and always with intention behind it. She had learned to crave the tender touches he granted her as reward for a job well done.

For the first two years she had stayed with him he had used discretion, flirting excessively to win her, but never threatening with an unwarranted touch. He had not pushed. Such constant attention had reduced her initial shy hesitation, so by the time he'd suggested they take their relationship further, she had literally flung herself into his arms. He'd taken her virginity on her sixteenth birthday.

Closing her eyes, Rachel fought a pleasurable shudder as his palm moved up, over her breast. Her nipple hardened mutinously. She thought to lunge up and kick him in the chest. That would bring the thugs on her like two rabid dogs chomping for raw meat. She didn't care. The more the merrier.

Drawing in a lust-thick inhale, Christian breathed, "I've missed you, Rachel Blu. Your body. Your scent. Your skill. This." He pinched her nipple. "This." He spread a palm across her stomach, stretching the thin cotton camisole. "You know you impressed the hell out of me that day you left me there in the courtyard."

She wouldn't speak. Separating her strange arousal from the pressing—the urgent—need to return the ruby to the States required utter power of will.

Why succumb to a man's easy power over her?

Just do it for yourself. That Jason would suggest something so…intimate, had stunned her. But why not? She didn't need to rely on a man for pleasure. Nor need she fear the accidental pleasure that came from a man's touch. It was just a touch, no promise, no real pleasure.

So get over it.

"I expected nothing less."

He walked around her, drawing his hand over her rib cage. At her back, he lifted her shirt. Smoothing over the tattoo, likely, admiring it. Three days of many two-hour sessions stacked throughout the day, she had endured the numbing drag of the needle. The feel of his finger tracing a short line along her spine made her cringe, but not enough to move away from his touch.

Because it wasn't about pleasure anymore. It was all about freedom.

"I created an incredible machine. And that machine rebelled against the teacher to prove its mastery. You needed to escape. To taste independence. That's why I haven't come after you." His breath dripped over her shoulder. Rachel closed her eyes as he came around in front of her. "I knew you'd return. It was much sooner than I had hoped. Once a thief—"

Oh, not that crap again! Pressing up on tiptoe, Rachel gripped the chains and kicked up, catching Christian in the gut. But he did not falter. He'd taken the blow as if a tap from a child.

Weren't strokes supposed to incapacitate?

When would she get a break?

The door on the far end of the warehouse creaked open.

"I see we have a guest!" he called.

Rachel twisted to face the door.

Stumbling between the two thugs, his face and chest bloody, was Jason.

Chapter 23

Saturday—2:35 p.m.

Blood trickled from Jason's nose and bruises darkened his eyes. His shirt was torn to reveal more blood, its source indeterminable. They'd worked him over. He must have remained exactly where he'd dropped her off.

"Marland! Are you all right?"

"Ducky, sweet. Just—*ouff!*"

She cringed at the sound of his pain, but took comfort in the fact that he could speak and was at least joking.

They walked Jason across the room to her. Rachel saw he could stand on his own, but one eye was completely shut with vicious purple bruising. He spat, landing on the floor before Christian's toes with a wodge of bloody spittle. Still in the game. She regretted that he'd been insinuated into what should have been a one-on-one match. Could Christian know their involvement?

Could it be considered involvement when they'd only kissed twice?

I'm crushing on you...

The only thing that had been crushed was likely Jason's nose, and not for the first time.

"I think this one is yours," Christian said to her. He shoved Jason's chin upward, and Jason whipped his head away from the unwanted touch. Fire daggers shot between the two men. "I always suspected the two of you had something going on, Marland. A liaison. I just could never be sure."

"He's got nothing to do with me," Rachel said. "Let him go."

"And you'll return to me?"

She sucked in her lower lip. That ultimatum had come from out of the blue, though it had been expected. Return to Christian? Not if all the stolen rubies in the world could be traced to her.

But if it would free Jason?

She caught the cracker's careful stare. The barest movement of his head from one side to the other sent the "no" signal her way.

But he didn't have a vote in this game. She had gotten him into this mess; she would get him out.

"Ah." Christian stepped right up to Rachel. Odor of sweat curled into her nostrils, a feral cocktail of musk, sex and power. "I discover the truth of your liaison with your lacking answer."

"There was no fucking liaison."

"Such language, Rachel Blu. Don't speak like a trucker, it uglies your pretty exterior. Do you want the cracker released or not?"

The weight of her body stretched the muscles in her biceps, making control of the chain difficult. Needles prickled in her fingertips. She tried to avoid Jason's stare, but it was impossible. But this time he didn't shake his head. Rachel caught his glance up to her chains—and his wink.

When Christian lunged for her, she instinctively lifted her leg to defend, but stopped herself. A calm head would work to her advantage. His left hand gripped the neckline of her shirt, while his right slid down her side. Not a controlled action, she sensed. He just couldn't get a grip with his right hand. Was he weakening? Had he expended all his strength?

"Did you fuck him?" The rage in Christian's eyes manifested in a growl. He pulled her down, her muscles straining against the manacles so they were eye to eye. "Tell me what happened those days I left you in Paris with Marland. Did he have you?"

She shook her head no. It was the truth. Much as she'd have liked it to be otherwise.

"Why did you go to him, then? The first person you run to upon your return is this bastard."

"I trusted him!"

"Why? I gave you everything!"

A drool of shiny spittle ran down the side of his mouth. The muscles on the left side of his face were so tense. Had she done this to him? If she had helped Christian that morning in the courtyard, would he have had a full recovery? Did she not owe him that small kindness for the years he had sheltered and fed her?

Help him to your own detriment! Don't fall into his seductive clutches.

"Rachel."

Jason's bark drew her up from the swirl of conflicting thoughts. At Christian's signal one of the thugs punched Jason in the gut. A spray of the cracker's blood spewed across the floor.

"So that is the way of it?" Christian released her and strode before Jason. "Is he the one you take orders from now? How'd you manage that, Marland?"

"I had no idea she was in Paris."

"You didn't answer my question." A thug gripped Jason's head and wrenched it up so he looked Christian straight on. "Tell me you fucked her."

"She's your whore, Lazar. Always has been, always will be. I wouldn't stir in those waters if I were drowning."

Jason's cruel retort cut Rachel. But like a slice from a blade, she shook it off.

"Maybe." Christian stepped back. "Maybe not." He released a swing, connecting his left fist with Jason's jaw.

Jason hung between the thugs, as if he was unconscious. Scent of blood overwhelmed. Rachel cautioned herself against verbal protest.

Christian turned to Rachel, a beaming grimace curled wrongly upon his mouth. He was growing weaker. His right side was wilting as the minutes passed!

"You give me the ruby," she offered. "And I give you the contact book. It's a fair deal, you know it. The names in that book are priceless."

"But you don't have the book."

"I can get it!"

"How? Do you know where Rousseau is? I didn't think so." He smoothed a thumb over a smear of blood on his rigid abs—Jason's blood. A slide of that thumb over his tongue sickened Rachel.

"You don't want to go legit," he spoke softly as he approached. All gentility now, he stroked the tips of her hair. "You can't. You know nothing but what I have taught you. You are a thief. I never taught you to go it alone. You need my protection, my connections. My love."

She looked away, closing her eyes. Christian's brand of love hurt. The small taste she'd had from Jason proved when one person cared for another it didn't have to hurt. It simply felt…right.

So why was it so difficult to just take him out and be done with him? He was crippled. Half her strength. The thugs she could obliterate with ease. Jason needn't move a muscle.

"Rachel Blu," Christian singsonged in that soft, teasing voice that had always promised a rare moment of lightness. Of maybe being held in his arms. Just like a real man and woman would do. Not two criminals. Not a thief and her psychotic mastermind lover who lived to control. To defeat. To hurt. To see her succumb when her inner being struggled merely to stand with dignity and respect.

Rachel lifted her head and stared at Christian Lazar. He had hurt her. So deeply that the scars of betrayal would never surface to show like the tattoo he'd branded into her flesh.

Just give back my dignity.

You want it, Rachel? Take it!

Right. She would not again fall into Christian's trap of twisted love and hate.

A glance to Jason found a verifying nod. He was ready.

Rachel looked up the length of chain. Her arms had stopped shaking. Numbness had settled at the back of her neck and was beginning to spread through her shoulders. She had to act now or risk complete loss of muscle control.

"I—I do love you, Christian."

Chapter 24

That announcement got his attention. Riveted, Christian moved closer. Close enough for that one morsel she had always craved.

"I want to come back to you." She looked over his face, the left side hard and tense, the right, soft. Cold elegance; weird madness. Not a bit of heart in this man. Or, if so, half was frozen, the other half desiccated. "Me for the cracker. Will you release him?"

"Just say the word."

"You won't put a bullet in his back?"

"Promise. Not even his ugly front."

His morbid humor stirred the bile in Rachel's throat. To keep from looking at Jason, she focused on Christian's mouth. The curve on the right side sagged. Hideous. How was it this was happening? Was he aware? Was he on medication?

Yes! He'd mentioned something about it at the apartment. Might it be something that improved his muscle control, a medication he needed to redose? Or lose his strength.

Praying for that small mercy, Rachel played her final move.

"But I want one thing from you."

"You're in a fine situation to be asking anything of me, Rachel Blu."

"Then kill him. But I'll escape again, and next time I won't come back."

To her side one of the thugs moved. He lifted a leather-garbed arm in preparation for Christian's command, his knife blade glinted. But the command didn't come.

"Not come back? Of course not! You can't return from a jail cell, darling. That's the way of it."

Christian glanced to the side. Rachel had forgotten the ruby; it lay on the floor still, near the wall where he must have kicked it when she'd watched Jason enter.

"If I'm in jail, I can't stand at your side. What's it going to be, Christian? Will you honor my request?"

"You still know how to play," he said. "I expect nothing less." Now he stood so close his breath danced with hers. Dangling on tiptoe, she matched his height. "Tell me, what do you require for your lover's release?"

"He is not—" Hell, why not allow him to suspect? "Fine. I will return to your command, and your bed, if you give me the one thing I have only ever wanted."

Christian tilted his head.

Rachel swallowed. Many times she had attempted to win the prize—why now did she expect he would relinquish it?

"I'm waiting," he said. "What do you want, Rachel Blu?"

"A kiss."

Her request unsettled him. She sensed the minute intake of his breath, even though he did not move from his close position.

"A kiss?" Christian repeated. "You know that is not allowed."

"Why?" she challenged. "Too afraid of your own heart?"

"You speak silly romantic babble."

"Oh, that's right—you don't have a heart. It rusted years ago. Probably why you had to kidnap a lover—"

Fire seared across her jaw, following the wake of his bared-knuckles smack.

"Has less than a year away from me polluted your brain so thoroughly? I suppose you've indulged in popular culture and molded your brain with television and theater and all that rot that preaches to the choir."

"Not at all." Rachel spat blood to the side. "I live in a spare warehouse with but a bed and some books."

"Books?"

"A reclusive pastime. Machines don't adapt well to popular society."

His grin tried to be normal, but it just wouldn't work.

"Machines are not supposed to desire either," he said. "Yet you desired freedom and you took it."

"And now I desire proof of your love for me." An impossible request, she knew, but she was buying time and hoped that he'd lose all control on the damaged side of his body.

"A kiss." His lips almost brushed hers now. He looked up and down her face.

Even with Jason standing but three strides behind her she fell into the intrigue of the moment. "All I've ever wanted from you was a kiss." Feeling her tension loosen and her mouth soften, she didn't flinch at the tear that trickled down her cheek. "You can have me with a kiss."

"But you're already mine."

"You've never had my heart, Christian. Don't you want all of me?"

He stared at her for the longest time. Working up courage? Had he ever kissed a woman? Yes, and Rachel had watched as he'd stroked his hands and moved his mouth over the bitch he'd brought home for a week to teach her the art of seducing a man. As if demonstrations were needed!

Just do it, she thought. Rachel tilted her shoulders slightly. One chain link moved soundlessly to the left. Her left heel touched the ground. She moved the balance to her toe, and simultaneously gripped the chain linked to the right manacle. Needles pricked at the numbing circulation in her left arm.

As Christian's mouth moved closer to hers, Rachel let out a breath. She inhaled, breathing a bit of his soul into hers. His lips, hot and quivering, pressed firmly. Something was wrong. The right side of his mouth hung loose. The morsel she had always dreamed of—meant nothing now.

Lifting a foot, she used her other to push from the floor. Her left toes hooked at Christian's waist and levered her body up. Gripping the chain with both hands, she swung up her foot and connected with Christian's face.

Meanwhile, one thug was leveled by Jason. A gunshot echoed. Heat impacted Rachel's upper left thigh.

No time to determine what the hell had just happened. Rachel gripped both hands on the chain and climbed inch by inch. When she was about a foot above the hook and the manacle chain had come free, she dropped to the floor in a crouch, wincing at the impact.

Her kick had not leveled Christian. It had merely been a slap to a bull.

Another pistol report kept her in a crouch. The whiz of a bullet shattered glass.

"Not her!" Christian shouted. "Take out the cracker."

Jason, his hands still bound behind his back, wasn't close enough to the thug to kick. He ran for the gunman, closing the distance and making the target more difficult.

Swinging the chains high above her head, Rachel lunged for Christian and lassoed him from behind. Success! She jerked him back, and they fell to the floor. Rachel tightened the chains about his neck, successfully immobilizing him. Feet secured at his shoulders, she torqued her grip.

"Cut him loose!" she shouted to the thug. "Or Lazar dies."

"Don't listen—" Rachel cut off Christian's retort. His face reddened. He lifted a leg to kick at her, but, kneeling above his head, she was well out of his attack periphery.

"Do it," she whispered.

The one standing thug hesitated. Jason turned and offered up his tied hands. The other thug, still out, lay close.

Christian struggled with the heavy chains. She shoved down each hand, tightening the chain across his throat.

She wasn't sure this would work. She couldn't kill Christian. Murder wasn't her game. And he knew it.

A slice of steel through the ropes binding Jason's hands— and the thud of thug hitting floor. Jason lunged for the Ruger that had landed a foot from the first thug's hand, a .22-millimeter, its long sleek barrel of black steel. He shadowed her and Christian, taking aim.

"You want me to put a hole in this wanker's brain?"

She loosened the chain and Christian choked in air. Swinging her leg around and over his body, Rachel moved onto his chest, framing her thumbs over his Adam's apple but not obstructing his air. Racked with coughs, each movement clanked the heavy chains that draped his throat. He was too drained to fight defensively, at least for a moment or two, which was all she needed.

"You'll never be free from me unless you kill me," Christian snarled. He reached up and slid a quick hand along her spine. "How do you think I found you? I knew the moment you arrived in Paris."

"There's another tracker on me, isn't there?"

He just smiled.

"Where is it?" Jason demanded over her shoulder.

"Hold." She signaled to Jason. This was her game. She would call the shots. "Your trigger finger secure, cracker?"

"There's a lot of blood on my hands."

"Don't let it slip."

Despite his dire position, Christian smiled up at Jason. "She'll never be yours, Marland. I live inside her. I made her."

"Yeah? Well, I can unmake you." The trigger cocked.

"You're wrong," she said to Christian. Pressing her palms on the floor at either side of his head, she sat on his torso, not fearing any sudden moves. "There's not a single breath of you inside me. Because you never gave me that kiss. Pity. You could have owned me with one simple act."

"But I just did—"

"That was a goodbye kiss, lover. Don't you know anything?"

With that, she smashed a right hook up under his jaw, knocking him out cold.

Untangling the chains from Christian's throat, Rachel stood and turned, finding herself in Jason's arms. The Ruger melded against her spine. Gold eyes melded to her soul.

"Sure you don't want me to take him out?"

"I didn't know you could take life so easily."

"I can't. I never have." He glanced to Lazar. "But this one would be bloody brilliant."

"Let's just grab the rock and get the hell out of here before they all come to."

"You're the boss, sweet."

"I am?"

"Yeah, you are."

"In that case—" she swiped the blood from her lips "—kiss me."

"I'm bleeding like a fountain, I don't want to get you—"

She silenced him with a quick, hard kiss to the corner of his mouth with the least bruising.

"You crushing on me?" he wondered.

"Yep."

"Wicked."

"Where's the rock?"

"It's over by the wall. We'll get the chains later. Probably be a good idea to get them off before you board a flight for the US."

Rachel stepped over Christian's body and paused.

"There's another tracker on me somewhere. I'm going to need a head start."

Shoving the rock into her front pants pocket, she turned her back to her nemesis.

Jason tucked the gun in the front of his pants. "If you don't take him out, he's going to follow you to the ends of the earth."

"Yeah? If he follows me that far, I'll just push him off—"

Clutched from behind, Rachel wobbled. Reacting by reaching behind, she paused as the slice of a blade opened her throat and hot blood spilled down her chest.

"Back off, Marland," Christian said.

Ramming his body tight to hers, Christian held Rachel, one hand wrapped beneath her breasts, while the other held a blade to her throat at the base of her neck. He pressed hard but did not drag the blade. Rachel remained still.

"If I can't have her," Christian started, "then no one can."

Jason dropped his hands that he'd been holding at his shoulders. Utter irritation crossed his bruise face "Besides sounding cliché, Lazar, you just don't get it, do you? I don't want her."

Rachel searched Jason's face for a signal, a clue he was bluffing. Not a glance her way.

"You were ready to walk out of here with my Rachel Blu." A firm press of the blade felt as though it cut bone. Rachel cautioned against swallowing.

"All I want is the bloody ruby."

"And you'll take off?"

Jason nodded.

The tight clamp about her ribs relaxed. Christian reached down with his left hand and shoved it into Rachel's pants pocket. Now she remarked their position. He held the knife to her throat with his *right* hand.

Feeling him claim the prize, she then saw the ruby take flight. Jason nabbed the sparkler with one hand. He gave it a look-over then pocketed it. "Nice doing business with you, Lazar." And he turned to walk out, whistling as he did.

He whistled that damn tune! The one Rachel had thought he only whistled when around her.

Anger didn't blip her radar. Jason Marland had never made promises.

The far door opened and closed. Thugs were sprawled like scattered puppets across the floor. Rachel listened as Jason's footsteps echoed farther away.

The blade tightened. An ooze of blood trickled between her breasts.

"I think he's got a crush on you," Christian said. His mirthless chuckle echoed in the vast warehouse.

"You're an idiot." All bets were off. "Crushes are for teenagers."

Thinking to swing up the chain and land it behind Christian's head, Rachel paused, chain suspended before her. The blade slipped from her neck—

"Damn it!"

—and found a new home in her side. Just below a kidney? The way her luck had been lately, it was very likely.

"Reach into my pocket."

"What?"

"The medication," Christian chuffed out in a forceful breath. "I need to dose. Do it, or I carve out a kidney."

Rachel reached back and slid a hand into the front pocket of his Armani trousers. A small vial fit into her hand, and she took it out and shook it before her. But three or four pills inside.

"Snap off the cap."

She did.

The blade clinked as it hit the floor. Simply following Christian's movements, Rachel went down with him as he landed on the floor in a crouch. Stretching her legs before her, she remained in Christian's grasp—though she sensed escape would be easy. Together they sat, or rather Christian might have had no choice but to go down. His fingers dug into her gut, not so much holding as...fighting an inner pain?

"What happens when you miss a pill?" she asked.

"Shut up!" He clung to her from behind, as a child cleaves to a stuffed animal. The blade lay just at the end of Rachel's toes. "Why did you leave me, Rachel Blu? I gave you everything!"

"I've never denied that." Keep him talking. Calm him, she thought. The pill vial still in hand, she vacillated between tossing it across the warehouse or handing it back to him.

"Then why?"

Now he would ask of her heart? Is that what desperation did to a man? Made him feel?

"I guess no matter how much you force a person, if their heart is not meant for it, the criminal life just won't stick. I don't like taking things from people, Christian. I never have."

"You're taking yourself from me."

A shake of the vial. Rachel handed it over her shoulder. "You'd better take one," she said. "Will you always need to medicate?"

"Yes." The pills rattled in the glass vial. Christian swallowed one dry, and again, his forehead hit her shoulder. Weak, and growing weaker.

A slide of her leg moved the dagger handle so it pointed toward her. He didn't notice.

"You," he began in whispers that gasped, "were once perfect. We were perfect."

She nodded. Tilting back her head brushed her cheek aside the crown of his soft hair. Spice. Not an awful scent. One ingrained within her, a part of her. She liked to place a person by their unique scent. It stayed in memory ever after. But all that filled her mind at this moment was that tune, hummed by Jason as he'd strode away without looking back.

Had *that* been the clue? The song?

"Give me another chance, Rachel Blu. I won't ask anything of you. I just...want you."

Yes, like a rare jewel kept beneath a glass case for all to look at but never touch. Not even Christian, for he hoarded his kisses like diamonds.

"I did love you," she offered.

The vial shattered on the floor beside her leg. It had not been thrown; fallen, slipped through fingers that just couldn't grasp. Christian Lazar's new chink. A shaky hand landed at Rachel's waist. The left hand reached for her throat. The clasp was hard and unrelenting.

Enough. This machine had played its last command.

"*Adieu,* Christian." Rachel twisted at the waist and shouldered him hard in the right bicep. He released the choke hold. An elbow caught him in the gut.

Christian fell backward, his body flattening to the hardwood floor. Lunging for the dagger, Rachel wielded it high, turned and stabbed him in the right shoulder. She pressed the blade until she felt the resistance of the floor beneath.

"Bitch," he muttered.

Rachel leaped to her feet. "Free."

Turning, she walked away, limping slightly at the pain in her thigh, past the fallen thugs, and out the door—where Jason stood, casually tossing the ruby into the air.

Ankles crossed and attitude airy, he winked at her. "Took you long enough."

Threading her fingers through his, the twosome fled the warehouse, chains clanking between them as they took the stairs.

For the first time, Rachel felt she was running toward something and not away from it.

Saturday—3:30 p.m.

"Not your apartment," Rachel said as Jason suggested they head toward the Sixteenth arrondissement. "Pull in to the alleyway up there, behind that hospital."

The Fuego managed the narrow cobbled passage with ease. Stacked barrels and ground coffee tainted the air. Jason switched off the ignition and turned to her. Twisting around on the seat, Rachel handed him the dagger she'd taken from the thug. "It's on my back somewhere."

"What?"

"A tracking device. Lazar ran his fingers along my spine when he said that creepy thing about always knowing where I am. I thought I got them all from my arm." She lifted her shirt and inched it up as best she could, manacled as she was. "Feel around. It's a thin narrow strip about half an inch long."

"Hell, I don't know, sweet."

"Just do it! Or they'll be on us in minutes."

"You think? Didn't you take Lazar out?"

"He's not dead. I'm not counting my eggs until I'm out of the country. The tracker, Marland."

"All right, all right. Christ, this is remarkable." Jason's fingers moved over her back, lightly at first, tentative, but then he really started to feel. Slowly he traced up her spine.

"Just don't view it from the side."

"Why? Will it hypnotize me into wanting to kill, kill, kill?"

"What?"

"Sorry. Too many horror flicks."

"Is there a space?" she asked. "A place where it looks like the ink is missing? A slot?"

Jason's fingers stopped just above her bra line. Unreachable with her own hands.

"Ducks and tattoos, oh my. Wait—I think I found something. There is a small section of skin here without ink, right in the middle of this slash. Is that a tiny scar? I feel it. It's definitely not bone."

"That's it!"

"You want me to cut it out? How deep does it go?"

"It lies just under the flesh. Cut the length and it should pop out."

The sudden heat of his forehead pressed to her back. Jason's breaths huffed down her spine.

"What are you waiting for?"

"I don't want to hurt you."

"Now is no time to get all mushy. You'll cause me greater pain should that bastard find us."

"Right." His palm smoothed over her spine. "This is a proper mess. Ready?"

The cut of the blade was like a bug bite, irritating but endurable. Especially when it meant she was once and for all cutting Christian Lazar from her life. Rachel prayed this was the last tracker on her body. He must have inserted it while she was getting inked—the needle numbed her flesh after a few minutes, so who would notice something like a little strip of plastic being embedded against her spine?

"You get it?"

Jason held the bloody strip up for her to see. She took it and bent it in half. It didn't break, being pliable enough to bend with her movements. Rolling down the window, she thrust it as far as she could.

"You're going to need a bandage."

"No time. I'll heal." She tugged down her shirt and turned on the seat, but winced at the ache in her thigh.

"What else?" Jason wondered.

"Nothing. How's my neck look?"

"It's bloody awful, but I think you'll live. He didn't cut too deep. Something wrong with your backside?"

She eased a palm over her thigh. "That first gunshot—I think I took a bullet to the ass."

"You're—let me take a look."

"Really, it's nothing serious. Just aches a little."

He chuffed a breath and gave her the "turn around" signal. So she did. Jason eased a hand over her thigh. "Looks like the bullet burned the suede clean off, but it didn't penetrate. What the hell?"

"High-tech fabric. Bulletproof."

"No bloody way." He slapped her behind and rubbed it soundly. "I gotta get me some of this stuff." He leaned back and switched the car into drive.

"I don't know where you can buy it. Probably can check into it for you, if you're really interested."

"Sure, sweet." He winked. "But that would mean I was talking about the trousers, instead of your bum."

Chapter 25

"What time is it?" Rachel tapped her watch. The crystal was cracked—the manacles had crushed it.

Jason pulled up a block away from his apartment. Partly for caution, the other reason, the Fuego was out of gas. The little pink machine puttered to a stop and nudged the curb with a sputtering sigh. He peered out the windshield at the clock set over the glass doors of a financial building. "Four-fifteen, Saturday afternoon."

"A flight to the States is eight hours."

"Yeah, but with the time difference, you'll still get there today."

"If de Gaulle has been reopened."

"Let's run up to the apartment and put in a phone call."

"What about these lovely bracelets?" The chains, heavy in Rachel's lap, clanked with a twist of her wrists. "No way to hide these from airport security."

"Or that cut on your pretty neck. You're going to need a—"

The thud of a palm upon the driver's-side window alerted them both. Pistol at the ready, Jason cocked the trigger. Rachel gripped the chain in both hands, ready to choke.

"I don't believe it," she whispered as the face bent and peered in. Vincent actually smiled at them.

At a tap of Jason's finger, the window rolled down. He pressed the Ruger to Vincent's forehead. "You've caught me at a particularly bad time, Rousseau."

"Got something you might need."

"I thought you were dead," Rachel said.

The Frenchman lifted his shirt, and the undershirt, to reveal a hastily bandaged wound just below well-toned abs. "Didn't hit any major organs. Those bastards dumped me in the trash bin, can you believe it?"

"I can," Jason said. "You reek."

"I landed in a pile of pizza boxes. Lots of garlic. I tried to follow Lazar, but they flattened the tires on my car. You got the ruby?"

Rachel looked to Jason's pants pocket. She hadn't asked to see the rock. That ruby had caused her enough trouble. She'd like to toss it into the Seine—good riddance—but she hadn't suffered the past forty-eight hours for nothing.

Now the final standoff remained—would Jason give the ruby to her or Vincent?

Jason jammed the pistol against Vincent's forehead. "You just wondering?"

"Maybe. You want help or not?"

"I don't need any help you can offer." Rachel opened the door and began to march toward Jason's apartment. Vincent followed with Jason, and gun, in tow. So close to escape, and yet again, the French menace managed to wend his way back into her face.

"Those chains a new fashion statement, or are you just into bondage, *salope*."

At that word, Rachel spun and dived for Vincent. Jason

caught her around the waist. Chains clanked furiously. "Just let me at him!"

Light on his feet, Vincent bounced out of reach. His cocky grin infuriated. "Let her at me, Marland. I know how to incapacitate this one."

"Asshole!"

"Salope!"

"Children? You two are worse than a couple of kids on the playground. I really should let her loose on you, Rousseau. I don't think there'd be much but shreds to pick up after. Would you chill?" he whispered to Rachel. "We're standing on a public street. See those tourists down the road? They've probably taken a lovely photograph of your little spat. Half an hour from now you'll be starring on their vacation Web site."

Jarred back to reality, Rachel relaxed in Jason's grip. "Sorry." She eyed the tourists. Dressed in matching Do the Louvre logo T-shirts and bright white tennis shoes, they were pointing at a shiny black Hummer 2.

A Hummer? Rachel blew a strand of hair from her face and tugged the cashmere sweater to her hips. What the hell was that Hummer doing back in this neighborhood?

Vincent approached, but stopped just behind Jason's wall of warning. "You don't need my help, Marie Antoinette?"

She didn't understand. Vincent drew a slash before his neck. "Don't lose your head."

Ah. Idiotic French humor.

"She's got all the help she needs," Jason said.

"So you side with her now instead of your partner in crime?"

Jason winked at her but turned a serious face to Vincent. "She's a helluva lot prettier."

"True. And a good—" Vincent pulled that sentence short. All three could guess what he'd been about to say. "Sorry. You know we Frenchmen—we like to boast of our conquests."

"Rousseau." Jason reminded he still held a gun at his friend.

Vincent beckoned down the street. A silver Peugeot waited. "Need a ride to the airport?"

"I thought you said they let out the air from your tires?"

"It's another rental."

"First—" Rachel focused across the street "—tell me what you know about a black Hummer with dark windows and thugs inside packing heat."

"What?" He swung a look behind him. Vincent's entire body tightened at the sight. The tourists began to snap pictures and point at the black-windowed monstrosity.

Rachel looked to Jason. Now he recognized the vehicle.

"What's your story?" Jason wondered with a careful shove of the pistol into Vincent's hip. "You don't think I'll blast your liver to Italy, if I have to?"

Vincent held up his hands. "She's got the ruby. I am—how do you say?—cool with that."

"Whatever." Rachel wasn't buying it. She nodded toward the Hummer. "Who are they?"

"Haven't a clue."

"Yeah?" Jason gave him that snarky I'm-pissed-and-I-don't-have-time-for-your-crap face. "Well, they look familiar to me and my aching jaw. They must know who you are 'cause they got a bead on the back of your head."

"*Merde.*" Vincent made to dodge to the right, but Rachel reached out—her left hand followed, attached as it was by a chain. A hand to his shoulder held him straight. Jason confirmed, with a nod, that the laser was still on Vincent's head.

"They got a hit on you?"

"I'll explain while we drive," Vincent offered. "You are in a hurry, no?"

"Probably as big a hurry as you are," Rachel said. Both men faced Rachel—she was the only one of the three who could see the Hummer. Jason knew better than to turn and gape. "You think they'll take him out with tourists to record the event?"

"Unlikely," Jason said. "But thugs, by nature, are just dumb, they're never too concerned with witnesses."

"Right. We could walk away?"

"Leave Rousseau to deal with his own rot?"

"I'm favoring that plan more and more."

"Do we really need to have a discussion?" Vincent hissed. "You need a ride. Let's move."

"Fine." She did need a ride, and wasn't yet prepared to release Rousseau. "But we're not going to shake that bead unless you do exactly as I say. Ready, gentlemen?"

Jason nodded.

"You're our captive," Rachel said to Vincent.

Vincent raised his hands to splay at his shoulders. Rachel eyed the Hummer. The black barrel of a gun poked out the back window. The tourists likely did not notice, for their proximity placed them yet behind the vehicle on the sidewalk. Their attention was drawn to the rear of the vehicle. What was so interesting about the ugly tank of a car?

"We'll walk slowly toward your car. Jason, stay at my side, eyes to the back of Vincent's head. Vincent, walk out in front. Keep your hands up."

They walked. Peripheral vision sighted the gun following their every move. The tourists crossed the street now. Do not approach the Hummer, Rachel silently prayed. Just walk on. There's a café down the street. Go there! She didn't want innocents involved.

Her prayers didn't take. Now the couple stood but ten feet from the vehicle, gazing over the rear bumper. The gun in the window remained.

When they arrived at the rental Peugeot, Rachel positioned herself behind the two men and the car. All the Hummer could see was the tops of their shoulders and heads. If she positioned herself just so...her center was blocked by Vincent's body.

Jason nodded. The bead was still on Vincent's head.

"Hand me your gun," she muttered and made a low gesture near her thigh. Jason slid the weapon into her left palm.

She hated guns. They were loud and dangerous. And bullets hurt like hell. But she wasn't afraid to use one. Her target skills were exceptional.

"Now, don't freak on me, Rousseau. Just hold position."

"Wha—"

Both hands gripping the gun, and chains hanging heavily, she aimed at Vincent's forehead.

The Frenchman made a little noise in his throat.

"Higher or lower?" she asked Jason.

"I'd say—" he leaned back, perusing the back of Vincent's head "—about eyebrow level."

"Merde," Vincent mumbled. But for his nervousness he held straight, not a flinch.

"You said you wanted to watch, Marland?"

"Yeah, but I wanted to watch…"

"Well watch this. If all goes correctly, this may give me some damn good pleasure. When I say 'go,' Vincent, you drop straight down. Climb into the front seat and fire up the ignition. Jason, drop and get in the back, close the door and roll the window down all the way. Yes?"

"Just give the word, sweet."

Sweat purled down Vincent's nose. He nodded minutely.

Sighting in her aim on Vincent's forehead, she lined up where she imagined the laser beam was to the back of his head. They could not be aware she held a gun, for Vincent's head blocked the view. It was as close as she could get without a better view. One chance—a quick one—was all she was going to get.

The tourists had moved closer. The woman ran a hand along the back bumper. This was not going to be pretty.

Heartbeats thundering, Rachel drew in a breath and exhaled apprehension.

"Ready, steady…go!"

Vincent dropped. The laser beam flashed in Rachel's vision. She squeezed the trigger.

Jason slid into the back seat and slammed the door.

Target hit. The gun flew out of the space in the back window.

Tourists shrieked and scattered. Good.

Another thug appeared from the opposite side of the Hummer.

Entirely expected. Rachel shot another round. She hit the shooter's hand. The gun went flying across the hood.

The Peugeot revved. The Hummer began to roll, turning toward them.

Rachel dived in through the open back window. She landed in Jason's lap headfirst and twisted her body to draw in her legs from the window. Lunging out the open window, she stepped up to sit on the door frame.

"Hold my legs," she directed Jason.

Vincent's driving swerved them around a corner, but she held a steady aim. One shot took out the front left tire. The Hummer did not even swerve.

The next shot shattered the windshield.

The driver's window rolled down. Rachel dodged a bullet that soared yards from her head. She took aim for the driver's head and squeezed the trigger. The Hummer spun and crashed into a concrete retaining wall.

"You're good," Jason said as Rachel slid back down inside the car.

All business, she tossed him the gun and nodded toward Vincent. "Keep it on his back the whole drive to the airport."

"Fine," Vincent snapped. "But you'll have to set the gun down to pick those manacles. I don't think she'll get through security with those on. Hell, that Marie Antoinette look will never do."

Jason looked to Rachel, gun at the ready. It was her call.

She was in no position to command much more from either of these men, manacled as she was. A quick hand to the back of her pants confirmed the passport was still there, hadn't slipped out.

But she did trust Jason. Sitting next to him, she actually felt relief knowing that he held the upper hand against the threat. Like he was protecting her, and that was just fine. She didn't need to protect herself. She could just draw in a breath and…relax.

For about two seconds.

"Let's go. I've got a plane to catch."

Chapter 26

Saturday—5:05 p.m.

According to the newscaster on the radio, the Charles de Gaulle had reopened two hours earlier.

Vincent navigated the late-afternoon traffic on the périphérique with minimal swearing. Rachel had become accustomed to his caustic mouth. Perhaps in his world *salope* was a term of affection, but never in hers.

Jason worked on the manacles. They were rusted and dirty. The hairs on her wrists had been ripped out. He hadn't the proper tools, so the makeshift pick, fashioned from the temple piece off a pair of Vincent's sunglasses, proved a challenge.

Rachel sat, her head against the back seat, staring out of the open roof at the blue sky racing overhead. Her legs, she had strewn casually across Jason's lap. Not really thinking, just exhausted, was all. And so in need of contact, a grounding touch, for right now she felt thirty thousand feet high with a dizzy head.

The events in the warehouse replayed. He had been but a hair from kissing her. Christian had been willing to surrender his power over her just to have her back at his side. At his side and one step back. Never equals.

Rachel had no intention of standing one step behind a man. Ever again. She didn't want to crave a kiss so badly she would commit crimes for the promise of catching that morsel. Because kisses didn't mean love, they were tricky and easily used to manipulate.

A glance to Jason focused on the crown of his shaved head. Intent in his work. He was not tricky. But manipulative? It was a thief's very nature.

But what was love?

Not Christian Lazar. At least not the embodiment of Christian Lazar. He was no longer inside her. The final tracker had been cut from her body.

But still he lived. And Rachel sensed that for every breath she took, somewhere out there, Christian would seek it. *You should have killed him.*

She had no right to take another life. Murder had no justification. Even if Christian had been the one responsible for the cruise ship going down at sea—taking the lives of her parents—Rachel still could not dredge up a single reason to want him dead. She just wanted him…away.

Could that ever become reality?

She'd thought starting a new life in the States would put enough distance between them. But it was apparent now Christian had been tracking her. He could know the exact location of her loft. America was no longer safe. Nor was France.

How far did she have to run to escape?

Jason lifted his head and smiled at her. Rachel realized she was still gazing at him. She smiled and he went back to work.

Did he really care for her? Who was she to be thinking such silly thoughts?

The girl is having fun. Everything you've been denied, you're going to want it, big-time. I'm crushing on you.

That was it—just a crush. A silly infatuation. Nothing more.

It had to be, because within the hour Rachel would board a plane to New York and never look back. Vincent had called ahead; a flight to New York departed at 6:03. Paris promised too much danger, too many memories both ugly and bittersweet.

"One down."

The heavy pressure of the manacle gave way from Rachel's left wrist. The sores from the handcuffs had been reopened and she moved to ease her fingers over it. Jason's kiss beat her to it. He looked up to her from where he'd pressed the tiny morsel. Rachel had to bite her lip to prevent a tear from rolling down her cheek.

"You'll heal."

"I always do."

"Save it for later, lovebirds," Vincent called from the front. "We'll be at de Gaulle in fifteen minutes. It took you that long for one."

"I'm experienced now," Jason said, and started on the other. "These rusty old manacles are no match to my master fingers. Five minutes, tops."

"We'll need the extra time for whatever Vincent's got cooking," Rachel said. "Plan to stop five minutes from the airport? A ride for the ruby?"

"It is yours," Vincent insisted.

"I thought it was yours? A family heirloom?"

"It is. But..." A twirl of his fingers near his head and a shrug. "You need it more desperately right now."

"Why the sudden change of heart?"

"You're a friend of Marland's? You're a friend of mine. Besides, I keep tabs on the thing. I'll give it a year or two, then take it back. Again."

"Seems like a whole lot of trouble for a woman who twisted your balls," Jason muttered.

"Increases the challenge. And she did just save my neck," Vincent offered. A wide grin filled the rearview mirror. "Besides, I've got something more interesting and valuable."

Rachel's instincts switched to alert. In the next moment she closed her eyes and let loose a long exhale. "You've got the book."

"Maybe I do, maybe I don't."

Of course he did, else he wouldn't have a clue what she referred to merely as "the book."

"That's why those men in the Hummer were after you?"

"Not saying."

"Keep it," she offered.

"What?"

Without seeking his expression in the rearview mirror, Rachel knew she had shocked the irrepressible Frenchman. For once she had gotten the upper hand on Vincent Rousseau. A small victory, but she'd take it.

"I don't want to see it. The names mean nothing to me. It's just a list of all the people I most want to avoid for the rest of my life." A tug of her wrist reminded her that Jason's name was in the book. "Ninety-nine percent of them," she corrected.

"And the other one percent?" Jason asked.

"Thieves and criminals we may be, but we can't all be bad, can we?"

"Which terminal?" Rachel asked as they exited onto the airport roads.

"Two-F," Vincent verified.

They pulled up across the street from the long-term-parking ramp at Charles de Gaulle. Vincent—wearing but his undershirt, after, at gunpoint, he'd been enticed to loan Rachel his blue silk shirt—pulled on a pair of silver Gargoyles sunglasses that sat at an angle on his face for the missing temple band. He walked around to the passenger side to join Jason and Rachel.

Rachel stood back from the two of them, backpack slung over her shoulder. She shoved her hands in her back pockets, thankful that Vincent's button-up shirt, though torn at the shoulder, was long enough to cover her bruised wrists. The collar actually covered the cut on her throat. It had stopped bleeding, but if she jerked suddenly it might reopen. She felt sure there were various small cuts and bruises on her face, but couldn't care right now. If she moved quickly, there would be time to stop in the airport bathroom for a concealing touch-up.

Jason looked the worst. His left eye was completely closed and his lower lip swollen. It must have hurt when she'd planted that kiss on him at the warehouse. Maybe the pain would cement the memory. Yes, she hoped it would. She would never forget Jason; the least he could do was pocket her into a little corner of his memory.

Vincent was the first to speak. "Can I see it before you leave?"

Thinking he'd finally revealed himself—now he would take the ruby from her—Rachel balked. But she didn't have it.

Vincent slid his sunglasses onto the top of his head. The sunlight served him well, flashing in his green eyes like a speck of sugar. For all he had suffered, his face hadn't taken a hit. A glance to his stomach showed the bulge of a makeshift bandage beneath the undershirt. A spot of blood stained the hem.

"You need to get that stitched up," she offered.

He dismissed her concern with a shrug. "Says Marie Antoinette. The ruby. Just a peek?"

"Let him hold it," she said to Jason, and turned her back on the exchange. If they wanted to jump her, knock her out and leave, do it now, while she wasn't looking.

She guessed the thief weighed the rock's volume in his palm, wrapping his fingers around the walnut-size girth. Probably he'd want to hold it up to the sun to catch the light—but no, he wouldn't. They stood in a public forum, packed with tourists, and likely, police. The buzz of passing cars and the occasional horn reminded her of the impossibility to act covert.

"Nice." Vincent's voice.

Nice. Some things in life were just too rich to be merely nice.

Rachel almost thought the whole experience of getting to know Jason just a little better would be worth them duping her and driving off with the ruby, leaving her to succumb to Christian's reign once again. But she knew better. The little girl had taken back her soul when she'd strode out of the warehouse. Behind, she had left her chink, never again to challenge her.

"Here."

At a nudge to her arm, Rachel turned and saw Vincent held the rock in his palm.

"*Merde!* Don't stare at it all day," he complained in a sharp hiss. "We're handling a stolen jewel in the middle of a crowded parking lot."

"You are the king of suave."

She took the jewel but froze when Vincent gripped her by the shoulders and pressed a kiss to either of her cheeks. A Frenchman's farewell. It was the kiss to her lips, quick, but enough to mean something, that brought her up from her dumb gape.

I won't forget, his dancing green eyes singsonged. And neither will you. *"Au revoir,"* he said.

Until they again meet?

He's one of the network.

They would meet again, if Rachel had anything to say about it. Because the whole idea of a network of innocent women, trained to their masters' bidding, did not sit well with her. If any were like her, they may just need a chance to walk away, to know it could be done.

"Thanks." She shoved the ruby into her pocket and watched Vincent walk around to slide behind the wheel. The engine revved. He would wait for Jason.

They'd already decided Rachel would enter the airport herself. Neither of them were too keen on advertising their bruised and battered visages to the Paris police. Alone, Rachel wouldn't draw half so much attention as the threesome.

She looked to Jason's swollen and purpled face. His attempts to smile resulted in a wince and a sheepish shrug. So this was goodbye? She'd never had a goodbye before. It was going to hurt more than a fist to her jaw. And it would probably never heal.

"So, do I get a hug?" he asked.

She shrugged. More contact would only make leaving harder. And she might cry. She didn't want to cry.

Feeling her entire body slip from the militant stance she'd been holding, and change into something loose and not entirely at her control, Rachel offered a wobbly shrug. "Maybe I should just get going."

"Yeah," he said. He shoved his hands in his pants pockets. "I suppose."

"Thanks for everything, Marland," she offered. One foot toed a crack in the pavement. Inside, her heartbeats raced. "I couldn't have done this without you."

"You could have. But every hero needs her sidekick, eh?"

"I certainly hope you are not implying that I am heroic."

"If the shoe fits."

"Please, I just did what I had to to save my own ass."

"A nice ass—"

"An ass which may yet see a jail cell if I can't place the ruby back in the Lalique without an entire army of policemen waiting to take me down."

"Well, I'm no bloody fool to toot the horn of honor, but I think heroism could be learning to be true to yourself, Rachel. You know what you'll stand for, what you won't abide. You wouldn't have stepped back to Lazar's side."

Raising her chin to meet his wondering gaze, she locked onto his gold eyes.

"Not even for a kiss?" he wondered.

The kiss that almost was. Her goodbye kiss to Christian Lazar.

"No, I wouldn't have." A heavy sigh was erased with a smirk. Keep it light, she coached. Calm, stay calm. Just walk away, and forget it all. Leave the crushing teenager here in Paris where she belongs.

"I'd better run. I don't want to miss the flight."

"You'll call me?"

She turned and studied the asphalt. Easy excuse, coming right up! "I don't have a phone."

"I can fix that." Jason opened the passenger door, said something to Vincent, then reappeared with a cell phone.

"That is mine!" Vincent shouted. "First my shirt and now—"

Jason slammed the car door.

He pressed the cool silver phone into Rachel's palm. "Now you do. You can ring me with speed dial number two. I'll wait for your call."

She nodded, clasping the phone to her breast. He'd wait. Those two words put a smile to her face. He wanted to hear from her.

Michele Hauf

"Thanks."

Giving a tug to the silk shirt, she began to walk away. Rachel could feel Jason's eyes follow her as she stepped toward the curb to cross to the airport check-in. Feeling as if a part of her were being stripped from her body to expose the raw nerves. *All I ever wanted was a kiss.*

Jason had given her kisses freely. Because he'd wanted to kiss her. Not to sway her or trick her or even to buy her alliance.

Should she stay?

Silly thought. It wasn't as though he had invited her. With Christian yet alive, France proved too dangerous. Even if she did stay, Jason had not made any promises. She didn't expect promises. Promises were not tangible currency.

She needed something she could touch and hold. Like a kiss.

Her future demanded she board the plane. Black and white. No options.

The gray was thick with subtleties and options. A lot to sort through. But…worth it?

Rachel stopped. The entrance to the de Gaulle buzzed with the hum of life. Men, women and children, intent on their destinations. Some arriving to experience a foreign land, others leaving for home. Some starting a new life, others perhaps fleeing an old memory.

Some memories were too rich to discard.

Rachel turned and stared back at Jason. Despite his battered condition, he stood tall. Handsome? Yes, in so many little ways a simple look could never discern. When he talked fast she couldn't understand him. His smiles were rare, and crooked. He hummed Elvis when around her. And he'd developed a penchant for ducks.

Sweet.

I could have a guy like him in my life, she thought. Is this how love feels? Kinda achy, certainly perfect, and a little bit…woozy.

She smiled.

As if he'd caught her mind message, Jason nodded. He kissed his fingertips and blew the morsel her way.

Walk away, Rachel. It's the easy choice.

Choose white, avoid the gray.

Since when have you ever taken the easy route?

Her footsteps increased to a run. Behind her the de Gaulle facade glinted in the evening sunlight like a jewel to entice a five-fingered free-for-all. Rachel plunged into Jason's body. Wrapping her arms about his shoulders, she kissed him. A good long I-think-I-might-be-crushing-on-you kiss. It didn't promise anything.

It didn't have to.

"I will call you," she said. "We've got lots to talk about."

"I agree. You'd better run, sweet."

"No more running. Not ever again. I'll miss you, Jason."

"Don't worry 'bout us blokes. We'll be ducky." He bussed her cheek with a gentle fist. "Don't lose that phone."

"I won't." Unwilling to withdraw from their embrace, Rachel slid her hand back and shoved the slim phone into her pants pocket. "It's more valuable than a flawless Burmese ruby."

Rachel turned and began to walk, this time with purpose. The phone weighed heavily in her pocket. It felt good. Jason was close, and would remain so, even when she touched down in the States.

First stop, the bathroom to make herself more presentable to airport security. Second stop, the States—but not for long.

Jason slid into the passenger side of the rental car. He and Vincent silently watched Rachel cross the meridian to the airport sidewalk.

"You just going to let her walk out of your life?"

Jason swung a crazed look at Vincent.

The thief shrugged.

"She said she'd call," Jason offered. He tapped his fingers on the door frame. Rachel's sleek form insinuated herself with ease between the crowd of tourists. She moved her head, taking in all but covertly covering half her face with her hair to conceal the bruises. Tough bit of luck she had bruises to contend with. There were drug shops in the airport; she could find some makeup to pretty herself up.

She would call. Hell, that kiss hadn't been for nothing. And he could wait.

Maybe.

"Why aren't you driving, Rousseau?"

The shift jerked into gear. "Thought I'd be driving home solo."

"Yeah?" Jason looked from Vincent's innocent stare back to the airport doors.

She was gone. No sign of those long legs clad in brown suede, or the swing of smooth dark hair. A trick of the trade. One minute you're there, the next gone.

Gone.

"So, let's ride?" Vincent prompted.

"Uhhh…"

Chapter 27

Saturday—8:00 p.m.—United States

"The Paris police did not locate her." Posada was surprised to get a call from the buyer and not Finley. He'd initially thought it better to deal directly with the buyer anyway, but now that everything was screwed up, this conversation was making him sweat. "Nor has my man been able to flush her out."

"What did he say?"

"I haven't heard from him. I haven't called to report the break-in yet."

"Be patient. She'll show up."

"Yeah, but will it be here? And with the ruby? I can't risk that. I need that insurance money. I have to call the police, if I wait any longer it'll look suspicious—"

"Hold your horses. I'll make a few phone calls. Actually, I'll make one call. I'll get her."

"And then what? Ms. Anderson will go to jail for robbery and I'll get the damn jewel back. I don't want it."

"Neither do I."

"What? But you—"

"Calm down. You'll get your insurance money, and I'll ensure the ruby is lost. Give me half a day."

"Very well. But no more than six hours. Then, I'm calling the police."

Posada clicked off.

On the other end of the line, Christian Lazar hung up the phone. "Idiot."

Sunday—12:00 a.m.

This combination dial moved jerkily. The average consumer would never notice the slight tug with each twist. Rachel did. It was stiff. But workable.

The third number gave up its secret and Rachel pulled open the safe door. Leaning forward, her body balancing precariously on the granite desktop, she studied the interior contents.

A small tray of stones—diamonds, rubies and emeralds—a mixed bag. Surprising to find jewels in this safe. There were a lot of authenticity documents, folded neatly and filed by inventory number. A small .22-millimeter pistol, loaded and ready for action. None of it interested her.

This was just a courtesy visit. One reserved for all clients who tried to fuck with her.

Sunday—2:00 a.m.

Rachel flicked off the hot water and trailed her fingertips through the bubbles in the tub.

She was in the clear. Nothing left to do but reap the reward. Oh, who was she kidding? There would be no reward. Unless she considered relocation to a foreign country a positive. To maintain operations in the States now would only raise suspicion. Time for a new location and a new name.

Padding out to the bed, she shed her shirt and unzipped her pants. They landed on the heap of blue silk still piled at the corner of the sisal rug.

So ready to dive into bliss but wanting to get everything ready for tomorrow, Rachel tossed her trusty backpack on the bed, and then sorted through the few pieces of clothing she had hanging outside the bathroom wall. Just the essentials. A few pairs of pants and shirts and maybe…a dress.

She wasn't sure of her destination, only that she could not remain in the States. There wasn't any particular country that called out to be visited. France was off limits until she had heard that Christian was either gone or…gone. Jason would find out.

Tossing some black jersey pants and a loose pair of blue jeans into a canvas duffel, Rachel topped that with a white T-shirt and a gray jersey dress. Jersey was key to a quick move; it didn't wrinkle and never lost its shape.

Ha! Rachel caught herself. Fabric queen? Maybe a bit of domesticity had begun to seep in.

Underthings she could find wherever she chose to roam. Toothpaste and a few cosmetics she'd pack after her bath. And the cell phone.

Leaning across the bed to study the pile of hardcover books stacked on the floor, she wondered which would make good airplane reading. Her nervous stomach hadn't dared rear its ugly head during the return flight. So much to think about. Maybe she'd gotten over her flight anxiety? Reaching for a copy of an erotic novel, she tensed at a familiar sound.

The tap of cold steel against her cheek alerted her—too late—to danger.

Rising slowly to stand straight, Rachel dropped the novel on the bed.

Michele Hauf

"Leaving again? But you just returned."

Oscar?

Blood draining from her extremities in a cold rush, Rachel slowly turned. Naked, she couldn't begin to worry about her lack of clothes. The tip of the semiautomatic, lengthened with a bulky silencer, stayed at her cheek.

"Nice tits." Bed-tousled hair spiked at odd angles around his face, Oscar readjusted the sucker stick in his mouth to the opposite side. Cherry. Rachel's new least favorite flavor. "But I've seen them once. They're nothing new."

Thoughts ran the gamut. First being: What the fuck? Second: Someone had played her well.

Who was Oscar allied with? Had he known about her the entire eight months she'd been living here? She had trusted him. Had considered him her only friend. An innocent. What was his play in this game?

"Oscar," she managed to say. Keep calm. She wasn't about to defend with the silencer pressing a dent in her cheek. "Interesting way to welcome me home."

"Couldn't be avoided. I know what you're about, Rachel Blu Anderson."

So he worked for Christian. Lazar was the only living soul who knew her middle name. Yet, he'd never known her last name, which explained why Oscar assumed it was Anderson.

"So, what are you?" she asked. Not really caring, but—yes. She had been duped by this man with such ease. A writer? "One of Christian's lapdogs?"

"I'm a freelancer. Assassin."

A gulp stalled in her throat. Assassin? Christian now wanted her dead?

"What do you want?"

"I just want this babysitting assignment over and done with. You got the ruby?"

"Babysitting? How long have you— You were here before I moved in."

"You think so?"

"I—" Well, was he? He'd introduced himself to her that first evening she'd moved in. She hadn't noticed him moving furniture into his own place after that. It might have been about a month before he'd invited her over to his place. "You don't like dachshunds, do you?"

"They were left behind by the former resident. Ugly little bastards. No reason to change the decor though, I hadn't planned for such a long stay."

"So you're not really a writer?"

"Oh sure. Isn't everyone? I work on my great American novel during the day, and at night, well…you know what it's like living a double life."

"No, I don't. What you see is what you get, Oscar. I thought I'd been living the hard way all along."

"No one ever goes clean, Rachel."

"I guess not." Clean was a relative term. Like kiss, and…chink. "So, did Christian put a hit on me?"

"First things first, you have the ruby?"

She shook her head. Long gone.

Oscar waved the gun in the air. "Your flight just arrived a few hours ago. You can't tell me you fenced it so quickly. I know you don't have connections in this city."

That everyone in her life seemed to know her every move bothered her more and more. Hell, she was pissed. An assassin babysitting her until Christian called the final shot? That she had so easily been tricked by this man. Had trusted him. Someone was going down for this one. And it wasn't going to be her.

She was so over taking crap from Christian Lazar.

As the gun swung toward her face, Rachel deflected it with a wrist and kicked high. The semiautomatic flew into the air. Oscar ducked into a defensive position and barreled a shoulder into her ribs. They landed on the bed, his thumbs pressed to her throat.

"This is my job, Rachel, don't take it personally." A jab of his knee to her gut forced breath from her lungs.

Groping to the side, she touched the canvas duffel. Not heavy. She'd use what she could before he choked the life from her. Raking the open zipper across Oscar's face, she managed to induce enough pain that he released her.

Slamming a foot into his chest sent him flying. Oscar landed on the hardwood floor but bounced right up.

Rachel dashed for the bathroom. Oscar loped on her heels. Good. He hadn't gone for the gun.

Feet slipping on the steam-moistened tiles, Rachel crashed into the vanity. Fists raised, she pounded them into the medicine cabinet. The mirror cracked but didn't shatter. Oscar grabbed her about the waist and flung her to the side.

She landed in the hot water in the tub and slipped under the froth of bubbles. Fingers wrapped about her ankle and tried to pull her out. Swallowing a mouthful of soapy water, Rachel emerged, spewing a hot stream directly into Oscar's face. He released her. The slick porcelain tub made escape difficult.

"If you kill me, you'll never find the ruby," she warned. Twisting to her knees, she rose from the water and grabbed the plastic toilet seat. "Christian will not be pleased if he doesn't have something to show for my death."

"You think very highly of yourself." Oscar stepped one foot into the tub and slipped. His body fell on top of her back. Rachel conked her jaw on the toilet seat.

A shard of the mirror slid from the cabinet and landed on the floor, shattering into long silvered pieces.

Struggling against the elusive slide of wet over tile and porcelain and the groping jabs and kicks from Oscar, Rachel managed to slip from his grasp and land on the floor like a mermaid on a rock. Oscar leaped from the tub like some kind of amphibious creature.

Rachel twisted her body, hoping to avoid the impact, but the vanity cupboard prevented her from moving out of position. Stretching out an arm, she took the weight of Oscar's body landing against hers with a grunt. Again her jaw clacked on a hard surface. She bit her tongue. Blood trickled down her throat.

"Some assassin you are." Gripping a silvered shard, she lunged her arm backward and connected the sharp piece of mirror with flesh.

Oscar immediately let go of her. Rachel scrambled for another piece of mirror. Her fingers drooled her own blood. Turning on her thighs, she slashed at Oscar's lunging face. Blood spurt over her eyes and mouth. She'd sliced him high on the throat. Not a life-threatening cut, but enough to buy her time.

He collapsed on his side, rolling to his back. A squeak landed the yellow rubber duck on Oscar's chest. Rachel pulled back her arm, ready to slash at the surprise attack, but then she smiled.

"Just ducky, I see."

Scooping up another piece of mirror, she then staggered out to the loft. The gun lay in the beam of a streetlight from outside her window. She ran for it and kicked it. It skidded behind the stack of books.

Panting, she looked about her empty loft. Laced with cuts, her fingers stung. Soap bubbles streamed down her arm. The heavy sliding door was open just enough to allow a man to sneak inside.

"I'm sick of this game," she muttered.

Behind her, Oscar slapped both hands to either side of the bathroom door frame. He stood. Blood ran down his neck and trailed to his waist.

"Whatever he's paying you—" Rachel called.

"You'll double it?"

"Hell no! It isn't worth your trouble, is all. You want to take me down?" Shard of mirror held like a dagger, she snapped back her shoulders. "Come and get me."

When he reached around behind his back, Rachel guessed the gun had not been his only weapon. The glint of steel swept before his face as Oscar did some ridiculous twirly move with the short blade he'd pulled from the back of his pants.

Theatrics didn't play in her book. Might and attitude were all she needed.

Lifting a defiant jaw, she waited as he made a few more fancy moves. Then he approached. If she could keep him moving for a while, the blood loss would eventually wear him down, maybe bring on a faint. She just needed him out. There was electrical tape under the bathroom sink.

"So, you do this often?" she asked. Dodging a swipe of blade, she spun on one foot and turned her side to him to reduce his target. "Babysit your targets?"

"Lazar wanted me to keep tabs on you. I knew every time you returned after midnight that you'd been on a job."

"And you reported them all to Christian?"

"Of course."

A sweep of the blade cut a wind across her belly, but no blood. Rachel spun once and landed a soggy fist to Oscar's shoulder. She dragged the mirror down his arm, opening it in a crimson gash. He let out a moan.

"So Christian was just content to wait for my return to Paris? Why didn't he have you take me out right away?"

"Don't know. Don't care. So long as the cash kept coming."

"He made payments? How much is my life worth?" She avoided a lunge with a deft dodge to the left. Oscar ran straight into the brick wall.

Before he could turn, Rachel gripped Oscar's head and smashed it into the wall. "How much?" She shoved. The brick cut into his cheek.

"A million."

"Really?" She let go. Quite a large sum for a hit. Christian put a lot more value in her than...

...she did?

The glint of a mirror shard flashed in her peripheral view. Oscar yelped. Blood spurt from his hand and splattered Rachel's face.

He'd been...shot?

Another click of the trigger—now she heard it behind her—drilled a perfect red hole through Oscar's skull.

Rachel stepped back, releasing Oscar to fall in a heap. She spun to find Jason Marland standing twenty paces behind her, his trusty Beretta held sure.

"A million for your hide?" He cocked the gun and tossed it to the end of her bed.

"I guess." Stunned to see Jason standing in her home, Rachel couldn't even bother with the dead man on the floor. Staggering, she stepped forward, then remembered her lack of clothing. Clapping her arms across her breasts, she said, "You...followed me?"

"And look how I'm rewarded. Naked death match." He chuckled and gave a shrug as he splayed out his hands. "I guess I'm a bit like one of those puppy dogs that follows you about, eh?"

"A puppy with smart aim."

"Yeah, well, I had a strange feeling things might go a bit pear-shaped for you."

Walking backward, she stepped into the bathroom and snagged a towel from the rack by the door. He was here! But in the nick of time? "I didn't need your help, Marland."

"'Course not. You could have taken him out."

"Damn right. But...I appreciate the intervention." Towel hanging before her soaking limbs, she scanned the damage. Water flooding out from the bathroom. Guns strewn here and there. Dead assassin on the floor to her right. "This has been a wild couple of days."

"About to get even wilder if we linger around the body. Don't your American police have a thing about bodies?"

"They do. We both need to put this country far behind us."

"I'm one step ahead of you." Jason took out a phone from his back pocket and flipped it open. "Gather whatever you need."

"But...Oscar?"

"Taking care of it, sweet. I've got a few connections in the States. Franko? Good to hear your voice, you wanker. Got a situation. Need a cleaner. Within the hour."

So he had it covered. Back to business. Stepping around Oscar's body, Rachel tugged a shirt from the closet. Eyeing her bullet-burned suede slacks, instead she dug out a thin pair of black nylon pants from a drawer. Stuffing clothes and passport and toothbrush back into her duffel, Rachel smiled as Jason took control. It was cool. She didn't need the upper hand now.

"The whole place can be flamed—" Jason paused and looked to her. Yes? he mouthed.

She nodded.

"Yes, take the whole warehouse out, if you feel so inclined. Thanks, Franko. I'll leave a little something for you in the usual location. All right, all right, a *lot* of something."

That the man knew someone who cleaned up murder scenes didn't surprise, it only relieved. One less mess for her to deal with. Rachel stared at Oscar, blood trickling from the hole in his head. It's not something she could have done— she still thought of him as a friend, damn it!—unless it had been a life-or-death situation. Which, it might have become.

Hell, all confrontations were life or death. She was usually cocky enough to believe she always had the upper hand. Maybe not today. The machine no longer existed. Sure, she walked, talked and acted like the machine Christian had created. But, inside, Rachel didn't feel the same. Inside, things had…evolved.

Striding back into the bathroom she looked over the floor littered with mirror shards and covered in water. Reward would have to wait. Leaning over the tub, she splashed water onto her face and ran it over her arms to wash away Oscar's blood. Quickly, she dressed. The duck squeaked as she stepped backward. "My lucky charm."

She plucked it up. Jason waited silently, sitting on one of the kitchen stools.

"Here!" She tossed the duck to him.

"Your mascot?"

"Maybe. Let's get out of here."

"Right behind you."

She retrieved her backpack, and with one glance to Oscar's inert figure, walked away from the loft—Jason in tow—leaving the door open.

"On to the airport?" Jason queried.

"We'll take separate cabs," she explained as they clanked down the metal stairs. "There's something I need to do. Some final ends to tie. I'll meet you in three hours?"

They landed the sidewalk and Jason slid his hand into hers. "Sounds fine with me, sweet. I'll pick up the tickets. Any preference to destination?"

She lifted their clasped hands and pressed the back of Jason's hand to her lips. The warmth of him, his presence, his being, felt ridiculously luxurious. But a definite improvement to her black-and-white life.

"Surprise me," she said.

Chapter 28

Sunday—9:10 a.m.

Rachel entered the Lalique museum and surveyed the elegant foyer styled in dark walnut paneling and crystal chandeliers. A couple reading through the promotional flyer near the doorway glanced her way, and then moved onward toward the sculpture room.

The receptionist, seated behind a massive granite desk, gave her more attention. Her eyes wide, she tapped her headset, muttering rapidly and in hushed tones. As Rachel's heels clicked across the marble floor, the receptionist made eye contact.

"Ms. Anderson?"

"Mr. Posada—"

"Is waiting for you."

"I thought so. I'll see myself in."

"Wait!"

Rachel strode down the hallway toward the office suites, aware of the receptionist's frantic attempts to get her to remain in the foyer. As well, she babbled into the headset. Calling the police right now?

Rachel counted on it.

Posada's office was not locked. Rachel walked right in and sat in the thick leather chair before his desk.

The tanned and coiffed curator choked on nothing more than his own breath. "Ms. Anderson, I am…stunned."

"I believe the term is gobsmacked."

He shot her the most incredulous look.

"Forgive me." She turned as the hairs on the back of her neck prickled. There in the doorway stood two armed policemen in full regalia: badges, guns, belts, hats, you name it. That was quick. Maybe they were security guards.

Calmly, almost too slowly, she turned back to face Posada. "I'm terribly sorry, I wasn't able to do the security check this weekend, as we had agreed. Life…interrupted."

"What are you talking about, Ms. Anderson?" The man's voice held a flame. Tension tightened his tanned flesh so that the white age lines at the corners of his eyes disappeared. "There has been a robbery!"

She glanced over her shoulder, but didn't make eye contact with the officers. "Oh?"

"Oh? You confessed to it in the e-mail!"

"E-mail?" She pressed her fingers to her chest. The soft red silk shirt was almost too thin in this air-conditioned office. To her left sat Posada's computer; the password had been an easy crack—Lalique. "Are you accusing me of something, Mr. Posada?"

"Ma'am?"

She shrugged, acknowledging the policeman's query. "I don't know what he is talking about. I don't even use e-mail."

"Liar!" Posada fisted the granite desk. "Cuff her!"

"How dare you!" Careful with her movements, Rachel stood and eyed the policemen. "He's making false accusations. I can't begin to guess why. Makes me suspect he hired me for...ulterior reasons."

The officers looked to Posada.

The curator twisted his face into a miserable crunch and gestured madly with his hands. "A ruby valued at two million dollars is missing from my office safe. And this woman, who was hired to check security, is the only one who has had access to my office. As well, she sent me an e-mail saying she had the ruby in hand."

"Was a report filed?" one of the officers said.

Rachel could feel them close in on her. But neither touched her, nor had she heard the snap of cuffs removed from a hip belt.

"Report? I, er…" Posada rubbed the back of his hand across his forehead. "I just noticed it was missing right before she arrived. I was going to call."

So these men were officers on duty, not called in to investigate. Which meant Posada hadn't had a chance to show any evidence, such as the e-mail. Not that it even existed…

"She sent an e-mail, and yet," one of the men queried, "you just noticed the jewel missing?"

"Where is the ruby?" Rachel prompted.

"What? You should know! You stole it!"

"Mr. Posada," an officer said. "Can you show me the e-mail?"

"Certainly, I kept a copy on my desktop." He tapped at the keyboard to his right. Tap, tap. A long moment passed as Posada stared at his screen. Then his stern mouth sagged. "I don't understand, there's not a single e-mail in my save file—"

"We did have another power outage early this morning," Rachel offered. "I've heard an electricity surge will zap computer files."

"She did it!" Posada accused with a thrust of his finger.

Rachel stood.

The officer stepped forward to parallel her, and addressed Mr. Posada. "Show me where the ruby was kept. Ma'am, please don't move."

"I wouldn't think of it. I want to see this. It should be good."

"Very well." Posada snapped his jaw shut and turned to remove the fake Picasso from the wall behind his desk. He spun the combination dial.

Rachel didn't watch. Instead, she kept an eye on the officer nearest her. He rubbed a thumb over the handle of his pistol. A smile wasn't appropriate, but she did manage a sheepish shrug. And she kept a keen ear peeled for—there it was—Posada's gasp.

"I don't understand." The curator's arms dropped at his sides.

"Is that the ruby?" one of the officers prompted.

"Er…yes."

Rachel leaned forward, propping her palms on the cool desktop. A tilt of her head spied the glinting red gem inside the small wall safe, nestled atop a stack of folded authenticity documents. Exactly where it should be.

"Why would you accuse this woman of theft, if the ruby is in your safe, Mr. Posada? If this is some kind of lovers' squabble—"

"He hired me to check security," Rachel offered slowly, and in a manner that would lead them to think she was just figuring things out. "Maybe…he had some weird insurance scam planned? Accuse me of theft, and then collect the insurance?" She pinned Posada with a solid stare. "Didn't exactly work, did it?"

"I…" Posada sank into his chair.

A flip of her hair over her shoulder and a part of her lips did not go unnoticed. "May I leave, officers? I'm on a schedule."

"We'll need to take a statement, ma'am."

"Oh. I've a flight…"

"It won't take long."

"Fine." She delivered a beaming smile to Sidney Posada, then followed one of the officers out of the room.

Europe—undisclosed location, Monday

Rachel pressed number two on the speed-dial menu.

After five rings a gruff male voice answered in a yawning sigh. "Sweet?"

"So," she drawled, feeling as lazy as he sounded, "what are you up to?"

"Hmm, I'd say sea level, at least."

Smiling to hear the Brit's voice, Rachel smoothed a hand along her naked belly. Sunlight beamed in through an open window across her legs and feet. "Is that a bird I hear?"

"Looks like some kind of eagle. It's got a hooked beak."

The squeak of a rubber duck chirped over the phone line. Jason chuckled and the low-battery beep sounded on Rachel's phone.

"You've only got a minute," he said. "Talk fast, sweet."

"Well, I've nothing to say, really. Just wanted to return that phone call you said you'd be waiting for. I suppose you've a right to know, I've…relocated."

"You don't say?"

Jason appeared in the doorway to the cabin and leaned against the fieldstone wall. He studied the bright yellow face of the rubber duck with intense interest. "Where to?"

Rachel sat up on the bed and tossed her hair over her shoulder. She leaned forward and caught a palm on the granny-square counterpane that dripped from the mattress to a pool on the stone floor. "What do you think of Wales?"

Jason glanced outside. "I hear it's dreary and dull, a nasty piece of rock and brambles."

"It is whatever you make it."

"Did you just say you want to make it?"

She nodded and closed the phone. Before Rachel could toss it, Jason took it from her hand and set both phones on the uneven stone floor. He stripped from his jeans in record time and climbed onto the bed beside her, fitting his body against hers the way he had all night.

He kissed her breast and nuzzled up along her throat, drawing his tongue along the fading cut. "So what's next for us, sweet? Can there be an us?"

"I think so."

"You think?"

"I want an us."

"So do I."

"But I've never done a normal us."

"I know. What's so keen about normal anyway?"

She sighed. "I don't want to keep you from…your profession."

"What if I say I like the idea of keeping it legit?"

"It's not easy to live the hard way."

"It can't be that hard if it promises I'll be lying next to this gorgeous body every night." Nuzzling his mouth to her neck, he hummed a few notes. That tune. Their tune.

"Sing it out loud," she said lazily. "Please?"

"I can't carry a tune, sweet." He nipped her earlobe, humming again. And his hums segued into words.

Rachel recognized Elvis's tender words about wise men cautioning fools who rush in. All this time…he'd been humming about falling in love with her?

A kiss to her cheek. Soft breaths tickled her eyelids. His smile moved across her forehead, and he kissed her again, a quick end to his tune. "Good then?"

"It's all good." And Rachel slid a foot down Jason's leg and tangled her toes within his. "You know I have plans."

"For the network?"

"I want to find those other women."

"I'm a bit of all right with that."

"We'll need Rousseau's help."

"Good luck to you, sweet. All bets say the man has gone deep into hiding."

"I'll find him."

He let out a frustrated sigh that ended in a hopeful wink. "After we have sex?"

She smiled. "Sure."

* * * * *

*Turn the page for an exclusive excerpt
from one of next month's releases,*
Invisible Recruit *by Mary Buckham.
On sale July 2007 at your favourite retail outlet.*

Invisible Recruit
by
Mary Buckham

Vaughn Monroe hesitated, unsure for a second, hugging the brick wall and peering into the darkness beyond. The smell of spring dampened the night air. A whip-poor-will's trill was cut off midnote with crickets playing beyond the mowed grass. Traffic far down the valley hummed past while her heart beat shallow and fast.

Had she killed him? Or should she have tried harder?

The run uphill had been rough, guided only by the moon glowing overhead and the vapor arc lamp in the opening between buildings that hunkered down in the stillness, obsidian slabs casting more shadows.

She'd trained for this, anticipated the drill inside and out. But knowing and doing were worlds apart. How many had he said? Five total? She'd counted four down. One to go.

Not bad for a deb. *Take that, Stone, and stuff it up your backside.*

She crouched lower, not wasting much effort on celebrating. Yet. Not while he could still be out there. Somewhere. Waiting.

Overextended muscles cramped in her lower stomach, mimicking those in clenched fingers cradling the modified Walther PPK. She ignored everything except the space before her. She hadn't come here to fail. This time she was going to win. Two hundred yards and she was home free. Another quick scan as she swallowed hard.

She should have made sure she'd taken him out back at the creek. Maybe it'd been enough. But the man was like Lazarus—killing him meant nothing.

She stepped forward, heard the brush of her crepe-soled boots against the gravel.

Damn!

She froze, breath stalling in her lungs, muscles quaking, sweat trickling along her lower back.

He was there. She knew it.

Waiting. Watching. Anticipating.

He wanted to stop her.

Tough. Let him want.

Nothing.

When pinpricks circled her vision she gave in, gulping a ragged fistful of cool air. Only then did she move forward into the shadows.

Wall to her left, steel building to the right. Objective at four o'clock.

Where would she hide if she were him?

Straight in front of her. Downwind. Easier to hear movement. He'd stay south of the objective, where the darkness deepened between two buildings.

She smiled, stood and crept forward. Ten feet. Eight.

Almost there. Stay focused, no time to get cocky.

Five.

A whisper of cloth against cloth. That was all.

Too late.

She whirled. The slam of a shoulder careened along her rib cage, twisting her, rolling, her back punched against packed gravel. She couldn't inhale, couldn't move.

A knee slammed to her chest. Hand to her throat. Pressing.

He had her. And there wasn't a damn thing she could do about it.

"You're dead," he whispered, leaning so close his breath warmed her face. "Mission failed."

Lights blazed on all around them. The exercise was finished. She swallowed the defeat clogging her throat, telling herself it was physical pain but knowing she was lying.

She noted only his eyes, inches from hers.

Death promised less pain than they did.

This wasn't over. Not by a long shot.

MILLS & BOON
INTRIGUE
On sale 15th June 2007

AT CLOSE RANGE
by Jessica Andersen

Can rival investigators Seth Varitek and Cassie Dumont set aside their differences to take down a serial killer who has trapped them in close proximity?

SOMEBODY'S HERO
by Marilyn Pappano

Jayne Miller moves to the small town of Sweetwater, and next door to sexy, brooding Tyler Lewis. Jayne makes Tyler want what he can't have...not with the secrets in his past.

A HUSBAND'S WATCH
by Karen Templeton

Darryl Andrews and his wife Faith were childhood sweethearts. But after a tornado hits, things don't seem right between them. Suddenly Darryl has to fight for Faith's love.

DREAM WEAVER
by Jenna Ryan

Someone, somewhere, keeps giving Meliana Maynard white roses. Will FBI agent Johnny Grand be able to uncover her admirer before his affection blooms into something more sinister?

Available at WHSmith, Tesco, ASDA, and all good bookshops
www.millsandboon.co.uk

MILLS & BOON
INTRIGUE
On sale 15th June 2007

PERFECT ASSASSIN
by Wendy Rosnau

Trained assassin Prisca Reznik was on the hunt for her mother's killer, Jacy "Moon" Maddox. Moon thinks Prisca could be the love of his life and she's out to get him too, but for very different reasons...

INVISIBLE RECRUIT
by Mary Buckham

Debutante Vaughn Monroe was working undercover for the IR-5 Agency and the seductive MT Stone was pretending to be her husband. How long would it be before the pretence became reality?

CHAIN REACTION
by Rebecca York

An explosion exposes Gage Darnell to a chemical that gives him the ability to manipulate matter with his mind. But on the run and looking to reconnect with his estranged wife, Lily, will he powerless to change hers?

DEAD RECKONING
by Sandra K Moore

Christine Hamilton travels to an uncharted island to rescue her sister and makes another discovery: DEA agent Connor McLellan, the man she confided in — and bedded, seems to have been lying to her all along.

Available at WHSmith, Tesco, ASDA, and all good bookshops
www.millsandboon.co.uk

0307/46/MB084

MILLS & BOON

INTRIGUE™
Breathtaking romantic suspense

NOW INCLUDING
Sensation
STORIES

Intrigue and Sensation series have now merged to form one supercharged, breathtaking romantic suspense series.

Called Intrigue, the new series combines the best stories from both Intrigue and Sensation. You'll still find all your favourite authors and mini-series – and still at the same great price.

Three brand-new hot and sexy stories that will make your summer sizzle!

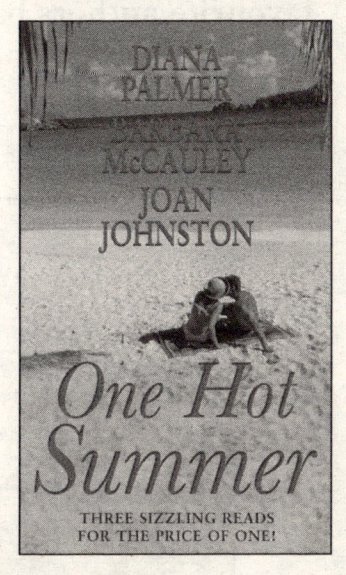

Marriages of convenience, men you can't resist and the guarantee of hot, sultry passion in these three novels:

Blackhawk Legacy by Barbara McCauley

The Founding Father by Diana Palmer

Hawk's Way: The Substitute Groom by Joan Johnston

Available 15th June 2007

www.millsandboon.co.uk

MILLS & BOON

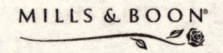

Bestselling novels by your favourite authors back by popular demand!

MEN TO MARRY

Spotlight

2-in-1 FOR ONLY £4.99

Featuring
The Groom's Stand-In
by Gina Wilkins

&

Good Husband Material
by Susan Mallery

MILLS & BOON

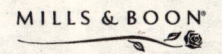

THE CONNELLYS: SETH, RAFE & MAGGIE

Spotlight

This month a 3-in-1 featuring

Cinderella's Convenient Husband
by Katherine Garbera

Expecting…and in Danger
by Eileen Wilks

Cherokee Marriage Dare
by Sheri WhiteFeather

2-in-1 FOR ONLY £4.99

On sale from 15th June 2007

Available at WHSmith, Tesco, ASDA, and all good bookshops

www.millsandboon.co.uk

FREE!
4 Books
and a surprise gift!

We would like to take this opportunity to thank you for reading this Mills & Boon® book by offering you the chance to take FOUR more specially selected titles from the Intrigue series absolutely FREE! We're also making this offer to introduce you to the benefits of the Mills & Boon® Reader Service™—

- ★ **FREE home delivery**
- ★ **FREE gifts and competitions**
- ★ **FREE monthly Newsletter**
- ★ **Exclusive Reader Service offers**
- ★ **Books available before they're in the shops**

Accepting these FREE books and gift places you under no obligation to buy, you may cancel at any time, even after receiving your free shipment. Simply complete your details below and return the entire page to the address below. You don't even need a stamp!

YES! Please send me 4 free Intrigue books and a surprise gift. I understand that unless you hear from me, I will receive 6 superb new titles every month for just £3.10 each, postage and packing free. I am under no obligation to purchase any books and may cancel my subscription at any time. The free books and gift will be mine to keep in any case.

I7ZEF

Ms/Mrs/Miss/Mr .... Initials ....
Surname ....
BLOCK CAPITALS PLEASE
Address ....

....
.... Postcode ....

Send this whole page to:
UK: FREEPOST CN81, Croydon, CR9 3WZ

Offer valid in UK only and is not available to current Mills & Boon® Reader Service™ subscribers to this series. Overseas and Eire please write for details. We reserve the right to refuse an application and applicants must be aged 18 years or over. Only one application per household. Terms and prices subject to change without notice. Offer expires 31st August 2007. As a result of this application, you may receive offers from Harlequin Mills & Boon and other carefully selected companies. If you would prefer not to share in this opportunity please write to The Data Manager, PO Box 676, Richmond, TW9 IWU.

Mills & Boon® is a registered trademark owned by Harlequin Mills & Boon Limited.
The Mills & Boon® Reader Service™ is being used as a trademark.